# ATALAN I
## BEGINNING'S END

# Future Perfect Series

*Commencement*

*Triplicity: The Journey to Adoraim City*

*Atalànt: The Beginning's End*

---

*The Lost Journal of Professor Rudy Geiger*
(FORTHCOMING)

STEVE CARLSON

# ATALÀNT

BEGINNING'S END

Book three of
THE FUTURE PERFECT SERIES

CARLSONWRITING.COM
PUBLISHED BY STEVE CARLSON

Copyright

Atalànt–Beginning's End
Future Perfect Series Book 3

Published by Steve Carlson

All rights reserved. Except for brief excerpts for review purposes, no part of this book may be reproduced or used in any form without written permission from the author.

This story is a work of fiction. Characters and events are the product of the author's imagination. Any resemblance to any person, living or dead, is coincidental.

Unless otherwise noted, all Scripture quotations are taken from the King James Version of the Bible. (Public domain); Scripture quotations marked NIV are taken from the Holy Bible, New International Version®, NIV®. Copyright © 1973, 1978, 1984, 2011 by Biblica, Inc.® Used by permission. All rights reserved worldwide.

© 2017 Steve Carlson
Cover design: Jeremiah Humphries 2017

www.carlsonwriting.com
Email: steve@carlsonwriting.com

Give feedback on the book at:
steve@carlsonwriting.com

Printed in U.S.A

For Lois Peterson, the most dedicated Bible teacher and most amazing evangelist I have ever encountered in our world. She chose to meet people where they were and loved them too much to leave them there.

# Contents

| | |
|---|---|
| Author's Note | ix |
| Epigraph | xi |
| Sons of Adam | xiii |
| Family Tree of the Ancients | xv |
| Foreword | xvii |
| Prologue | xxi |
| I | 31 |
| II | 39 |
| III | 49 |
| IV | 61 |
| V | 65 |
| VI | 73 |
| VII | 77 |
| VIII | 87 |
| IX | 101 |
| X | 111 |
| XI | 119 |

| | |
|---|---|
| XII | 125 |
| XIII | 137 |
| XIV | 141 |
| XV | 145 |
| XVI | 155 |
| XVII | 165 |
| XVIII | 173 |
| XIX | 181 |
| XX | 189 |
| XXI | 201 |
| XXII | 221 |
| XXIII | 229 |
| XXIV | 233 |
| Epilogue | 249 |
| Concluding note From Author | 253 |
| About the Author | 255 |
| List of Characters & Terms | 257 |

# Author's Note

As I was thinking about the story arc for the Future Perfect Series, I imagined a pathway with a number of sign posts strewn about. Some of the signs were fixed in the ground and completely unmovable, while others could be picked up and moved to different places. These sign posts represent different pieces of information handed down to us regarding the Antediluvian era. The immovable signs represent the events and genealogies found in the Old and New Testaments, while ideas coming from sources such as the Jewish historian Josephus are the moveable ones. I thought it would be interesting to craft a story which would weave in between these signs and provided plausible answers to some intriguing questions that arise from the first five chapters of Genesis.

I have created a way for my readers to learn more about these "sign posts" and how they fit into the story. At the end of certain chapters you will see QR codes like this:

These QR codes will lead you to a page where there is a deeper discussion about different topics from within the chapter.

*The future perfect is a verb form or construction used to describe an event that is expected or planned to happen before a time of reference in the future.*

Wikipedia

# Sons of Adam

1. Cain*

Abel* (deceased, no children)

2. Seth**
3. Ono
4. Zimmah
5. Susi
6. Adoraim
7. Zilthai
8. Zior
9. Rohgah
10. Hermon
11. Okra
12. Ulai
13. Zirci (deceased)

**The Line of Cain***

Cain begat Chanokh (Enoch)
Chanokh begat Irad
Irad begat Mehujael
Mehujael begat Methushael
Methushael begat Lamech
Lamech had two wives:
    Adah who gave birth to Jabal and Jubal
    Zillah who gave birth to Tubal-Cain

**The Line of Seth****

Seth begat Enos
Enos begat Kenan
Kenan begat Mahalalel
Mahalalel begat Jared
Jared begat Enoch
Enoch begat Methuselah
Methuselah begat Lamech
Lamech begat Noah
Noah begat Japheth, Shem, and Ham
 *Genesis 4 / **Genesis 5

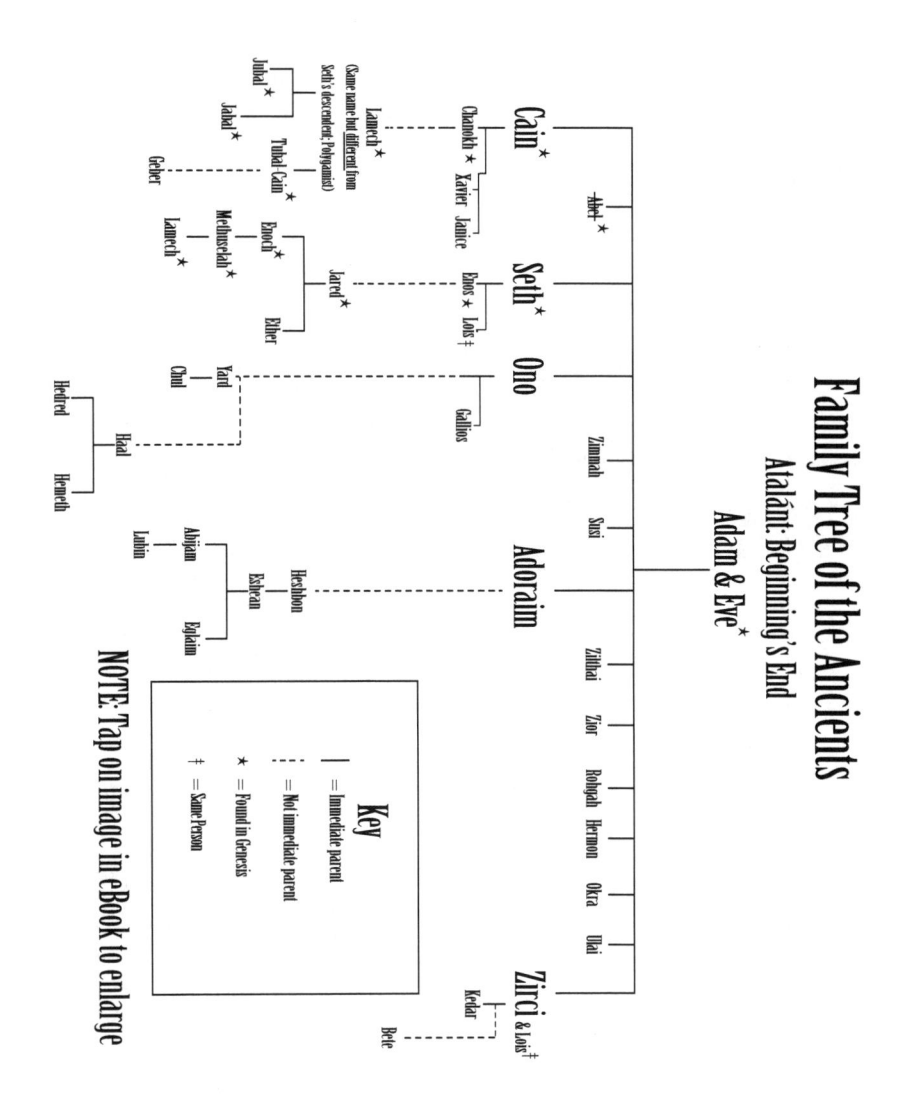

# Family Tree of the Ancients

## Family Tree of the Ancients
### Atalânt: Beginning's End

**Adam & Eve** *

- Abel *
- **Cain** *
  - Chanokh * — Xavier, Janice
    - Lamech †
      - Tubal-Cain *
        - Geber
      - Jabal *
      - Jubal *
  (Same name but different from Seth's descendant; Polygamist)
- **Seth** *
  - Enos * — Lois ‡
    - Jared *
      - Enoch *
        - Methuselah *
          - Lamech *
      - Esther
- **Ono**
  - Gallius
    - Yard
      - Chul
        - Heal
          - Hedrel
          - Hemeth
- Zimmah
- Susi
- **Adoraim**
  - Hesbhon
    - Eshean
      - Abijam
        - Lotin
      - Eglaim
- Zilthai
- Zior
- Roliyah
- Hermon
- Okra
- Ului
- **Zirci** & Lois ‡
  - Kedar
  - Bete

### Key
| = Immediate parent
--- = Not immediate parent
\* = Found in Genesis
‡ = Same Person

NOTE: Tap on image in eBook to enlarge

# Foreword

In the first two installments of the Future Perfect series, thirteen-year-old Logan Doss traveled to Israel with his mother, Lois Doss, an accomplished archaeologist, to study newly discovered evidence of ancient life. This evidence was found inside a cave on an island that had recently resurfaced during an earthquake in the Mediterranean Sea. Because of strange magnetic readings coming from a large rock formation inside the cave, world-renowned physicist Dr. Rudy Geiger was also called in to investigate. Tragedy struck the night Dr. Geiger arrived. As Lois was showing Dr. Geiger and his assistant around the cave, another earthquake struck and the rock formation Dr. Geiger was sent to investigate began to pulse with radiant light. Before the earthquake subsided, Dr. Geiger and Logan were thrown into the glow of the stone structure and vanished. Dr. Geiger's assistant sent a robotic probe into the strange phenomenon, and it too disappeared.

Dazed, Logan found he had been transported thousands of years into the past, where he encountered a famous, mysterious prophet named Enoch. Together with Enoch's grandson Lamech, Logan was able to escape capture by Tubal-Cain, a leader of the intelligent, ruthless Cainite clan. Logan found many amazing differences between the Earth he knew and the one into which he had fallen. Both the earth's atmosphere and humanity were different. Instead of rain, water rising from the ground, called the mists, bathed the land with moisture. The planet appeared to be much more protected from the harmful rays of the sun. Perhaps because of these and other differences, humans aged at a much slower rate, so that people who looked thirty years old by modern standards might be more than two hundred years old in the Ancient world. People also seemed to be able to access more parts of their brains than is common in the modern world. Some even possessed unique abilities called Gifts. A Gift might be the ability to project one's thoughts or even to read minds. Other people, such as Lamech, had the ability to fight with profound speed and accuracy.

For the first few weeks after being transported, Logan lived peacefully in Enoch's city of Parvaim, learning the Ancient world's customs and history, including how the sons of Adam had begun to spread out and inhabit the world. Logan's time in Parvaim was cut short when agents of Tubal-Cain kidnapped him and took him to an outpost just outside the Tortured Mists, an unstable area where the natural mists of the world turned violent and dangerous. Having been warned in a vision, Enoch sent Lamech to follow and rescue young Logan from his captors. During his rescue attempt, Lamech burned down the outpost but got lost with Logan inside the Tortured Mists. Through a series of miraculous events, Lamech and Logan found their way into a land hidden deep within the Tortured Mists. In this land, called Pellios, the two travelers found the remnants of the Line of Zirci, who, forced into the Tortured Mists by the Line of Cain, had been left for dead. By God's grace, they had survived and even flourished in their new home. However, the Zirci's days were numbered. With only one exception, no children had been born to the Zirci for more than two centuries. That one exception was a young woman named Bete, who befriended Logan and Lamech.

After several months of recuperation, Lamech returned to his people while Logan remained among the Zirci. For thirty years he learned from them the skills and knowledge he would need to survive in the Outside World of Men. These decades were important not only to Logan but also to other forces in the Ancient world who had designs on the future.

At the conclusion of this time, Enoch send Lamech to retrieve Logan in order for him to attend a Firstborn Council set to take place in the port city of Adoraim. During their journey, the two travelers encountered a precocious young man named Hemeth, who had found himself caught in one of Tubal-Cain's grand schemes. After helping him escape, Logan and Lamech had to flee with him from pursuing Cainite warriors and were saved only by the last-minute intervention of Enoch. Once inside Adoraim, Logan, Lamech, and Hemeth found themselves in the middle of an inter-Line conflict and had to defend themselves in the Council of the Firstborns. While the members of the Firstborn Council were occupied with their deliberations, Tubal-Cain took matters into his own hands and brutally assaulted Lamech using his powerful Gift of the Mind. While Lamech was trapped within Tubal-Cain's mental grasp, Hemeth stumbled into this mental connection and found that although he was a Lowborn, his mind was every bit a match for Tubal-Cain's. In rescuing Lamech, Hemeth created and trapped Tubal-Cain in a mental labyrinth and left the Cainite to find his own way out.

After the assault on Lamech, the Firstborn Council, unsure how to proceed without war erupting, sent the three young men to the island of Atalànt, where they were to seek an audience with Adam, the Created One. Despite last-minute resistance from Cainite factions and their allies, the three weary travelers succeeded in boarding the ship *Tomorrow's Destiny*, commanded by its young captain, Lubin, and set sail for the mysterious island of Atalànt.

And so the story continues.

# Prologue

"Is this not great, sister?"

Sara stood looking out the window of the room they had been shown to after arriving in Nod that morning. The sun shone low in the sky. Frowning, Sara did not answer.

"I still cannot imagine that we are here in Lord Cain's first city," Hedred continued, ignoring her silence. "And I think Geber is quite taken by you, my sister. You should not ignore him the way you do. This could mean great things for me."

Sara's eyes widened and she turned to him abruptly. "Is that all you care about, Hedred? Raising yourself in the eyes of these Cainites?"

Now it was Hedred's turn to frown. Taking her arm in his massive hand he spun her back toward the window and pointed. "Look out there, Sara! See those magnificent structures? Do we have anything to compare to them in the Ono lands? No! We do not. Even the most humble homes out there are like mansions compared to what we have. And you cannot deny that the food we have been served is the most amazing we have ever tasted. Look at the way the Cainites dress and hold themselves, moving about with their heads held high. Ono could learn from these people."

"Yes, Hedred," Sara replied sharply, "these Cainites possess so many things we do not, including the greed and envy that fill their hearts. Every Cainite covets what every other one has and is constantly scheming to gain an advantage."

"I admit they are very competitive, but that is what makes them so successful in their endeavors. Look at what they have accomplished. What do we have to compare with them?"

"We have our honor and dignity," Sara replied.

Hedred snorted. Letting go of her arm he walked away, shaking his head in disbelief. Sara's expression softened. "Do you not think our patriarch Ono kept us away from these people for a reason?"

"Ono is obsessed with keeping us away from all other Lines, not just the Cainites. He does not think clearly anymore.

Our influence in the world is falling behind the other Lines. That is why the younger Firstborns had to move in secret. We must be brought closer in line with the Cainites to keep our influence strong."

"But do you not see that by aligning the Ono with the Cainites we will lose influence, not gain it? They wish us no goodwill. They wish only to dominate others."

"Clearly, sister, you do not understand the Cainites." Hemeth flexed the muscles in his forearms. "You fail to see how the Cainites value strength, and despite Ono's foolishness, we are still strong. Together the Ono and Cainites can control more of the world. You and I, we are only the beginning of many more connections between our peoples."

Sara chuckled sadly. "What I see is Tubal-Cain manipulating our younger Firstborns and Geber wanting something from you and me, and I am pretty sure that something has to do with Hemeth."

Fury flashed in Hedred's eyes at the name of his younger brother. "Why must you bring up Hemeth?"

"Why must you hate him, Hedred? Is he such a threat to you?"

"Of course he is a threat, but not just to me. He has put at risk everything our Line has been working toward with the Cainites! Don't you see what he has done? Hemeth is—"

Sara ceased hearing what her brother had to say as her head began to spin. She tried to concentrate, but at that moment her vision blurred and she felt herself falling to the ground. *Oh no*, she thought, *it is happening again.* It felt like she was trapped in what she imagined the Tortured Mists must be like, though she had never been there. Just when she thought she might be sick, the mists started to dissipate.

*Where am I?*

Soon Sara's vision cleared and she found herself standing in a large tent. A man lay before her on a bed of many fine blankets. Blinking her eyes, Sara looked more closely at him.

*It is Tubal-Cain*, she mused. *How did Tubal-Cain make it to Nod so quickly?*

A moment later the answer came to her.

*He is not in Nod. It is just a vision. But my visions have never been this clear before.*

Just then Tubal-Cain spoke. "Servants! Attend me!" His voice sounded unusually weak. His servant entered the tent with a look of relief on his face. It was Talaon, the Sethite traitor who served in Tubal-Cain's house. Sara had met him during her brief stay in Adoraim.

"My lord," said Talaon, "I am so glad you are back. I was beginning to worry—"

"Be still," Tubal-Cain croaked. "Get me water, quickly!"

"Yes, my lord."

Talaon disappeared behind the curtain and returned moments later with a jug of water, which Tubal-Cain took and began to drink feverishly. Halfway through the jug, he paused to order some food. When he had sufficiently revived, he turned his attention back to his servant. "How long have I been out?"

"Five days, my lord."

"Five days!"

"Yes! Much has happened that I must tell you about."

"Where are my regular servants?"

"That is part of what I must tell you," Talaon replied. "They are occupied elsewhere."

"What? How are they occupied with anything but serving their Firstborn?"

From behind them came a voice from the tent's entrance, followed by the figure of man. "That is just it, dear brother. They *are* serving their Firstborn."

"Jubal!"

Jubal smiled and turned to Talaon. "Leave us, Sethite! I must talk to my brother."

The servant looked to Tubal-Cain, who reluctantly assented.

"Do not stand near the entrance listening," Jubal warned, "or you will regret it." Once Talaon had left, Jubal turned a malevolent gaze to Tubal-Cain. "May I be the first to inform you, dear brother, that you no longer need to concern yourself with the office of Firstborn for our generation."

"What?" cried Tubal-Cain, rising quickly but immediately falling back on his elbows.

"Do not exert yourself, brother. You have had a rough time of late, and we would not want anything to happen to you now that you are awake." As he spoke, Jubal's hand gently caressed the hilt of a dagger attached to his belt. "No one was sure how deranged you might be when you awoke from your trance."

"Of course you have taken advantage of my absence to promote yourself."

"Your absence?" Jubal said with a laugh. "I took advantage of much more than your absence. You have barely lived down your blunders with the Okran camp thirty years ago, and now you have gone on to embarrass our entire line with your mess at the artisan camp. Added to that, you were caught assaulting another Firstborn in the hallway while the Council was deliberating. Worst of all, you were bested by a Lowborn boy in mental manipulation, the one area you were supposed to be strongest in." Jubal laughed again. "No, brother, your absence was the least of what I took advantage of."

"You cannot hold the title of Firstborn, Jubal. Your brother Jabal was born first, not you, and he shuns the responsibility."

"It seems both my brother and our forefathers have had a change of heart. With your many defeats, Jabal felt forced to challenge your claim to the position, and our forefathers readily agreed to his demand. Because Jabal has neither the time nor the inclination to lead, he gave me authority to act in his place. Although it is unusual, our forefathers once again agreed. Drastic times require drastic measures, after all."

Tubal-Cain dropped his gaze to the floor, unsure what to say.

"It is a shame my own descendants are not set to inherit the title, but I am working on that, too," Jubal continued with a wolfish smile. "It was gratifying, however, to see your son removed from the Council proceedings these last few days. As for your grandson Geber, it seems he shares your incompetence. He did not even attending his first Council meeting, which is odd because I saw him here a few days ago. Where did he go off to in such a hurry?"

Tubal-Cain raised his eyes and smiled for the first time, refusing to answer.

Jubal returned a cold smile. "I will find out soon enough. Now I have other duties to attend to, but I did want to personally share with you the news of my good fortune." He gave a short nod and turned to leave. As he reached the exit, he faced Tubal-Cain again. "I should also inform you that the artisan camp as well as your other experiments are being shut down. With all the questions raised by the other lines concerning the artisan camp, we decided to disband it and send the participants back to their lands. I am sure those ventures were expensive. I trust this development does not inconvenience you too much."

With those smug words Jubal left Tubal-Cain alone in his tent. A minute later Talaon reentered and set a fresh jug of water on the small table.

"Why are you still here, Talaon?" Tubal-Cain asked. "Everyone else has left me. Why do you choose to stay?"

"It is simple, my lord. I have nowhere else to go. As I told you before, my own people will not have me back, and I will never be accepted into Cainite society."

Tubal-Cain nodded. "Where is Hemeth now?"

"He set sail for Atalànt four days ago with Lamech and Logan. They left on an Adoraim ship."

"I feared the Firstborn Council might turn to Adam for help. But they got passage to the Blessed Isle on an Adoraim ship? That line is wary of Sethites."

"True, but it seems Enoch arranged the transportation in advance with Lubin, the youngest of the Firstborn Adoraim captains. Lubin has a particular grudge against us and was happy to oblige them. Once the Firstborn Council agreed to seek Adam's help, Enoch dispatched them immediately."

"Enoch! That magician always seems to be in the middle of things. Has anyone followed the ship?"

"No. Shortly after they departed a strong storm was sighted off the coast, and it has continued to rage ever since. It took everyone by surprise, since we are not in the season of high storms. The Adoraim fear that it may be weeks before vessels can safely leave the harbor. Meanwhile, the Council has been discussing other topics."

"They will continue to meet on mundane matters for weeks. I do not suppose we can hope Lubin's ship was lost in the storm."

"We can hope, but I doubt it, sir."

"Did Geber make it out before the storm?"

"Yes, my lord, he did. Before he left, he arranged to take Hemeth's brother and sister with him."

"Good. That may give him leverage over Hemeth. Perhaps by alerting Lord Cain of impending danger, I may yet regain favor among my line."

The curtain covering the entrance to the tent moved again. Emerging from behind the curtain was an exceedingly beautiful woman who appeared to be from the Zior Line. She walked straight up to Tubal-Cain as if the tent were her own.

"Lord Cain, I have a message for you."

"Young woman," said Talaon, "I do not know how you got in here, but you are not—"

The woman silenced Talaon with a vicious stare. "Be still, Sethite. My message is not for you." Turning back to Tubal-Cain she said, "My message is for this one."

Tubal-Cain's motioned for Talaon to remain silent. "Continue, woman."

"Those who sent me wish you to know that both the metal creature and the strange Zirci boy came through a door. That door will open again, and if you are there, you may have what comes through."

As she spoke, the young woman reached out and gently caressed Tubal-Cain's forehead with the tips of her fingers, straightening a few strands of hair that had fallen over his face. "You would be wise to listen to those who sent me," she said softly. With that, she walked out of the tent without another word.

Talaon watched incredulously as the woman departed. "I do not know who that woman was, but I will find out and have her punished!"

"You will do no such thing," replied Tubal-Cain with an odd expression on his face.

"What do you intend do, then?"

"We have been given a message, and I intend to find out what it means," Tubal-Cain said with a smile.

"You mean you believe her? You are planning to go to the Sacred Cave and just sit there waiting for something to come through?"

"When that woman touched me, I sensed something very different about her, something that makes me want to investigate what she has told me. Jubal has made it clear there is nothing for me to do here anymore, so why not? Twice the Sethites have cheated me out of what came from that cave. If what this woman says is true, it is time I received something for all my trouble!"

At this point, Sara's vision dimmed and the mists overtook her again. After a few moments of nausea she opened her eyes and found herself lying in bed across the room from where she had been standing when the vision overtook her. The room was dark, lit only by a single glowing gourd on the far wall. A figure whom Sara took to be Hedred stood in front of the gourd, silhouetted by the light.

"I am sorry, Hedred," Sara said weakly, thinking of how Tubal-Cain had looked when he woke up in her vision. "All this excitement must have made me faint. Would you be so kind as to give me some water?"

The figure walked over to the table not far from her bed, poured a cup of water, and handed it to her. Sara realized the figure was not Hedred, as she had supposed, but Geber.

He smiled. "I am glad you are finally awake, my dear," he said in a tone that actually sounded sincere.

"Thank you, sir," she said awkwardly, having never been served by a Firstborn before. Her eyes widened as she thought about the vision and how Geber did not know he was no longer a Firstborn.

Geber saw the change of expression on her face. "What is wrong, my dear? You do not look well. Was your vision disturbing?"

Sara remained silent. She heard the shifting of a stool. In a dark corner of the room she saw another figure stand up and approach her. As he came closer, she recognized the familiar face of her brother.

"Tell him what you saw, Sara," said Hedred.

*Of course Hedred went to fetch Geber*, she thought. *For years he thought I was just odd, but now he thinks my visions will help him.*

"I told you," she said uncertainly, "I was just overcome by all we have experienced lately."

"Tell him!" Hedred said. He walked over and firmly grasped her shoulder. There was a new look in her brother's eyes. While she and her brother had often argued, she had never been fearful of him. That was not the case now.

She looked from Hedred to Geber, who smiled at her. "You have nothing to fear," he said. "But your Hedred has told me of your odd behavior over the years and what recently occurred between you and Logan, the young Zirci you met in Adoraim. While it is very strange in a Lowborn family to have Gifts, perhaps like your brother Hemeth, you too have been touched by the gods. I think you may very well be a seer. So, my dear, be so good as to tell me what you saw."

Coaxed as much by Geber's gentle tone as by Hedred's suppressed ferocity, Sara relented and explained everything she had seen in her vision, including how Tubal-Cain had awoken from five days of unconsciousness that had somehow been induced by her brother Hemeth. To Sara's surprise, Geber gave no outward sign of shock or irritation when she told him how Jubal had used Tubal-Cain's absence to usurp the Firstborn title. The only time Geber showed surprise was when she told him of the Zior woman's message to Tubal-Cain and his grandfather's decision to travel to the Sacred Cave. When she finished, Geber walked over to the window, gazing out for several minutes.

Finally, he spoke. "If what you told me is true, then I am doubly pleased my efforts to convince Lord Cain to travel to Adoraim have been successful."

"What of Lord Tubal-Cain?" asked Hedred.

"What of him?" asked Geber.

"He is no longer Firstborn," replied Hedred.

"True, he is no longer Firstborn, which means I am no longer Firstborn. But no one here knows that yet, and it will remain that way," Geber said with an edge in his voice. "Understood?"

"Yes, sir."

"Besides, my grandfather can take care of himself," Geber said. He turned to Sara with a warm smile. Sara smiled sadly in return. While she was sure she had made the right choice in telling Geber about the vision, she could not help but feel fear in the pit of her stomach. By telling Geber what she saw in her vision, Sara knew she would not be leaving his side anytime soon, and that frightened her. She had become too valuable to him, and because of that, she just might yet see her young brother again and find a way to help him.

"It looks like you and your brother will be joining me on another voyage," Geber said, still smiling. "This time, however, we are going to Atalànt."

# I

*"He loads the clouds with moisture; he scatters his lightning through them. At his direction they swirl around over the face of the whole earth to do whatever he commands them. He brings the clouds to punish people, or to water his earth and show his love."*

Job 37:11-13 (NIV)

Logan lay quietly in the bow of the ship watching the waning starlight dissolve into dawn. The vessel beneath him, aptly named *Tomorrow's Destiny*, was unlike the massive ships he had seen in the harbor of Adoraim City. It was small and insignificant, with a very young captain named Lubin. Yet, Enoch had chosen this ship to transport Logan and his friends to the mysterious island of Atalànt, where they were to meet Adam, or "the Created One," as Enoch referred to him. As he looked up at the remaining stars in the early-morning sky, Logan could not help but think that somehow he too had been chosen, but for what reason he could not fathom.

Logan smiled as he considered how the harrowing life Lamech had dragged him into had become almost normal to him. He still missed Pellios, where he had lived for thirty years among the Zirci, protected within the lands hidden deep inside the Tortured Mists. Since leaving Pellios, he and Lamech had met and rescued the young but brilliant boy Hemeth from one of the Cainites' bizarre schemes. Despite being chased by Cainites, attacked by hyenas, and nearly turned over to the Cainites by Enoch's own brother, the three friends had made it safely to their destination—Adoraim City. Logan had thought being near Enoch and the Sethites would provide protection, but events proved him terribly wrong. Lamech had been viciously attacked by Tubal-Cain and was rescued only by the combined intervention of Hemeth and their ship's captain, Lubin.

Once on Lubin's ship and away from Adoraim City, Logan had hoped they would finally be allowed to take a break from their troubles. He smiled to himself again at how wrong he had been. In fact, as he reflected on the events of the past two weeks, he could not imagine how things could have gone any worse.

They had left the harbor in a hurry and once at sea, Captain Lubin ordered the crew to quickly prepare for a great storm he predicted would soon be upon them. Logan remembered wondering at the strange command as he looked about him and saw an abundance of clear sky.

However, Lubin's storm prediction proved accurate. Within an hour of leaving Adoraim City, the weather changed dramatically. The wind picked up and the harmless, wispy clouds in the high atmosphere began to swirl. Logan saw them transform into intricate patterns. Glancing over at Lamech and Hemeth, he had seen how both were feeling the effects of seasickness. Having often sailed with his father, Logan was untroubled by the swaying of the ship, but his friends who had never been on a ship were not faring as well. That moment, Logan remembered, had been the first time the three of them were together after setting sail, because each had been busy working on separate parts of the ship.

Hemeth looked up toward the swirling mass and cringed. "I have never seen anything like this before!"

"Neither have I," Logan agreed. "The weather has always remained the same on land. What do you think, Lamech?"

Lamech gave no reply, and instead turned his back on Logan and stared out at the water. Logan had tried conversing with Lamech when their paths crossed while they were working on the ship, but to no avail. Silence was the only response he had thus far received from his friend.

Suddenly, the wind stopped and everything became deathly still. While ancient weather patterns were vastly different from modern ones, Logan could see one element was the same: the calm before the storm. At that moment, Logan saw Lubin's first mate, Huppim, heading toward them.

"Captain Lubin has ordered you to lash yourselves to the masthead. The sea will be getting very violent soon, and he does not want you, his cargo, washed overboard," he said with a chuckle.

"Won't we be dropping the sail?" asked Logan. "If the storm hits, I do not want to be under it when you do."

Huppim smiled at him. "Do not worry. The captain knows how to judge the storm. He will ride before it, keeping the sails high to give us greater speed away from Adoraim City. I saw him do it when I served with him on his great-grandfather's ships." Throwing an armful of rope at Logan, the first mate turned and left.

Logan looked at Hemeth and shrugged. Not knowing anything about tying knots, Hemeth asked Logan to help tie him to the masthead not far behind where they stood. Hemeth watched while Logan worked on a complex knot he had learned from Kedar years ago.

"Lamech is still under Tubal-Cain's influence," whispered Hemeth. "I tried to release him, but he would not let me help."

"I know," said Logan. "You did the best you could. We'll just have to give him time to snap out of it."

"I am not so sure," said Hemeth. "Tubal-Cain taught him what it means to be weak and defenseless. That is something I have felt my whole life, but for Lamech, I think it was a new experience. When I released him, you should have seen how he looked at me. I am not sure if what has been done to him can be so easily undone."

When Logan was finished with his knot he called over to Lamech.

"Come over here, Lamech," said Logan, keeping an eye on the storm that continued to swirl in the upper atmosphere. "Let's get set for this storm; it looks like it is almost here." Lamech ignored him and stood stock-still looking out at the water. Frustrated at his friend's continued silence, Logan walked over to the side of the ship where Lamech stood.

"Look, Lamech," Logan said, placing a hand on Lamech's shoulder. "I know you must think this is—" As fast as lightning, Lamech turned, grabbed Logan's wrist, and wrenched it behind his back. Then, with one foot he swept Logan's feet from under him, landing Logan hard on the wood of the deck. After this, Lamech turned back toward the sea as if nothing had happened.

Logan groaned in a heap on the deck. He had never been on the receiving end of one of Lamech's attacks and hoped he never would be again. The commotion of the men around the ship ceased as they took in what had happened. Logan sat up on one elbow to try to talk some sense into Lamech. Before he could say anything, he heard rapid footsteps approach.

"What are you doing?" cried Captain Lubin.

"It is all right," said Logan, trying to stand up. "Leave him to me."

Lubin glared at Logan. "You may be my guest, but do not presume to tell me what I should and should not do on my own ship," he said curtly.

"I mean no disrespect, Captain," said Logan quietly. "But if he chooses not to lash himself, we cannot make him."

"I will find a way!" Lubin countered. "I cannot get paid if he gets himself washed overboard."

"You will also not get paid if he kills you," whispered Logan so the other crew members could not hear. "Please, let me talk with him. I will convince him."

"You will not convince me," Lamech said, still with his back to the others. "But you are right about one thing, Logan—if I don't want to be lashed to the post, none of you can make that happen."

Just then, Logan saw a small dart lodge itself into the back of Lamech's neck.

"That's not true," Logan heard Hemeth say quietly. Everyone turned to see Hemeth holding a small reed near his mouth. Lamech reached to the back of his neck, pulled out the dart, and glared at Hemeth.

Logan cried, "Lamech, don't do anything stupid—"

Lamech ignored him and strode toward Hemeth, who tried to back away but found he could not because he was tied to the mast. Logan was sure Hemeth would not have survived the next few minutes had not the drugged dart begun to take effect. Logan watched Lamech stumble just before he reached Hemeth. Taking that as a cue, Lubin and five crew members jumped on Lamech and held him down. They would have had a very difficult time of it if Lamech had had full control of his faculties, but the combination of the drug in his system and exhaustion from having not slept for days allowed them to overwhelm him. After a few tense moments, Lamech surrendered to the drug and fell unconscious. The ship became eerily quiet except for the labored breathing of the crew members who had held Lamech down. The next moment, however, the ship shuddered, knocking Logan and some of the others off balance. The tempest was upon them.

"We don't have any time! Get to your stations," Lubin shouted to his crew, who immediately dispersed. "And you," Lubin shouted at Logan and Hemeth, "secure him now!" Leaving the two young men to their task, Lubin sprinted back to the quarterdeck and grabbed the wheel from his first mate.

"Lamech is not going to be happy when he wakes up," yelled Logan to Hemeth over the wind as he struggled to move Lamech's limp body closer to the masthead.

"Did you see any alternative?" Hemeth yelled back while tying the rope around Lamech's waist.

"No," Logan said. "Did Methuselah give you the reed and dart?"

"Yes. He was worried Lamech might do something to put himself or us in danger. So he gave me these things and told me—"

But that was all Logan could hear as the howling wind became all-encompassing. He moved quickly to finish securing the rope around Lamech. He noticed Hemeth had already recreated the same knot Logan had just tied him with. In Pellios, it had taken Logan many tries before he could tie that knot as well as Kedar. Hemeth was able to recreate it perfectly after watching Logan do it only once.

Both young men took hold of Lamech's unconscious form with one arm and awkwardly grabbed onto the masthead with the other. Their muscles ached as they held on for all they were worth. Rocking violently back and forth, the ship endured walls of seawater washing up on the deck, the first of which sent Hemeth sliding as he lost his grip on both the masthead and Lamech. Fortunately, the rope that bound him held. Struggling to pull himself back, he reached the masthead before the next wave came. As the storm raged on, Logan and Hemeth began to figure out how to manage the position of their bodies, and they took turns holding on to Lamech. While his fear of being washed overboard subsided, Logan could not help worrying about what the temperature might do to Lamech. Logan prayed he would not go into hypothermia as he himself almost had during his first trip through the Tortured Mists years ago.

After what seemed like an eternity, the rocking of the ship lessened and the wind, while still strong, lost it violent demeanor. As they reached what appeared to be the edge of the storm, wind filled the mainsail and moved the ship forward at a solid clip. While the storm still raged behind them, the ship broke away from it. The sun was a welcome sight as it emerged and shone its warm rays down upon the three travelers. When Logan and Hemeth could finally stand, they looked aft and saw in the distance the dark, disastrous clouds and the churning sea beneath them. The two young men were silent for several minutes.

"So that is a storm?" said Hemeth at last.

"Yes, Hemeth," said Logan. "That is a storm. But I have to admit, it is a kind I have never seen before."

"You better get used to them," said Lubin, who had come up behind them. "They have a habit of popping up, and they have been getting worse over the last few centuries."

"Really?" asked Logan.

"Yes. But I do not sense any coming soon, and in the next few days we will not be hitting any others in the direction we are heading."

"How do you know that?"

Lubin tapped the temple of his forehead. "I just know."

"You are a Storm Seer," said Hemeth. "That is your Gift, isn't it?"

"Yes," replied Lubin. "That was one of the reasons we wanted to leave as quickly as possible this morning. Both my great-grandfather and I knew this storm was approaching. I told your master, Enoch, that it would be harsh but we could outrun it. He agreed, knowing that we would be out and away before other ships could follow. Now all the Adoraim and Zior vessels will be stuck in port for days while the storm runs its course."

"Does your crew know about your Gift?" asked Hemeth.

"Up until recently, no. My great-grandfather had me keep it a secret until my first voyage. He wanted my crew to respect me first and foremost for my skills at piloting the ship. But this crew is very clever, and many of them have served alongside me for years before I was made captain. No doubt, they had their suspicions." After gazing at the storm for another moment, Lubin turned to look at the prone figure at his feet.

"The question now is, what will we do with this Firstborn Sethite?" said Lubin. "If his Gift of Combat is as powerful as I have heard, how will we control him when he wakes? He did not look very pleased with you, Hemeth."

"No, he did not," agreed Hemeth. "But perhaps he will be more reasonable when he wakes."

"I do not think so," said Logan. "I have known him many years and, yes, he is as powerful as you have heard. He is not well, and for now we cannot trust him—not even with his own life."

"So, what do you propose?" asked Lubin.

"We must bind him for his own safety," Logan replied reluctantly.

"You want me to lock up the very passenger whose grandfather is paying me a fortune to transport him? He is a Firstborn Sethite, second-eldest among all the sons of Adam. This could bring war between his people and mine if they find out. If he were a Cainite, I would be threatened with death for even entertaining such an idea."

"Sethites are noble, very different from their Cainite cousins. War will not start when they learn the truth," said Logan. "Enoch told me to allow nothing to hinder us from reaching Atalànt—that includes Lamech himself. I will take full responsibility for it."

Lubin smiled grimly. "Because you are a foolish land-dwelling Zirci, I will let that comment pass. At sea, an Adoraim captain may ask for suggestions, but he—and only he—makes the decision and takes the responsibility. To suggest otherwise is a great insult."

"I apologize, Captain Lubin," said Logan, realizing his mistake.

"Your apology is accepted," said Lubin. "As much as I do not like it, I agree with you. Lamech must be protected from himself if we are to complete the voyage. Take him below deck and bind him in the hold. Make him as comfortable as possible."

"Yes, sir," replied both Logan and Hemeth.

"Captain Lubin," said Logan, "may I be with him when he wakes?"

"Yes," Lubin said. Turning to Hemeth he asked, "How long will he be out?"

"Methuselah told me this dose would keep him out for about two hours," Hemeth replied.

"Well then, get him secured below deck, then report to my first mate for your tasks until he awakes, understood?"

"Yes, sir" both said.

"Good, let's get going."

# II

*"If I rise on the wings of the dawn, if I settle on the far side of the sea, even there your hand will guide me, your right hand will hold me fast."*

Psalm 139:9-10 (NIV)

Logan was indeed by his friend's side when he awoke, and he remained there for the duration of the journey. They stayed in a dark room with only a small porthole through which light could enter. Lamech was bound hand and foot to the bulkhead. Although Logan had placed a blanket underneath him to provide some comfort, it was still a hot, uncomfortable space. Logan always placed himself as close as he could to his friend, but just outside the length of the ropes that bound Lamech.

Several times throughout the day Lamech was allowed to eat and relieve himself. With his bonds still secured, he was escorted to the deck above during these breaks. While each time he was given the option to walk around the deck, he chose not to, preferring to return to his little room in the hold instead.

Logan and Hemeth sat with Lamech as often as they could. Lamech continued to say little to nothing. Often, Logan felt like walking over and shaking his friend's shoulders to wake him from this disquieting depression. Feeling the bruises from his encounter with Lamech on the first day of the voyage, he always thought better of it. Instead, he sat in silence with his friend.

When Logan and Hemeth were not with Lamech, they had jobs to accomplish on the ship because the crew was so small. Being the stronger of the two, Logan took the more physically demanding tasks. He assisted with raising and adjusting the sails, moving equipment, and coiling the heavy ropes. Hemeth assisted wherever he could, but most often his job was in the galley helping the cook prepare meals. Early in the voyage, Hemeth sought out the first mate and followed him around, asking questions to understand the purpose of each piece of equipment on the ship. Logan could see that Hemeth was like a sponge, soaking up knowledge from his observations of all the new things around him.

Because of his great interest in the ship, Hemeth became a favorite of the first mate, Huppim. After the tenth day at sea, Hemeth surprised Huppim by suggesting they create a four-sided fore-and-aft sail to be flown above the main staysail to maximize drive in light winds. After thinking about it, Huppim agreed the idea had merit. Then the two began figuring out how they could rig the new sail even while they were at sea.

The past two weeks had been tranquil, with a good, strong wind to pull the ship along. Lubin elected to head straight for Atalànt without any of the subterfuge Kedar had used when he had traveled to the island centuries before. With as few people as he had to man the ship, Lubin did not want to extend the voyage a minute longer than he had to. Logan guessed that the presence of a potentially violent Sethite Firstborn with the Gift of Combat also made a quick trip desirable. Still, Captain Lubin did not abandon all caution about protecting the island's location. Sethites were known for being able to follow the constellations, and Logan noticed that Lamech was never allowed out at night, making it difficult for him to track their direction.

There were, however, no such restrictions on Logan and Hemeth. The two young men were too valuable as crew members to be kept below out of fear they would figure out the way to Atalànt. It helped that neither the Zirci nor the Ono were known for the ability to read the stars. Thus, the boys were left to roam the ship unimpeded as they saw fit, night or day.

Logan, however, *could* read the stars, and it was this ability together with a sextant Methuselah had given him that allowed him to track the progress of *Tomorrow's Destiny* against Kedar's map. Concerned about a discovery he had made, Logan decided to confide in Hemeth. For this reason, Logan was waiting for him in the early-morning hours.

When Logan saw how well Hemeth got on with first mate Huppim, he made a point of encouraging Hemeth to help him discover the average speed per day of their journey. Armed with this information, Logan took out his map every night and quietly charted, as best he could, the ship's course. For the first several days, Logan thought that perhaps his calculations were off, but he had doubled- and triple-checked them each night and was sure he had made no mistake. They were moving five degrees to the south on a trajectory that, despite the massive size of Atalànt, had caused them to miss it by at least a hundred nautical miles. According to Kedar, the trip should take no longer than two weeks. Now, thirteen days in, they were making a beeline in a direction that was wrong and with no land in sight. Despite Hemeth's occasional questioning glances, Logan had kept the matter to himself. Now, without Lamech to rely on, Logan felt he had no choice but to bring Hemeth into his confidence.

After visiting Lamech in the early morning, as was his custom, Hemeth climbed up to the forecastle and sat down next to Logan.

"How is Lamech doing?" Logan asked.

"The same," Hemeth replied glumly. "Every day I become more afraid he will never snap out of the strange state he is in. He just sits there and does not say a word."

"I know what you mean. We will have to figure something out," said Logan. Looking around to make sure there were no other crew members in earshot, Logan continued, "Right now I am afraid we have more immediate concerns."

"What do you mean?"

"I am pretty sure we have missed the island completely."

"What? How could you know that?"

Drawing the cloth map out of its hiding place in his pack, he showed it to Hemeth. Though it was still early, there was enough light for Hemeth to know immediately what he was holding.

"This is a map to Atalànt," he whispered. "Where did you get it?"

"That is a long story, Hemeth, which I do not want to go into now. But based on our average speed and direction, it appears we have been several degrees off course since we left Adoraim.

"So that is why you wanted to know the average speed every day."

"Yes. I have been charting the course every evening, and from what I can tell, we have missed the island because we have been traveling along this trajectory." Logan drew his finger across the map.

"Huppim has been rather edgy in the last day or so, but he insists everything is fine. Perhaps he is worried."

"Has he been to Atalànt before?"

"Yes, he said he has been there numerous times to transport cargo."

"Perhaps he is worried because he knows we should have spotted land by now."

"Are you sure this map is correct, Logan?"

"Absolutely."

"Well, I can tell you one thing. It is different from the one Captain Lubin is using," said Hemeth. "At least a little bit."

"What? You have seen Lubin's map to Atalànt?" asked Logan in surprise. "Did Huppim show it to you?"

"No, of course not," replied Hemeth. "He does not have access to it, but I followed Huppim into Captain Lubin's quarters a few days ago when we needed his permission to raise the new sail. When we entered the room the map was lying on his table. Lubin quickly placed something over it and scolded Huppim for entering without knocking. But I still saw it."

"You saw it for a second, but you can still recall it?" asked Logan.

Hemeth shrugged. "I have always had a good memory."

"Well then, how is it different?"

Hemeth's brow wrinkled in concentration. "The maps are very similar, though your map has a bit more detail. The one major difference, of course, is that on Lubin's map Atalànt is about here."

Hemeth pointed to a portion of Kedar's map where there was only sea and no island. "So, based on our trajectory, it appears Captain Lubin thinks he is going in the right direction."

"Why would his map be different?" said Logan, more to himself than to Hemeth.

"I have no idea, because I have been told the map was his father's. His great-grandfather gave it to him, and according to Huppim, Lubin and his great-grandfather are very close. Why would he want us to sail off the end of the world and die?"

Logan looked up from the map in surprise. "What are you talking about?"

"The edge of the Earth, of course," said Hemeth. "I for one don't want to sail so far that we fall off."

"That cannot happen, Hemeth," said Logan.

"Why not?"

"The Earth is round, like a ball," said Logan, laughing. "You can't fall off it."

"Really?" asked Hemeth. "Are you sure?"

"Yes. Didn't you know that? Everyone I have met in the Ancient world—at least from the Lines of Seth and Zirci—knows the Earth is not flat."

"Well, obviously I did not," said Hemeth in embarrassment. "That fact is not something my rulers think is important to mention to Lowborns like me who are destined to make Cainite art for the rest of their lives."

"I am sorry, Hemeth. I did not mean to insult you."

"It is what it is. I am terribly ignorant of the world."

"You have learned a lot the last couple of days." Logan smiled. "Who knows what you might learn after we make it to Atalànt—that is, if we ever make it there. But you bring up a good point: Lubin's great-grandfather may not wish to harm him, but there are many others who would not mind seeing him killed if it means getting rid of us. Perhaps we are meant to be lost at sea."

"I suppose we need to bring this matter to Lubin's attention, don't we?" said Hemeth.

"I am afraid so, but he won't be happy to see we have a map to Atalànt. I wish Lamech were able to help us. He is so much better at this kind of thing than me."

"You are sure the map is accurate, though?" asked Hemeth. "Perhaps your map is faulty and we will reach the island just as Captain Lubin is intending."

"I am absolutely sure this map is accurate, Hemeth. The man who made this map would never steer me wrong. I'd bet my life on it."

"You *are* a mysterious man."

"Mysteries are overrated," replied Logan with a sad smile. "We had better speak with Captain Lubin now before he takes over steering the ship."

A few minutes later, Logan saw Lubin come out of his cabin. He took out his spyglass and looked off the starboard side of the ship. Logan offered a quick prayer and looked at Hemeth, who nodded. Together, the two young men approached Captain Lubin.

"Good morning, Logan, Hemeth," Lubin said. "I trust you are well."

"Yes, Captain Lubin. We are fine," said Logan. "Are you expecting to sight land soon?"

Lubin did not answer immediately, but instead kept looking through his spyglass for a few more seconds. "It is something I am expecting to see very soon."

"I know that I mistakenly questioned a couple of your orders when we first departed, and I apologize for that," Logan began. "However, I have to bring something to your attention that you might not be pleased with."

Lubin looked at Logan curiously but said nothing.

"I have reason to believe that the course we are on will never get us to Atalànt."

Lubin's eyes narrowed. "And how would you make such a determination?"

Logan paused. He swallowed then answered, trying to sound as much like Enoch as he could could. "As you have observed, Captain, my two friends and I are ... different. Would you not agree?"

"I know that you are all more trouble than you are worth," replied Lubin, motioning to the hold where Lamech was tied up.

"That remains to be seen." Logan tried to sound confident. "I think it is safe to assume that Enoch will pay you handsomely on the explicit condition that all three of us make it to Atalànt safely."

"True enough."

"To that end, I feel I must show you something that came into my possession." Logan took out his map and laid it out before the captain.

Lubin's eyes grew wide. "Where did you get this?"

"I am sorry, Captain, but that is something I cannot tell you."

"No one but the captains of the Adoraim and Zior may have such information. This could mean great trouble for you."

"Yes, I understand," said Logan. "However, I have sworn to let nothing prevent us from reaching Atalànt, not even your faulty map that is leading us in the wrong direction."

"What? How have you seen my map?" cried Lubin.

Logan looked at Hemeth.

"I saw your map on the table a few days ago, Captain," said Hemeth quietly.

"When you and Huppim barged in? It was open for only a moment, and I did not think you saw it."

"I did, though."

"And you remember it."

"I have a good memory for detail," Hemeth said.

"That may not bode well for you."

"None of that matters," interrupted Logan. "We must make it to Atalànt. Even if Adam does not pardon us for this action, anything done to us will be worth it."

Logan expected the captain to react with anger. But Lubin just stared at him for a long moment. Finally, he spoke. "You are an odd man, Logan. Why is it so important you make it to Atalànt? Is it because a Sethite prophet commands you to?"

"No, Captain," said Logan. "It is because the Head of Days commands it."

"I do not believe there is a Head of Days," admitted Lubin.

Logan smiled sadly. "Do with us as you wish, but may I show you what I have discovered and what I fear has happened?"

"Yes, you may."

Logan laid out the map and pointed out the ship's trajectory, starting from the port of Adoraim and ending about where he thought they were that afternoon.

"So," said Logan, "as you can see, we are going to pass the island by a great distance to the east and never see it, even with your spyglass."

"Your calculations are very good," said Lubin. "Perhaps I should have turned the ship around a few times to confuse you as my forefathers used to do."

"But then we would not have known we were going off course," countered Logan.

"We are only off course if your map is accurate," Lubin replied.

"I have absolutely no doubt that it is correct. But can you say the same thing of yours?"

"I received it directly from my great-grandfather," said Lubin. "It was the very one my father received from his father. From its tattered condition, I can assure you it is very old, but still readable. I am sure he would not have given me a false one."

"Have you had it in your possession the whole time since it was given to you?" asked Hemeth.

"No," said Lubin. "I left it on this ship while I was at the Firstborn Council meeting the night before we departed. But it was sealed. I would have noticed if someone had tampered with it."

"Really?" asked Logan. "Would you really have known the difference between seals if another Firstborn had created the seal?"

Lubin was still for a few moments and Logan watched the blood drain from his face. "No," he finally said. "I would not have noticed it. And my uncle was on the ship the entire time preparing for departure. He only stomped off just before we departed." Lubin looked even paler as he grabbed Logan's map and ran toward his cabin. "Both of you, follow me—now!" he shouted over his shoulder.

Logan and Hemeth ran after Lubin, drawing stares from the nearby crew. By the time they entered the captain's cabin; Lubin had already opened a locked box and was pulling out his map.

"Shut the door, Logan," Lubin called. Logan obeyed while Lubin cleared the table and laid out the two maps.

"Should we be seeing this?" asked Logan, surprised at the captain's complete change of protocol.

"It doesn't matter much now, does it?" Lubin replied without taking his eyes off the two maps. "Look at this." Lubin pointed to a smudge next to a hole in the map he had pulled out. "I thought this was odd, but I assumed the map had been damaged. This is right where Atalànt is located on your map. I am afraid you might be correct."

Clearly, Lubin's mind was racing as he pieced together how his uncle and grandfather had conspired against him. "But why?" Lubin asked himself. A moment later the look on Lubin's face showed he had figured out the answer.

"Oh no," is all he said before running out of his cabin.

# III

*"There is the sea, vast and spacious, teeming with creatures beyond number—living things both large and small. There the ships go to and fro, and Leviathan, which you formed to frolic there."*

Psalm 104:25-26 (NIV)

Running after Lubin, Logan emerged on deck to hear the captain shout to the navigator currently at the wheel, "Turn the ship starboard as fast as you can! Head due east. I will be right up to check the course."

"Aye, Captain," said the man.

Lubin then ran to the men on deck, shouting orders to adjust the sails to compensate for the new direction. Logan was pleased to see that his advice had been accepted, but was unsure why the captain was so quick to adjust their course. It took several minutes to set the ship on its new course, and once it was, the wind direction pulled the ship even quicker than before.

In the meantime, Logan and Hemeth waited for an opportunity to speak to the captain. About a half hour later, the activity subsided and Logan found Lubin and Huppim speaking quietly together in the bow of the ship, both with grim expressions.

"Captain?" Logan approached him with Hemeth behind him. "May we speak with you?"

"Yes, in just a moment," Lubin replied. To his first mate he said, "Gather the crew, Huppim. I must speak with them."

"Aye, sir," said Huppim as he went off to fetch the crew.

"Why are you so keen on changing the ship's direction so quickly?" asked Logan.

Lubin hesitated. "The voyage to Atalànt can be very rough and dangerous," he began. "At a certain point in the journey, a captain must aim his vessel directly toward Atalànt at a very specific angle. It is not easy, because there are usually great storms and rough water along this route. To be honest, from all the stories I have heard I have wondered why we have encountered so few issues on the sea. I now know why. We are not on that route. We are on one that is easier to sail, but much more dangerous."

"Why?" asked Logan.

"If your map is correct—and I now believe it is—we may have entered the waters of the Leviathan!"

"Leviathan?" asked Hemeth. "What is that?"

"It is a kind of sea monster, isn't it?" said Logan as he felt his heart rate increase.

"It is indeed," said Lubin grimly. "Very early stories told among my people say that shortly after Adam taught my forefathers to build seafaring vessels, we began to explore the deep oceans. We soon encountered these powerful sea creatures which Adam named "Leviathan." They attacked some of those early seafaring vessels. The few men who survived told tales of monsters of enormous size and hideous strength. My people quickly learned, however, that Leviathans prefer to live in very specific waters of the deep and rarely leave them. With Adam's help, we painstakingly charted where they lived so we could avoid them. It was during this time that Adam discovered Atalànt. I was told he chose to live on Atalànt because it was so difficult to reach and afforded so many natural barriers. One of those natural barriers is on the east side of the island, where we long ago charted the waters of a Leviathan."

"And that is exactly where we are going to sail?" asked Hemeth.

"I am afraid we are there already," said Lubin. "And at this point, we are so deep within the region, it only makes sense to head straight toward the island with all speed. Fortunately, the wind is with us."

Captain Lubin turned his attention to his crew, now assembled below the forecastle, with the exception of Huppim, who had taken over the responsibility of steering the ship. After taking a deep breath, Lubin explained the situation and the grave danger they found themselves in. Logan was impressed by the captain's strong sense of calm during such a difficult situation. It reminded him of Lamech, or at least how Lamech used to be.

Logan and Hemeth were impressed with the crew's reaction to the news. Watches were set on the fore and aft decks with clubs and swords. The captain also placed lookouts in the two crow's nests.

The ship moved on throughout the day at as fast a clip as the crew could muster from it. They made good time, and Logan could see that Lubin was pleased. But it was clear to Logan that the captain, with his spyglass constantly out, was keeping a very close eye on the seas all around them. He seemed particularly keen on watching waves aft of the ship.

As night approached, Lubin ordered that only a few lanterns in the bow of the ship be lit. He did not want to take a chance on attracting the attention of anything that might surface from the depths.

"You might as well sleep now," Lubin told Logan and Hemeth. "There is nothing you can do. We must sail through the night and hope your map is correct. If it is, we will make it sometime tomorrow."

"You have seen something aft of the ship, haven't you?" asked Logan.

"Good night, Logan," said Lubin. "As I said, there is nothing for you to do now." He walked away, leaving the two alone.

"I do not think we have to worry about the Leviathan attacking right now," said Hemeth after a moment.

"Why is that?" asked Logan.

"Huppim said they normally attack in the very early morning, just before sunrise."

"It is always darkest before the dawn," Logan said to himself in English.

"What is that?" inquired Hemeth.

"Oh, it is just a saying we had at home," said Logan as he walked toward the quarters he and Hemeth shared. "It just means that things are always darkest before the breaking of dawn."

That night Logan slept fitfully. He kept hearing the words of Lubin, "There is nothing you can do," repeating in his mind. After several hours of restless sleep, Logan rose from his hammock and got down on his knees to pray. His quarters were almost completely dark, except for the faint light of one small candle near the entrance to the small quarters. While he could only make out the basic outlines of the others, he could tell from their breathing they were fast asleep.

"Lord," he said, speaking quietly in English. The words sounded funny to his own ears because he rarely if ever spoke it. "For the millionth time, I don't know why I am here. At night in Pellios you know I used to wish I might wake up at home in bed. But I am no longer that little boy, and I know you must have your reasons. Please show me what they are. I do not know why I have been placed in this dangerous situation, but may we please make it through the night and safely to the Blessed Isle of Atalànt."

From behind him he heard Hemeth's voice. "How do you do that?"

Logan looked up into the darkness. He was surprised that the rhythmic breathing of the other men in the room had stopped. "Do what?" he asked.

"Glow like that," said one of the other men.

Logan looked around, and except for the candle, he could only perceive darkness.

"For the last two weeks you have hardly glowed at all," said Hemeth. "And now, tonight, you are lit like a torch. It is a strange light, though, because it casts no shadows."

Logan looked around him but still could see nothing but the outlines of the other men. It frightened him to know that others could see him because of some kind of glow he himself could never see.

Reluctantly, he answered, "I do not control whatever it is you see. I was praying to the Head of Days as I have done many times during this voyage. Only this time, something is different. I believe it has something to do with the Spirit of God Most High."

"Whatever it is," said the same voice that had spoken earlier, "would you do something about it? Even with my eyes closed I can see it!"

"Very well." Logan stood up and left the others to sleep. It was a waste of time for him to stay there.

The moon was bright and high in the sky when he stepped out on deck. Moonlight bathed the ship in a pale luminescence. The lookouts Lubin had placed on guard looked at him as he approached. As he crossed the ship, Logan decided he would head toward the hold to see if Lamech was awake. Logan had informed him of the situation earlier that night, but as usual Lamech had given no sign he heard anything Logan said. Logan missed his friend desperately. Though he was physically present, it was if someone had stolen his real friend and left a shell of a man behind. After all the two had been through together, Logan had been completely unprepared for Lamech shutting him out.

Logan took a candle, lit it by one of the two lanterns still shining on deck, and went down to see his friend. After lighting the room's lantern, he sat down by Lamech, who as always was lying on the floor. Logan was surprised to see him awake, his eyes wide open. For the first time in many days, Lamech spoke first.

"I see we are still alive."

"Uh, yes," said Logan. "Yes, we are."

"I do not think we will be for long. I have heard that the Leviathan attacks in the early morning, only after a frightening night of restless sleep. Just before sunrise its prey is most exhausted, vulnerable, and coveting dawn. It is then that it attacks."

"You make it sound as if it were human," said Logan.

"They are far cleverer than us, I suspect."

"I don't think so."

"You are very bright tonight," said Lamech. "That only happens when trouble is upon us."

"And if it is upon us," said Logan, "what will you do?"

Lamech said nothing.

At that moment, Logan made up his mind about something he had been considering. He got up and walked out of the hold. Taking the keys off a hook just outside the door, he returned and unshackled Lamech.

"Lamech," said Logan, "I know you are not well, but we need you right now."

Lamech just stared at him.

"We need you, Lamech," Logan repeated. "You stopped the Great Reptile in Pellios. You can help us fight this creature. I think you may be the only one on this ship who might have a chance of defeating it."

"No."

"Why not?"

"Why?" cried Lamech in a burst of emotion, as if something broke within and every thought came spewing out of him. "Why? Because nothing matters. It never does, it never has, and it never will. You weren't there, Logan! You don't know what Tubal-Cain did to me."

The scene for Logan was surreal. The only man who might save them from the creature that was probably stalking them outside was crumpled on his knees before him, sobbing like a child.

"I fought so hard and for so long, but if evil men like Tubal-Cain can do unspeakable things to others—to me—what is the point? The world is corrupt and evil. I came face-to-face with evil and I was not strong enough. The painful toil, the very labor of our hands, means nothing. We think we are strong, but that is an illusion. We are not. We are all weak. More than that, we are nothing. So tell me, why would I bother to fight this creature? Why not die and be at peace?"

"Lamech," said Logan, "I cannot say I know what happened to you, but I do know the dread of facing Tubal-Cain. I have spent the last thirty years trying to overcome my fear. Maybe that is why I had to go through it first; to show you that you can make it through."

"It does not matter, Logan."

"That is where you are wrong, Lamech, son of Methuselah. It does matter," whispered Logan. "I think I was sent into the world by the Head of Days himself to see to it that this world survives, and in this moment, you are far more than nothing. You are the most important man in the entire world. I have never told you this, but I know the future better than any prophet, even Enoch. A son will be born to you who will comfort us in the labor and painful toil of our hands caused by the ground the Lord has cursed."

Logan guessed that the glow around him must have grown in intensity as he paraphrased the passage from Genesis, because Lamech covered his eyes as Logan continued. "But if you don't fight now, you will never live to bring that child into the world. Help us, Lamech. You heard the prophecy by Hemeth's sister. Now—in this moment—you must fulfill part of that prophecy. The Mind and the Spirit needs the Body!"

"Get away from me!" Lamech pushed Logan away.

At that moment, a huge jolt shoved the ship to starboard, flinging Logan and Lamech across the room like rag dolls. When Logan recovered, he looked over at his friend.

"Well?" he said.

Lamech looked away. Without another word, Logan ran upstairs to the deck. Other men were emerging from their quarters and looking about in all directions. Because the moon was so bright, Logan could see clearly those around him, including Hemeth, who was running toward him.

"It's the Leviathan, isn't it?" Hemeth shouted, but Logan did not have the chance to answer. Without warning, another jolt sent everyone flying toward the port side. Though it was a close call for some, no one fell overboard. Logan heard Captain Lubin barking out orders and saw Huppim handing out clubs and sticks. Over the next several minutes, three more jolts occurred from different sides of the ship. While the fear was palpable among them, the disciplined crew did not cry out or even make a sound.

Hemeth directed Logan's gaze to a point just off the starboard bow. Logan could see a large eddy of water forming. Suddenly, up rose a large, scaly, egg-shaped head with dark eyes protruding from both sides. The creature's long, thin neck rose higher and higher until its head came almost to the height of the mast. Its massive body began to surface, and Logan could see fin-like limbs that rippled with muscle.

The creature opened its mouth to reveal double rows of razor-sharp teeth. It plunged toward the deck and let out a shrill scream that made Logan's ears ring. Men dove out of the way of the monster's head as it crashed through the floorboards of the deck, momentarily getting stuck. The men around the monster recovered quickly and began beating it with swords and clubs, but they could not pierce or even bruise its armor-like hide.

The Leviathan broke free of the deck. The men around the monster jumped back, some of them being thrown by the force of its powerful neck. Screaming, the creature recoiled and disappeared into the dark depths, unhurt and preparing to strike again.

"It won't make that mistake again," said a voice from behind Logan and Hemeth. They spun around to see Lamech standing grim-faced and determined with two bows and two quivers of arrows in his hands.

"Lamech!" said Logan.

Lamech threw him a bow and one of the quivers. "Get up to the empty crow's nest and keep the monster distracted. Shoot at its eyes. They are the only vulnerable part of its body we can get at. Those eyes are gigantic targets—even you ought to be able to hit them."

Turning to Hemeth he said, "Show me where you keep the drugs my father gave you. I will need all of them. I have some, but this is much bigger than anything we saw in Pellios. Let's get going."

Logan swung the bow and quiver onto his back and ran toward the main mast, while Lamech and Hemeth ran toward Hemeth's quarters. The rest of the crew was too busy trying to spot and react to the Leviathan to take any notice of Logan. Grabbing hold of the ratlines, Logan climbed into the predawn sky high above the ship. As he progressed to the top, another jolt shook the vessel, nearly causing him to lose his grip. After a few tense moments, he finally made it into the crow's nest. Finding it empty, he took a deep breath and prepared for his next move. He did not have long to wait. Just as he hefted his bow into position, the creature reemerged, rising from the water like a demon from hell. The monster paused before darting toward a group of men in the stern of the ship. The pause was long enough for Logan to get off two shots aimed at the creature's left eye. Both shots missed by several meters, glancing off the creature's face but succeeding in distracting it from the crew members who were its intended target. But now the Leviathan was alerted to a presence above him. Quick as lightning, it shot upward, extending itself as far as it could reach toward the masthead. In an instant, Logan had his bow up with another arrow nocked to the bowstring. Shooting off one well-aimed arrow, Logan hit the creature in its right eye as it sprang toward him. Instinctively the Leviathan reared back, screeching in agony and falling back into the sea, producing a massive wave that rocked the ship.

Grabbing the sides of the small crow's nest, Logan braced himself and barely kept from falling to the deck below. After the wave passed, Logan could hear cheering from below. Then he heard Lubin's voice over the cheer.

"Stand ready, men. This is not over yet!" Lubin shouted.

As pleased as he was with his shot, Logan agreed. From below he saw activity on the port side where Lamech and Hemeth were lighting a dozen lanterns in a semicircle. Lubin and the crew members on the starboard side noticed and began approaching them. After a word from Lamech, Hemeth ran toward Captain Lubin and began arguing with him. Logan could not hear what anyone was saying, but he guessed Hemeth was explaining that

Lamech wanted to draw the creature's attention toward himself so that he could shoot the monster in the mouth the way he had shot the dinosaur that attacked Pellios. From his gestures, it appeared that Lubin had doubts about the plan. Logan could not help sympathizing with the captain. After all, he had locked up Lamech for two weeks for trying to kill himself. And now it must look to Lubin like he was about to try again.

Logan watched as Lubin ordered two crew members to restrain Hemeth while the captain and five of his crew proceeded toward Lamech. Looking toward his friend, Logan could see Lamech staring straight at him. He was shaking his head clearly, indicating "No."

Logan knew what he had to do. Nocking another arrow to the string, he raised the bow and shot an arrow just in front of Lubin.

"Do not go any farther, Captain Lubin," Logan shouted. "Lamech knows what he is doing. We have to trust him in this!"

"Are you crazy?" Lubin shouted. "I'll kill you myself if you don't put down that weapon."

Logan responded by nocking another arrow to the bowstring. He hoped he was doing the right thing and that Lamech really was trying to save them and not trying to get himself and all the rest of them killed. Logan didn't need to make another threatening gesture, because in the next moment the monster shot out of the water with a heart-piercing scream. Its intended target was the crow's nest, but with one of its eyes blinded, it misjudged the distance and snapped its razor-like jaws several meters away from Logan. Logan's heart pounded as his mind raced to figure out what he could do to save himself. From below, he heard Lamech's loud taunts as an arrow shot up, hitting the Leviathan's face. As before, it lost interest in its original target and focused its one good eye to the deck. Catching site of the loud little man illuminated by a ring of lights, the creature darted toward him with teeth bared. From his perspective above the scene, Logan saw Lamech wait until the last second, shoot off an arrow with a very large bundle attached to it, and jump as far as he could outside the ring of light. The arrow went straight up into the monster's mouth and its head crashed once again into the boards of the deck. From the strange sounds the creature made, Logan surmised that the arrow must have lodged itself in the soft flesh of the creature's esophagus. Darting forward, Lamech raised his bow and shot an arrow directly into the left eye of the creature, completely blinding it. The Leviathan reared back, howling in pain and defeat, before disappearing into the dark depths of the sea.

This time there were no cheers, only a stunned silence as the men considered what they had witnessed. Nobody moved for a long time. Logan could not think or feel anything. Slowly, he began to notice the feeling of the wind on his cheek and the smell of the salty sea air in his nostrils. When his heart stopped pounding like a hammer inside his chest, he was not sure what to do. They had survived, but what would Lubin do to him for threatening his crew? Logan decided he would find out later unless they wanted to come up and get him, because he suddenly felt too tired to climb down the ratlines. Sitting down in the base of the crow's nest, he closed his eyes. Though exhausted, the adrenaline running through his veins prevented him from sleep. To soothe his mind, he recited out loud to himself, in English, the book of Genesis, much of which he had memorized during his decades in Pellios. By the end of the second chapter, he had drifted off to sleep. He slept soundly through the morning, and while he slept he emanated a glow so bright no one dared approach him.

**Click or scan the QR Code to learn about the sign posts in this chapter.**

# IV

*"You make known to me the path of life; you will fill me with joy in your presence, with eternal pleasures at your right hand."*
Psalm 16:11 (NIV)

LOGAN OPENED HIS EYES FROM WHAT FELT LIKE A VERY DEEP SLUMBER. Expecting to wake up in the crow's nest of *Tomorrow's Destiny*, he was surprised to find himself on land.

*Could we have made it to Atalànt already? No, that is impossible. I must still be dreaming.*

Looking around, he saw two men nearby whom he recognized immediately from previous dreams he had experienced. Those dreams always brought him new insight into the life he had left in the future. One of the men before him was his father, Joshua. The other was none other than the prophet Elijah who mysteriously appeared and had saved his father from death by pulling him from the wreckage after his plane was forced to make an emergency landing in a mountainous region.

Logan observed that night was fast approaching and his father and Elijah were not in the same camp where he had seen them in his last vision. The two men stood in a clearing at the edge of a forest, looking down on the lights of a city far in the distance. The beginnings of a beard on his father's face indicated to Logan that many days had passed since he last saw them. The two men were attempting to communicate with hand gestures. Logan tried to hear what the men were saying, but besides a few words here and there, Logan could not understand the language either man spoke. Nevertheless, he could tell from his father's tone of frustration that they were not communicating well.

"How am I to explain microorganisms and vaccines to a man born nine centuries before Christ?" Joshua suddenly said out loud to himself in English. Looking toward heaven, Joshua continued, "How can he bear witness to the people if he cannot bear to live among them? How can I explain this to him when I don't know words or where to begin?"

Logan had never thought about this problem. In the pre-Flood world there were few diseases. In fact, Logan could not recall hearing of any disease in the Ancient world. But when Elijah had been transported from the past into the modern world, his body would have had no defenses against modern diseases and would thus be susceptible to serious health issues.

From his experience with previous visions, Logan knew his father and Elijah would be unable to see or hear him. While this had always disappointed him, he found comfort in knowing his father had not died in a plane crash and was undoubtedly involved in something greater than either of them could imagine. He only wished he could tell his father how much he loved and missed him.

While Logan was lost in thought, something began to happen. A warm breeze picked up, and the air filled with a kind of energy Logan had never felt before, making the hair on the back of his neck stand on end. Elijah jumped to his feet and instinctively reached for his missing cloak. At least, that is what Logan presumed he was doing, because, not finding anything to place over his head, the old man simply covered his eyes and bowed his head low.

"What is it, Eliyahu?" Joshua said, standing up as well and looking around.

Suddenly, the wind turned violent and the flames from the campfire winked out. Logan could hear nothing but the powerful sound of the wind. To his amazement, he found it was hard to stand in one place, and his clothes fluttered fiercely against his body. Whatever was happening in this vision, he was very much a part of it.

From out of the wind Logan saw what could only be described as tongues of fire burst into existence and settle upon Joshua and Elijah. As the fire rested upon the two men, a brilliant light shone all around them. Logan could see that his father and Elijah were speaking, but with the wind so loud there was no way for him to hear what they were saying. Then, all at once, the wind ceased and everything became still.

The scene in front of Logan faded to black.

**Click or scan the QR Code to learn about the sign posts in this chapter.**

# V

*"Some went out on the sea in ships; they were merchants on the mighty waters. They saw the works of the* Lord, *his wonderful deeds in the deep. For he spoke and stirred up a tempest that lifted high the waves.... Then they cried out to the* Lord *in their trouble, and he brought them out of their distress."*

Psalm 107:23-25, 28 (NIV)

As THE SUN ROSE HIGHER INTO THE LATE-MORNING SKY, Logan awoke—for real this time—to a drum-like sound banging close by. Stiff and groggy, Logan opened his eyes to see Lamech's familiar face peering down at him. Standing on the ratlines outside the crow's nest, he was hitting the side of the small compartment with the palm of his hand. The expression on his face, though not quite normal, was far happier than Logan had seen for many days.

"Finally, you're awake!" Lamech said to him.

It took Logan another few moments to fully rouse himself.

Standing, he said, "Hello, Lamech."

"Good morning, Logan. You have been keeping us all awake the last few hours."

"What?"

"I mean you have been glowing so brightly, no one aboard could even look this direction until just now."

As his memory of the morning's events came back to him Logan asked, "The captain? Does he want to kill me for threatening his crew?"

"I don't think he was pleased about your threats, but under the circumstances, he let it slide. You have more to be concerned about from the rest of the crew for keeping them awake when all they wanted was to get some sleep the last few hours."

"I don't understand."

"Really, Logan? When you have one of those episodes, it makes no difference if our eyes are closed or open. We still see the light, and it is very hard to ignore. This time we could see it even below deck, and instead of lasting a few moments, it just kept going."

"Sorry, I guess," said Logan. "I don't exactly control it. It just seems to happen."

An awkward silence ensued. Logan remembered and felt guilty for being the one to suggest locking Lamech up. Not sure what to say, he looked down at the deck and saw some of the crew members taking care of their morning duties. Occasionally, one of them looked up at him.

"I am sorry, Lamech. For binding you, I mean."

Lamech shrugged. "I do not know what to think. Tubal-Cain's words keep repeating in my mind, telling me how weak and useless my life is. I have never been so afraid in all my life. I know now why you reacted to Tubal-Cain the way you did years ago."

Logan shivered as he remembered that day on the edge of the Tortured Mists. Thirty years before Tubal-Cain had gone to a lot of trouble to have Logan kidnapped and brought to him so he might learn more about Logan's strange and sudden appearance. It was only by the grace of God that he had escaped.

Lamech continued, "But then you told me my son would comfort us in the future. I don't know why, but I believed you. Your words are the only ones I heard and continue to hear over the mantra of Tubal-Cain."

"You hear the mantra even now?" asked Logan.

Lamech looked down, and a shadow flickered across his face. "Yes."

For a few moments there was silence between them. Finally, Lamech asked, "Who or what are you, Logan?"

Logan paused. He had always wondered why Lamech had never asked him this question.

"I don't know exactly, Lamech. I just know I am a stranger in a strange land."

"Are you a prophet like Enoch? Is this how prophets of the Most High begin?"

"I don't think I am prophet, at least not like your grandfather," said Logan. "Yet, like him, I do carry the burden of foreknowledge, like that of your future son. I don't know if I should tell you this, but I know that he will be a man who will change the world."

For a third time silence ensued, but this time it was not awkward. Instead, it was the kind of silence one feels when he is at peace with another and no words need to be spoken. A moment later, Logan spotted Hemeth climbing up the ratlines opposite those Lamech was standing on.

"Good morning, Logan," Hemeth said when he reached the crow's nest. "You and Lamech were amazing last night. You are lucky; I think the captain will probably let you live even though you threatened his crew ... because you helped save it ... in the end." Hemeth cocked his head, thinking. "That sounded better in my head."

"Hemeth," said Lamech coldly, "what is it you want?"

"Well, there was not much space down there." Hemeth pointed toward the mess of broken boards that used to form the deck. "So I came up here to get a good look at Atalànt. The ship is pretty heavily damaged, so it is good we are not so far away."

Logan, who had been facing away from the direction the

ship was sailing, turned around to see a landmass looming in the distance. He could see what looked like complex geometric structures dotting the island, set at all kinds of improbable angles. The architecture was far more intricate than any Logan had seen in either the modern or Ancient world.

Hemeth crawled into the crow's nest with Logan, took out a spyglass, and gazed into it for a long time, gasping in surprise and wonder. Lamech became impatient and crawled into the now-crowded crow's nest.

"Okay already," said Lamech. "Let me see too." He took the spyglass from Hemeth while he was still looking through it.

"It is amazing," said Hemeth. "Those structures are so large yet intricately designed. I never dreamed of seeing such beautiful art in all my life."

"It is a shame we cannot see the Created One's residence," said Lamech, lowering the spyglass from his eye and handing it to Logan. "I have heard that it has thirteen unique spires, one for each of the sons of Adam—even one for Zirci."

Logan raised the spyglass to his eye. Hemeth was right. Each structure was truly unique, though all together they seemed to have a coherent style. One building seemed to have been made out of a spider's web, while another was a massive obelisk, and still another had such an intricate pattern of lines and circles that it gave the impression it was moving. Looking toward the southwest part of the island, Logan caught sight of several spires soaring into the blue sky. Each one was unique and beautiful. Logan could not make up his mind whether the spires complemented or dominated the buildings in the foreground.

"If you mean the spires on the southwest side of the island," he said, "I can see them fine, or at least six of them at this distance."

His two friends looked at him in surprise.

"What do you mean you can see them?" asked Lamech. "No one has seen them for more than 175 years. It is believed that the Created One values his privacy, so he has created a haze over his entire residence, shielding it from view."

"I don't know about you, Lamech," said Logan, looking

again at the island. "But I can see three of them now, even without the spyglass."

Lamech and Hemeth looked toward the island and back at Logan.

"So, you're telling me you cannot see the glow that blinds the rest of us," Lamech said, "but you can see something that no man has laid eyes on for almost two centuries."

Logan shrugged. "I guess so."

From below Logan could hear the voice of Huppim calling, "Hemeth! You and the other two need to get down here! The captain needs everyone as we approach the island. We're starting to take on water and we need all hands-on-deck to keep us afloat."

"Yes, sir," Hemeth called back. Turning back to his companions he said, "You are a strange fellow, Logan. I wonder what else you will see in Atalànt when we get there. But now we had better help the rest of the crew."

Captain Lubin said nothing to Logan after he climbed down the cargo net. A stern face and a short nod were the captain's only acknowledgement of the previous night's terrible events. Spooked by Logan's bright glow while he was sleeping, the rest of the crew now did their best to ignore him. Logan did not stand around for long. He joined the crew in working feverishly to keep the ship afloat. He and Hemeth were part of a group of men hauling and throwing overboard bucketfuls of water handed up to them through the holes the Leviathan had made in the deck. Together, the men were keeping the water leaking into the hold to a minimum, but the effort was backbreaking.

As the ship drew closer to Atalànt, two small outcroppings of land came into sight. They jutted outward and created a small natural harbor. Inside the harbor low cliffs stood above a beautiful sand beach surrounded by lush, colorful trees. Captain Lubin gave a sigh of relief and spun the ship around to head straight for the outcroppings.

However, just as he gave the order something strange happened. Everyone stopped their work and cocked their heads as if listening to some faint noise. Logan felt an odd sensation of danger, and the hairs on the back of his neck stood on end.

Looking over the port side, he saw a tall figure standing atop one of the cliffs. The person was frantically waving at the ship and seemed to be motioning for them to swing southwest. Logan felt a very strong urge to turn the ship in the direction the figure was pointing. Hemeth, who was standing next to Logan, dropped his bucket. Running over to the poop deck where the captain stood, he began speaking animatedly with Lubin.

The captain listened to Hemeth and then stared at the figure for a few seconds before countering his previous command. He turned the wheel and pointed the ship in a southwesterly direction, parallel to the island. Hemeth returned to Logan's side wearing a much-relieved expression. As the two resumed their work hauling buckets Logan asked, "What just happened?"

"We just avoided catastrophe," replied Hemeth. "Didn't you feel it?"

"I felt danger and a desire to turn away.

"Yes, that was it," said Hemeth with a smile. "But there was more. We just missed a submerged coral reef protecting the east side of the island."

"How do you know that?" said Lamech, who had run over when he saw the two talking.

"She told me." Hemeth turned around and pointed to the cliff, but the figure had disappeared.

"How do you know it was a she?" asked Logan.

"I cannot explain it," said Hemeth. "It just felt like a 'she' and that she could be trusted."

"I hope you are right. We had better not have passed up our one chance to land safely," said Lamech. "We are not going to keep this ship afloat much longer. I was just down below and it is not looking good."

Hours later another harbor came into view, this one much larger than the last. Two massive walls jutted out toward the sea, forming a thirty-degree angle. Each wall was comprised of some unknown vegetation and rose twenty meters into the air. Because the tide was low, Logan could see that this sturdy hedge grew on the foundation of a huge coral reef. From the precise dimensions and angles of the two walls Logan concluded they must have been man-made.

When Lubin had first sighted the island, he had raised the signal flag as his great-grandfather had instructed him to before leaving Adoraim City. Even with the storms they had encountered, the carrier pigeon should have made it to the island with the announcement of their arrival. Even now, however, no counter flag had been raised anywhere on the island in response. Because the ship was in such bad condition, Captain Lubin had no choice but to enter the harbor without permission. He hoped the islanders, whom he was told were very skittish of outsiders, would see his ship could not possibly pose a threat. Thus, in the early afternoon of their fifteenth day at sea, Lubin guided *Tomorrow's Destiny* safely into the harbor of Atalànt.

# VI

*"Woe to those who call evil good and good evil, who put darkness for light and light for darkness, who put bitter for sweet and sweet for bitter."*

Isaiah 5:20 (NIV)

XAVIER COULD FEEL THE POWER OF THE SHADOWS swirling about him as he stood alone atop the Cainite tower high above the harbor of Atalànt. He could see lightning flashing intermittently across the black clouds that hid him from his brethren on the other side of the island. With the combined power of the Dark Ones around him he had long held great influence over the mind of the Originator, and for that he was pleased. While Xavier admired the power of these Dark Ones, he never enjoyed direct contact with them, because they filled his mind with dank, oily thoughts.

He smiled contemptuously to himself. The Dark Ones had grown restless of late; he could feel it. They would love to possess him if they had it in their power, but both he and they knew who was stronger. Important events drew near, and like it or not, these creatures would do his bidding.

Xavier spoke out to the storm around him and the beings within it. "We must prepare for the ascension of the Originator. Adam believes his days are coming to an end, and he commands that word be sent to his sons instructing them to come at once."

The dark clouds responded in Xavier's mind like many garbled, high-pitched voices speaking in unison. "Yes, my lord," the Voices said. "If you will but open the way, we shall dispatch some of our own number."

"No!" said Xavier. He would never allow any of the Dark Ones to leave Atalànt. Even if he knew how to release them, once freed they would assuredly never return. Xavier had a better idea. "The men of the world would never see you as I do. They are weak. We shall send the message with Azazel and Samyaza. As Watchers, they are easily observed by ordinary men. They visit the island often and will be pleased to serve me in this errand."

"Yes, my lord," replied the Voices.

Xavier turned his attention to the recent unexpected arrival to the island. He scowled as he watched a rowboat filled with men who had left a ship that had just entered the harbor. The ship from which they came was listing to one side, and Xavier guessed it was taking on water.

Once again, he spoke to the swirling clouds about him. "Tell me about this vessel that has entered my harbor. No shipments are due, and these travelers look like young men. Why were they not destroyed when the approached the island unbidden?"

"We do not know who they are, my lord," said the Voices. "We know only that they were not attacked because they approached from the east."

"They came from the east?" said Xavier, turning pale. "How is that possible?"

"Once again, we do not know, because you do not allow us beyond the boundaries of this side of the island."

"Does the Originator know of their arrival?" asked Xavier.

"We have tried to keep the knowledge from him, but we

fear he has sensed them, my lord. He begins to ask questions."

"Are you so incompetent? Very well, I will deal with Adam."

"Yes, my lord."

"These visitors are uninvited," said Xavier. "Callos will know what to do. He will discover why they are here and kill them."

"Yes, my lord," said the Voices.

After this exchange, Xavier expected the Dark Ones to disperse, but they did not. Instead, they remained with an unsettled rumbling permeating Xavier's mind.

"Is there more you wish to say?" asked Xavier.

"Yes, my lord."

"Well, what is it then?" Xavier said in exasperation.

"There is one among them who is different from the others."

"Different?" He looked more closely at the men coming ashore. "How so?"

"One of them bears a light," said the Voices. "He was ... He was the source of the light in the eastern sky last night."

"What? You dare to speak of my sister's absurd prophecy in my presence?"

"No, my lord." The sound of fear rippled through their shattered voices. "We only know there was a light over the eastern horizon last night, and that the light came from one of them."

"The light came from a man?"

"Yes, my lord."

"But why can I not see it today?"

"It is being ... suppressed ... for the moment, but it is there, my lord," the Voices said.

"Who is suppressing it? You?"

"No, my lord. As you know, we have no power like that."

*Or you would not submit to me*, Xavier completed their statement in his thoughts. "Then who?"

The Voices remained silent. Tension filled the air, and the frightening answer dawned on Xavier. "Could the Master be among us and I not know it?" asked Xavier. Again, the Dark Ones brooded in silence. "If the Master is here, then we are blessed," Xavier continued, trying unsuccessfully to feel confident. "And it is no matter. The prophecy of the Light in the Eastern Sky is nothing but wishful thinking arising from the broken dreams of my mad sister. You will ignore it."

"Yes, my lord," said the Voices as the brooding clouds around Xavier began to fade.

When the Dark Ones were gone, Xavier looked again at the visitors, willing himself to discern who they were. Their timing did not bode well, but if the Master had truly come, he would certainly not allow anything to disturb the next few weeks.

Xavier was shocked for a moment when one of the men in the small boat appeared to look directly at him. Xavier told himself that what he saw was just a coincidence, because such a thing was impossible on account of the barrier that hid the entire residence from mortal eyes. Still, he quickly turned away and walked down to talk with the Originator.

**Click or scan the QR Code to learn about the sign posts in this chapter.**

# VII

*"Where there is no vision, the people perish: but he that keepeth the law, happy is he."*

Proverbs 29:18 (KJV)

Hemeth felt the back-and-forth movement of the small craft as the oarsman rowed the boat toward the shore. Captain Lubin had left Huppim to supervise the evacuation of the crew and the repair of *Tomorrow's Destiny*, while he joined Lamech, Logan, and Hemeth aboard the rowboat. Two weeks ago, Hemeth would have wondered why the ship had been moored so far out in the harbor. Now he understood. The harbor quickly became too shallow for a sailing vessel to dock. This arrangement was clearly a defensive measure which forced visitors to come ashore in small boats. Lubin had decided it would be wise to take only a few people ashore at first so as not to alarm the island's inhabitants.

The depth of the harbor was not the only defensive

measure employed by the islanders. Inside the harbor large stone piers stretched out several hundred meters, and it was to one of these piers they were now heading. Behind that pier lay a small, sandy beach, which Hemeth felt sure was submerged during high tide. The beach ran directly into a sheer cliff rising high into the sky. Anyone wishing to attack the island would need to first scale the massive cliff. Though he could not see anything atop the cliff from the angle he was at, Hemeth knew the fantastic structures he, Lamech, and Logan had seen earlier stood just beyond the cliff's edge.

It appeared that boxes on pulleys were let down to haul people and supplies up to the top of the cliff. Hemeth could count ten boxes and knew they must be used mostly for supplies brought here by the merchant ships of Adoraim and Zior.

Hemeth wondered how long they might have to wait until someone either came down or hauled them up. He did not have to wonder for long. As the small boat approached the pier, a box loaded with ten men began descending quickly.

Hemeth looked at Logan and saw his friend staring intently into the mist that shrouded the other side of the island. Everything to the north and east of the harbor could be clearly seen in the bright sunlight, but everything to the south and west was shrouded in an impenetrable mist. Strangely, the mist seemed to billow out from that side of the island.

"What are you looking at, Logan?" ask Hemeth.

"There is a man in the tower closest to us. He seems very interested in our arrival, because he has not taken his eyes off us since we left the ship."

The oarsman looked nervously up into the mist and shivered slightly before making a sign that Hemeth knew was meant to ward off evil spirits.

"Keep your mind on your rowing," Lubin said to the oarsman. Turning to Logan and the others he said, "You three are a strange bunch, no doubt, but we do not need to talk of such things now. There are more important things to consider at the moment."

Hemeth looked again toward the main pier and observed

the men who were now coming down to the pier to meet them. From the expressions on their faces, he had the distinct impression they were not here to welcome them. Most of the men were young, appearing to be only a few hundred years old. Clearly, they were some of the select few of the Elder Born's descendants allowed to stay on the island to work for their progenitors. Hemeth saw that some of the men held clubs and swords. At the front of the group strode a very old man with gray hair and deep wrinkles around his eyes. He was neither a warrior nor a sailor. Unlike most of the fierce men Hemeth had encountered since leaving the artisan camp, this one seemed smaller and not at all muscular. Nevertheless, when Hemeth looked into the man's dark eyes, he knew instinctively the man should not be underestimated. From the mark on his arm, Hemeth could tell the man came from the sons of Zimmah.

When the boat docked, the group of men from the island came and stood above the craft, blocking any attempt Logan and his companions might make to disembark.

"You are not welcome here. Know that if you attempt to attack us, we have the means to destroy you and your ship," the very old man said without any attempt at introduction.

"Does my ship really look like it could do any damage to you?" asked Lubin.

"Who are you, and what do you want here?" the man said, ignoring Lubin's comment.

"I am Captain Lubin, son of Abijam, Firstborn in the Line of Adoraim, and I was contracted to transport these young men here for an audience with the Originator. The Firstborn Council has approved this journey."

"Even a captain of your tender years ought to know the Firstborn Council holds no authority here. This is Atalànt!" said the man with such an air of superiority that Hemeth thought he might be a Cainite.

"Still," said Lubin, undeterred, "they directed us here, and they indicated that you would accept us. You should have received a message by carrier pigeon. We bore the colors on our vessel as we were instructed."

"No such message has come to us. Have you no other evidence to validate your claim?" asked the man.

"No," replied Lubin. "However, we were told that if there was a problem a man named Gallios from the Line of Ono would vouch for us." Hearing this, Hemeth looked over at Lamech and Logan, who simply shrugged in return. Clearly, the name was new to them, but not to Hemeth.

"Gallios holds no sway in these matters," said the man. "So you need to turn—"

"No sway in these matters, Callos? I would beg to differ," said a voice from above them. Everyone turned to see a rather stout man with curly gray hair and dark, bushy eyebrows standing in another box that was rapidly being lowered to the harbor.

"Gallios? What are you doing on this side of the island?"

"I came for a stroll earlier today when I saw we had visitors."

"You are full of surprises, my friend," Callos said coldly.

The newcomer smiled at Callos, but his dark eyes betrayed a stern fierceness. "It is true I have a sense of humor," Gallios replied as his box reached the ground. "But I am certainly not your friend, Callos. I was told we would have visitors whom I might want to meet." Gallios marched down the pier and through the assembled group of men to stand face-to-face with Callos.

"Another vision from your crazy seer?" sneered Callos. Looking at the assembled group of men he said, "Then again, perhaps you are the mad one because you listen to such gibberish and visions of folly." The men around Callos snickered.

"Mad or not, strange things have been happening of late—rumbling around the Originator's hidden residence and ... a light in the eastern sky."

The collective gasp from those on the pier and the look of disbelief on the face of Callos were enough to make Hemeth and his companions sure Gallios had said something dreadful, though they could not imagine what it was.

"You come very close to uttering the forbidden prophecy, my cousin," said Callos.

"Not at all, Callos," said Gallios with an impish grin. "For a prophecy to be a prophecy—forbidden or otherwise—it must describe the future. I am only relating what happened this past night."

"You are a trickster, Gallios," replied Callos. "And one day it will cost you dearly."

"Perhaps. But now I am more interested in these visitors arriving from the east."

"No one said they came from the east," said Callos quickly. "It is impossible to approach the island from that direction."

"Clearly that is not the case, because I saw them from my residence."

"And you told no one of this?" said Callos. "You simply let them enter our harbor?"

"What would you have had me do, Callos?" said Gallios. "There are no defenses on the east side of the island."

"Well, you could have—"

"Lord Gallios!" Lubin had grown weary of all the chatter. "Enoch, prophet of the Most High, salutes you and says your debt will be repaid this very hour when you accept us on the island and mark this Firstborn of Seth for his meeting with the Originator!"

All eyes turned to Lubin.

Even Gallios was speechless.

"What is he referring to, Gallios?" asked Callos when he found his voice. "What debt?"

Gallios remained silent, looking as if he were making a very weighty decision and unsure what to do. His gaze fell upon Logan, whose marking had not yet been noticed by anyone. A look of determination crossed the old man's face. "I sponsor their entrance to the island. Including the one with the Zirci mark!"

"Zirci?" Callos turned to look with new eyes at the men in the boat. "This is some new trick! I will not allow you to sponsor the entrance of this diseased man to our island!" The young men around him became agitated.

"Do not tell me what I can and cannot do, Callos." Gallios said angrily. "It is my ancient right, and I will exercise it! You know there is nothing to fear of the Zirci, and there never was."

"You go too far! Zirci or not, the Originator will not meet with them," growled Callos. "And Xavier will have your head!"

Gallios stood a little straighter and replied, "I am tired of caring about what our power-hungry cousin likes or does not like." The reactions of the others in the group gave Hemeth the distinct impression that people were not allowed to utter the sorts of things Gallios was saying.

"Besides," continued Gallios, "we do not really know what Adam wants. We only know what Xavier tells us he wants. If this Firstborn or this Zirci wishes an audience with Adam, I will not stop them from trying to obtain one."

The crowd began shouting and brandishing their clubs and swords. Just as Callos seized Gallios, someone brushed past Hemeth. Before he could fully register what was happening, Lamech jumped up from the boat, grabbed Callos, and threw him back, knocking him into the men standing directly behind him. Drawing his sword, Lamech held it just below the tip of Callos's chin.

"I am Lamech, son of Methuselah, Firstborn among the Sethites," Lamech said with a chilling calmness. "We have traveled many days and endured many hardships to seek an audience with our father, Adam. Since we have now been sponsored as your rules seem to require, do you have any further objection?"

Callos, whose eyes showed nothing but shock, opened his mouth to protest, but when he did the tip of Lamech's razor-sharp sword pricked the man's skin. A drop of blood fell upon his chest. Callos stopped and instead shook his head.

"I think that it is settled, then," said Gallios, looking down at his adversary. He continued, more to himself, "Who would have thought we would have seen a Zirci and a Sethite Firstborn with the Gift of Combat?"

Lamech brushed past the group and headed toward the boxes that would lift them atop the cliff. Hemeth and the others quickly exited the boat and followed him, with Gallios bringing up the rear. The islanders parted to make way for the travelers, but stared hard at Logan and his mark.

After being helped to his feet, Callos yelled to Lamech, who was entering one of the elevating boxes. "It seems your people are once again choosing to defend the diseased Zirci. I would be careful if I were you, young Sethite. This will not go unchallenged, and your line has not been welcome here for many years. Sponsored or not, that does not change for you."

Lamech glared at Callos but remained silent.

When Gallios had entered the box, he closed the gate and pulled a long rope. From far above Hemeth could hear the faint sound of a ringing bell. A moment later the box began to rise off the ground as they were pulled up the cliff face. As they rose higher, Captain Lubin took the opportunity to briefly introduce Logan and Hemeth, but did not bother introducing the oarsman from his ship, who stood quietly in the back. Hemeth was not used to being introduced to anyone. He had never been important enough to be noticed. So he was not surprised that after greeting Hemeth with standard courtesy due to their familial relations, Gallios ignored him and addressed only the Firstborns in the group.

It appeared to Hemeth that although the old man was very interested in Logan, he was not altogether comfortable being near him. Hemeth saw Gallios glance at Logan's mark. For an instant, a look of surprise came to the old man's face, as if he recognized something in it, but then it was gone.

When the group was halfway up the cliff and out of earshot of the others, Lubin asked, "Did you come down by yourself, Lord Gallios?"

"Yes."

"How did you know you would be allowed to sponsor us? After all, the men seemed rather hostile to you as well as us."

Gallios smiled. "I am sure you are a fine captain, particularly if you approached Atalànt from the east and lived to tell about it, but you could use some work on strategy."

Lamech slapped Lubin on the back and pointed to the top of the cliff, where several young men stood with bows and arrows covering them should anyone wish to cause trouble. "He did not come by himself," Lamech said with an admiring smile.

"No," said Gallios. "I thought it would be wise to take precautions by bringing several of my younger descendants with me when I came. Sometimes Callos can be a bit hardheaded."

"I thought only the Elder Born lived on Atalànt," said Lamech. "How is it that your younger descendants live here with you?"

"Many of us need them to help us. This island and its inhabitants are very productive, and only the highest-quality goods are produced here. Silk, perfume, spices, artwork, and so much more are shipped to the Highborn families in all the different lines of Adam. Most of the island's population lives in the city of Tipharah, just up from the harbor. It is a magnificent city, which you will see when we reach the top. I am sure you saw some of the architecture as you approached the island. Artisans of all types live there, constantly creating innovations. Those of us who live outside Tipharah have large estates where we grow the best produce and flora. Besides fruit, I sell the most exquisite perfumes to all the best families. Like others, I choose some of my descendants to help me maintain the grounds and do the work. It is quite a privilege among the Highborn Ono to be chosen to work for me."

"Could Hemeth here ever be among your descendants to join you here?" asked Logan, forgetting he had no right to ask the question. Lamech and Lubin stared at him in surprise. Because he was not a Firstborn, Logan was not supposed to address an Elder Born without being granted permission first. Realizing his mistake, Logan quickly looked down and said, "Sorry, sir."

Gallios smiled politely. "It is no problem, my young friend. I suppose wherever you grew up, it was not around a civilized society. I would like to hear more of your history, so you may address me and speak freely if you wish."

"Thank you, sir," said Logan, looking up.

"But as for your question, Logan," Gallios said without a glance at Hemeth, "it is true your Ono servant is of my same line, and he is welcome here as Lamech's attendant, but his mark indicates he is the progeny of my youngest brother. Thus, he is not directly my offspring and far too low in my line's society to be allowed such a privilege. It is miraculous that someone of his stature is even able to set foot on Atalànt. He will be content with that."

Hemeth, who wished he was not the subject of this conversation, had been used to such treatment his whole life and was not surprised by his kinsman's attitude toward him. Logan, however, looked like he was about to respond until stern looks from Lamech and Lubin stopped him.

The elevating box cleared the top of the cliff, bringing into full view the city of Tipharah. What Hemeth saw took his breath away.

# VIII

*"Perhaps I will stay with you for a while, or even spend the winter, so that you can help me on my journey, wherever I go."*
1 Corinthians 16:6 (NIV)

At the crest of a gently sloping hill Hemeth saw dozens of structures of intricate design. Some towered high with sharp angles while others were lower to the ground with graceful curves. Frescos and sculptures lined every part of the building in front of him. From just the portion Hemeth could see, the artwork was different from structure to structure, yet it all flowed together from one building to the next.

"The city itself is like a piece of art," Hemeth whispered to Logan, unable to contain himself. "Never in my life have I seen such beauty. I could stand here and look for days at this view."

"I agree," Logan whispered.

A small crowd of curious onlookers stared at the travelers.

After Gallios greeted his young descendants waiting for him at the top, he turned to Lubin.

"The rest of the islanders will be hospitable to your crew, Captain Lubin. The Adoraim are welcome on Atalànt, and your crew may stay in those barracks there." Gallios pointed to a small structure not far from the edge of the cliff. "The crews of trading vessels are allowed to stay there when they arrive, and as you can see from our harbor below no others are presently here."

"Thank you, Lord Gallios. My oarsman and I will make preparations for the crew to come ashore," said Lubin. Turning to Lamech, he said, "I trust you are well here, Lamech?"

"Yes, Captain Lubin. You have nothing to fear from me."

"Very well. If you need anything, you know where to find me."

"That I do, Captain. Thank you for bringing us here safely."

"Yes, well, now I have to see to repairing my ship."

"We have the best engineers and shipwrights here on Atalànt, Captain Lubin," said Gallios. "I will send my head steward back to introduce you to some of them and to help you negotiate what you need to repair your ship."

"Thank you, sir."

Just then the elevating box carrying Callos and the others made it to the top of the cliff. Gallios made a motion to the men he had brought with him from his residence. "Now I must take Lamech and the others to my residence on the east side of the island. I have more allies there, and I do not wish to have another confrontation here."

Gallios instructed his young descendants to fan out around the group and keep a watchful eye out for any possible trouble. To Hemeth's disappointment they did not head in the direction of the beautiful structures of Tipharah. Instead, they took a path away from the main plaza of Tipharah and headed toward the interior of the island.

After they walked a short distance Hemeth could see the swirling mists that covered the western part of the island. A bridge extended out and disappeared into the mist. Lamech asked Gallios about it.

"That?" said Gallios. "Why that is the path leading directly to Adam's residence. That side of the island used to be beautiful with luscious gardens and lovely fountains. Now it is probably all overgrown."

"I guess you don't go over there much?"

"Me?" said Gallios. "No. It has been more than a century since I have even considered it. Adam has made it clear he wants his privacy; we are not welcome there. Only Xavier, who is eldest on the island, is allowed there. In fact, he spends most of his time in the western portion of the island, although he makes his wishes known through Callos, whom you have already met."

"I would bet those spires behind the first one were all magnificent years ago," Logan commented. "I do particularly like the green one next to Adam's residence."

Gallios stopped abruptly and turned around to face Logan. Lamech also turned and gave his friend an exasperated look as if to say, "Did you have to say that?"

"You can see the spires?" asked Gallios.

"Uh, yes, sir," replied Logan timidly.

"What color is the building nearest us ... the one that has a portico with seven pillars?"

Logan took a moment to look over toward the swirling mists. "It looks a pale brown to me, sir."

Gallios made the same hand motion to ward off evil spirits that the sailors had made around Logan. He turned around and increased his pace.

"You have a strange companion with you, Lamech. Promise or not to your grandfather Enoch, I hope I did not make a mistake sponsoring you on the island."

"I understand, sir," said Lamech, shooting Logan another sharp look. "Logan is unusual, but you have made the right decision to honor your pledge to my grandfather. You will see."

"I hope so," replied Gallios. "But I did not sponsor you solely based on my promise to Enoch. I recognize Logan's mark as well. He is a descendant of Kedar, whom I knew many years ago. He was a good man and deserved better than what he got from the Cainites." Hearing this, Hemeth looked at Logan to see his reaction, but saw none. However, he noticed for the first time something different about Logan, something he could not quite place his finger on.

The group continued walking in silence. A short time later, Hemeth noticed Lamech taking particular interest in one stretch of their journey. He supposed Lamech found it as beautiful as he did. Two large hills rose up on either side of the trail, each with trees and vegetation bursting forth, displaying flowers of all imaginable colors. The valley in which they walked contained rock formations of various sizes, colors, and shapes. Hemeth could not imagine living in a place with such natural and man-made beauty. Past the valley, the group entered a plain that gently rose toward the east. A soft breeze blew at their back, and Hemeth felt more content than he had ever been in his entire life. As they walked through the plain, Gallios relaxed and resumed talking.

"It is highly unusual for a ship to make it so far as you did in your voyage," he said. "Normally, if there is an unscheduled ship coming a carrier pigeon is sent from the mainland prior to its arrival to alert us and tell us what color flag it will fly. No communications have been received from the mainland, so your flag meant nothing to us. You are fortunate we did not attack when you approached the island. We may not be fighters like you, Lamech, but our defenses are formidable."

"What defenses would those be?" asked Lamech.

"Nothing you need to concern yourself about now," Gallios remarked with a sly smile.

"We were assured our ship would be welcomed. It seems we were not expected to make it this far," said Lamech. "But if no message arrived, why weren't we stopped from entering the harbor?"

"No one expects a ship to approach from the east," said Gallios. "Even if someone did make it through those waters as you did, they would be dashed upon the hidden reefs that protect the eastern side of the island."

"You were right, Hemeth." Lamech turned to his friend, who was walking with Logan several steps behind. At the mention of his young relative, Gallios turned as well and eyed Hemeth.

## Chapter VIII

"What do you mean?" asked Gallios.

"Someone on the island stood on the eastern cliffs and warned us not to try and harbor there even though it looked like a perfect place to land," said Lamech. "The person used a mental technique reminiscent of my grandfather Enoch. The person who warned us must possess a powerful Gift, because we were still more than three thousand cubits off the coast, but everyone on board felt the same thing—that we were in grave danger. Hemeth here was the only one who understood the message clearly. He convinced the captain to change course."

"You, my son, presumed to tell an Adoraim captain what to do?" asked Gallios with unmistakable disdain in his voice.

"Yes, Lord Gallios," said Hemeth, looking down. "It was ... necessary."

"What has become of our world when a Lowborn is allowed such privilege?" Gallios asked.

"Was it not good that he intervened, Lord Gallios?" said Lamech in Hemeth's defense. "Otherwise, we all would have been lost."

"That is a point in his favor, I suppose," said Gallios. Changing the subject, he continued, "Most of the original inhabitants of Atalànt are second- or third-born children to Adam's original children, so we certainly have many people here who can project their feelings to others. Yet, I know of no one who can project their thoughts that far and to so many people—well, besides Xavier and the Created One. I doubt either of them was on the shore early this morning."

"You told Lord Callos that someone told you about our ship," said Lamech. "It would make sense that he is the same person who warned us."

A strange look crossed Gallios's face. "The person who asked me to come to the dock was not a man. It was a woman named Janice. Callos ridiculed me because most people on Atalànt feel she is quite mad. However, I knew her years ago when she was sane. She looked after me when I was young. We remained close until the death of our ... our Mother." Gallios grew silent and made another gesture to ward off evil. Hemeth had seen older members of his own line become reluctant to speak about Mother Eve, but he never understood the source of their reluctance. Most of his elders had never even met her, yet they always acted the same way. On those rare occasions when she was mentioned, it was only briefly and in hushed tones. Then, like Gallios, they would make the sign across their chest to ward off evil spirits.

"Janice was the handmaiden to Eve and cared for her during her last days. The death of our Mother deeply affected all of us, but none more than Janice. I do not know how it could have been she who warned you. She certainly would have had the opportunity, because she lives on the east side of the island near my estate; but her Gift—while quite useful—is purely physical, not mental."

"What can she do?" asked Lamech.

Gallios chuckled. "It is her nose that makes her special. I believe there is no son or daughter of Adam who can smell as many different fragrances as she."

"On the mainland women are not taught to use their Gifts, if they have them," said Lamech.

"There are many differences here on Atalànt," said Gallios. "We are all much older here, and because we are Second- and Thirdborns, the Gifts are much more prevalent. Unlike the Firstborns who rule the mainland, we dedicate ourselves to learning of all kinds. To that end, Janice's Gift has been profoundly useful. It is the reason why people here put up with her insane behavior." Gallios pointed to the rich variety of flowers all around them, which dwarfed the number of flowers on the mainland.

"There is no way to count the types of perfume that have been created because of her Gift. We trade them with all the sons of Adam, but particularly with the Cainites. Despite her madness, she is an amazing woman."

Hemeth felt as if Gallios must really have cared for Janice in the past. Gallios continued, "But Janice acts so strangely, and her hallucinations have been increasing the last few decades. This morning she was worse than I have seen her in ages. She came to my residence and insisted I come to the harbor immediately and would not take no for an answer. But she would not tell me why

I had to come. It was only because of my compassion for her and my love for who she was that I agreed. Well, I suppose I also came because of the light in the eastern sky last night."

Lamech stopped walking.

"What is it, Lamech?" asked Gallios.

"That is the second time you have mentioned a light. I think it was us that you saw last night. You must have seen Logan's glow over the horizon."

"Logan?"

"Yes. The light came from him. He does that from time to time."

"Is this true?" Gallios asked Logan.

"Yes," replied Logan quietly. "I believe it was me."

"Why are you not glowing now?" Gallios asked.

That is when Hemeth realized what was different about Logan: his glow was gone. Since the time Hemeth had seen him come over the ridge by the artisan camp, he had been aware of the odd brightness that hung about his friend. Most of the time it was barely noticeable, but occasionally, like the night before or when the hyenas attacked, the aura became brilliant. But it was always there. Now, however, it had disappeared.

"He is right, Logan," said Hemeth. "I have never seen you without that glow. What happened?"

"I have no idea," replied Logan. "You know I cannot see what you are talking about, so how am I supposed to know why it is not there?"

"We must talk further about you, my young Zirci. We will hear more about this when we arrive at my estate," said Gallios. "And we are almost there."

The group walked up a slight incline and came to a ridge overlooking another broad plain. To the left was the sheer cliff overlooking the sea where the figure had stood. Down from the cliff stood a beautiful building that was clearly Gallios's estate. A large courtyard in front of it held trees bearing dozens of types of fruit. What shocked Hemeth, however, was not the beauty of the estate, but the churios sculpture that towered over the middle of the courtyard. It was at least a hundred times larger than the pieces he had been taught to make. It reminded him of the mental maze he had created to trap Tubal-Cain, only this maze was in the physical world.

"Oh my! That is amazing, Lord Gallios," Hemeth said without thinking.

"Hmm?" said Gallios, who was deep in thought. Hemeth looked to Lamech for permission to speak. Lamech smiled and nodded back.

"Yes, sir," said Hemeth. "I was taught to make replicas of your original churios designs, or at least something similar to it. They were intricate pieces of art we made for the Cainites. I never dreamt anyone had ever made a life-size version of them."

"Where do you think the idea for that artwork came from? Certainly not from the Cainites!" scoffed Gallios. "Ha! They know only cunning, intrigue, and fighting. But they have an eye for art, I will give them that. No original art comes out of their minds. I was the first to conceive of the design back when I lived on the mainland. The sons of Cain fell in love with my work and begged me to teach them. Finally I agreed, and their people spent years coming to my studio to learn. Still, I never felt they quite got it quite right."

"They taught me, sir," said Hemeth. "I mastered the technique."

"Really? That seems unlikely. It would take decades to master, and you are far too young for that."

"The Cainite artisan masters believed that as well," said Hemeth.

"I see. Now they teach Lowborn boys my art. Really, what is the world coming to?" Without waiting for an answer, he turned around and motioned for the others to follow him.

"Building my estate was my first achievement here on the Island," said Gallios as he led them into the courtyard. "But it certainly was not my last." Several people were tending the trees and picking fruit as they entered the courtyard. Hemeth could hear the faint sound of someone singing.

"Grandfather!" an older man said as he came running up to Gallios. He stopped and pointed back toward a large tree near the entrance to what Logan figured was Gallios's residence. "We came out to pick the fruit this morning after you left, and *she* was here. Somehow she got up in the tree and refuses to come down. She has been sitting there singing that strange tune over and over. We do not know what to do."

Gallios gave a sad smile. "Don't worry. Tell your sons to continue their work." He looked at Lamech and said, "Let me introduce you to Janice." As he peered in the direction of the tree, Hemeth could see an extremely old woman sitting in the lower branches of a fruit-bearing tree. She had beautiful dark eyes and a round, dirty face. Her long gray hair, which Hemeth felt sure had once been jet black, fell down the length of her back. She wore a simple brown frock that was so long Hemeth wondered how in the world she ever got into the tree without getting it caught on the branches. She was gazing up at the sky, ignoring everyone, and singing to herself as if no one were around.

As they approached, Hemeth heard the song more clearly. Looking over at Logan he saw a strange look on his friend's face. "What is it, Logan?"

"That song," said Logan. "It somehow sounds familiar." Hemeth felt sure it was nothing he had ever heard before.

"Janice, my dear, what are you doing in my tree?" said Gallios in a tone that held only sadness. "Please come down. I will get you something to eat, okay?"

Janice stopped singing and looked down at him. A look of recognition came to her eyes, but then they glazed over and she gave him a toothy smile. "I like trees," she said in a faraway voice. "They change our destiny ... from one hung the knowledge of good and evil ... from another will hang the Bread of Life!" She began to sing again, and this time they could hear the words, which sounded a lot like the strange speech Logan and Enoch used.

"*Zacchaeus was a wee little man,*
*And a wee little man was he.*
*He climbed up in a sycamore tree,*
*For the Lord he wanted to see ...*"

Janice paused with an unsure look upon her face.

"*Zacchaeus was a wee little man,*

*And a wee little man was he.
He climbed up in a sycamore tree,
For the Lord he wanted to see ..."*

Before she repeated the lyrics again, Logan spoke up and sang what sounded like the next verse of the song for her.

*"And as the Savior came that way,
He looked up in the tree,
And he said, "Zacchaeus, you come down from there,"
For I'm going to your house today.
For I'm going to your house today."*

Everyone stared at Logan.

"Why do you taunt her?" asked Gallios. "She is just babbling noises."

"No, Lord Gallios," said Logan. "No, she is not. She is singing a children's song, but I cannot imagine how she knows it."

The old woman stopped looking up toward the sky and began staring intently at Logan. A hint of a smile crossed her face and she angled her head toward him, the way an animal does when it is trying to catch the scent of something. Her eyes seemed to gain a new light, and an expression that could only be described as joy came to her face.

"My dear Lois still lives! And she delivered you to me. That girl is blessed!"

Hemeth saw Logan's and Lamech's eyes meet when they heard these words. Hemeth figured whoever this Lois was, she must be someone of great importance to the Zirci.

"Now what is she on about?" asked Gallios. Before anyone could answer, Janice began speaking again as her eyes glazed over in confusion.

"But there is something wrong," she said. "What has happened to you?" As Janice spoke she shifted her weight and let go of a branch she was holding in her right hand, causing her to lose her balance and begin falling.

Hemeth, who was closest to the tree, reached out and stopped Janice's fall. Immediately, everything around him went out of focus. The thoughts and emotions of everyone around him splashed around his mind—Logan's fear that the Zirci's existence might be discovered; Lamech's depression still licking at the edges of his mind; and Gallios's deep compassion for Janice mixed with a childlike curiosity about what was happening around him.

Suddenly, a voice spoke to him. "Hemeth, son of Haal, Lowborn of the Ono, you have a worthy mind. You may speak with me later."

Hemeth returned to his senses and the world snapped back into focus. He let go of Janice and almost fell himself. Lamech moved over and helped the old woman out of the tree. When both her feet were firmly planted on the ground Janice's attention turned to Hemeth. The two looked at each other for long moment.

"What is it, boy?" asked Gallios.

Startled, Hemeth looked away and suddenly became pale. "I don't know exactly. She is a very unusual woman."

"This one has a strong mind," Janice said to no one in particular. "I wonder what part he has to play in all this. But there is something still not right here." Turning abruptly to face Logan, she fixed a frightening gaze on him. "Where is your glow?" she demanded.

"Come, my dear," said Gallios, taking her hand. "Let us find you something to eat."

"No, I am not hungry!" She impatiently pulled her hand away and said to Logan, "I must know. Why do you not glow?"

"How do you know about that?" said Logan.

Janice placed her hand on his cheek. For a moment, Hemeth saw in the old woman's eyes a profound intelligence, sane and strong.

"Beloved, your arrival was promised to me ever so long ago," she said. "And your glow ... Oh! I *can* see it. But it is so faint, as if it has been hidden. How can that be?" A look of sheer terror shot across her face. "Of course! It is the Bright Dark One," she gasped, looking around wildly. "He ... he must be here. He is intervening!"

Her agitation grew and her hands began flying in all directions. She started to fall, as her legs seemed no longer able to bear her weight. Logan caught her as she fainted.

"What happened to her?" asked Lamech, who looked

thoroughly confused.

"I have no idea," replied Gallios. "But let us quickly bring her into my residence." Together, Lamech and some of the men who had been picking fruit carried her through the main entrance and into the first room they came to. It was a large room with a high, vaulted ceiling and a fireplace. Stained-glass windows flanked either side of the room. Brilliant light filtered in through the windows in a radiance of rainbow colors. The furniture was made with solid wood and fine silk. Paintings and sculptures graced every nook and cranny.

"Lay her down here." Gallios pointed to a kind of padded bench. Once Janice was safe, all the men quietly left the room. Gallios directed Lamech, Logan, and Hemeth to another room down the hall.

"I am sorry you had to see that," said Gallios.

"Will she be all right?" asked Hemeth, still shaken from his experience and forgetting he should not speak to an Elder Born without first being spoken to.

Gallios looked at him with irritation and spoke to Lamech. "She is clearly not well. I will have my sons see to her comfort. In the meantime, I will show you where you will sleep. Then we will talk."

The elaborate ranch-style home had a mazelike feel to it. Gallios led them through a set of winding passageways past many doors until they came to a large room near the back of the house. There Logan saw a dozen or so bedrolls on the floor. About half looked as if they were being used, as there were blankets piled on top of them.

"This is where my grandsons and great-grandsons stay when they are called to work in my orchard," Gallios said. "Since it is not yet harvest season, there are fewer of them here at present. You may find a place to sleep among them."

"Thank you, Lord Gallios," said Lamech. "We appreciate your hospitality."

"I made a promise to your grandfather a long time ago," said Gallios. "It is time I fulfilled that promise."

"Lord Gallios," Lamech said, "why are there no sons of

## Chapter VIII

Seth on Atalànt?"

"I suspect your grandfather would be able to answer that better than I, young Lamech," replied Gallios. "So I will let him tell you why. But for now, drop your things here. You and I will talk and I would also like to speak with your Zirci companion, if I might."

"Certainly." Lamech nodded to Logan. Turning to Hemeth he said, "Will you be okay here for a while?"

"Yes," he replied.

"Very well," said Gallios. "Let's get going."

# IX

*"At that time Jesus, full of joy through the Holy Spirit, said, 'I praise you, Father, L*ORD* of heaven and earth, because you have hidden these things from the wise and learned, and revealed them to little children. Yes, Father, for this is what you were pleased to do.'"*

Luke 10:21 (NIV)

ONCE ALONE, HEMETH TOOK A FEW MOMENTS to place his meager belongings in order and then proceeded to retrace his steps to the room where they had left Janice. Hoping she had awoken, he was disappointed to find her still unconscious. Although it was highly inappropriate for a male to be alone with a woman, not to mention someone of his low rank, Hemeth was intrigued by what had happened in the courtyard and decided to remain with her until she awoke. While he waited, he looked at the intricate works of art that adorned the room. In one corner, he found a churios that was far beyond anything he had ever made. The ridges and shafts that made up the mazelike piece were paper thin and supremely intricate. He spent a long time just gazing at it, memorizing every curve and line. Once finished, he sat down on the floor on the other side of the room and waited for Janice to regain consciousness.

He considered what had happened when he touched Janice to prevent her from falling. A thought came to him. *Would it happen again if I took her hand now?*

At home he would be whipped for even accidentally touching a Firstborn. How much more would he be punished for intentionally touching an Elder Born? Yet, she had told him she wished to speak with him. Perhaps that was only his imagination. With the exception of Enoch, he had never intentionally connected with someone's mind; it had always been accidental. He did not know whether he could replicate what had happened.

Hemeth walked over to look at the unconscious woman. Her left harm was hanging limply from the side of the bench. She was the oldest person he had ever met in his life. She must have been from one of the first generations to live on the earth. He sat down on the floor facing her, took a deep breath, kept his eyes on the old woman, and took hold of her hand.

Nothing happened.

He waited a few more seconds, but still nothing happened. Feeling rather silly about what he was doing, he let go of her hand. He was about to give up when he figured he had better give it one more try. So, plucking up his courage again, he took hold of Janice's hand. This time he closed his eyes and cleared his mind. *Please, let me speak with you.*

Thinking he was just being foolish again, he opened his eyes and received a shock. He found he was no longer sitting in a drawing room in Gallios's house but instead was seated in a grassy field near the elevating box he and the others had used to reach the top of the cliff when they arrived on Atalànt. He was near the bridge he had seen earlier, the one connecting the Elder Born side of the island with Adam's side. Only now, no mist was covering Adam's residence, and he could see several massive spires stabbing the sky. However, the bridge dead-ended into a wall at least forty cubits high.

Hemeth noticed a woman about fifty years older than himself standing on scaffolding about halfway up the wall. He could not see her face because her back was to him. She seemed to be working on the wall, repairing it in some fashion. However, as hard as he looked he could not see how she was doing it. As he continued to watch, he saw small holes opening up all around the wall. Whenever he blinked, more holes appeared near the woman. She seemed to fix them as soon as they appeared. He was about to speak when he heard the woman say something.

"What took you so long?" she asked bluntly without turning around, keeping her focus on repairing the holes. Hemeth, who was still seated, rose to his feet and looked around to see if there was anyone else to whom she could be speaking. He saw no one.

"Are you talking to me?" he asked.

"Of course I am talking to you," she said in an exasperated tone. "Do you see anyone else here?" Despite himself, Hemeth began to look around again.

"Don't bother looking around. There is no one there." She still had her back to him.

"How did you know ...?"

"It is my mind you're in," she said. "I am not blind."

"Yes," he said, "but you are not looking at me."

"Really, Hemeth," she said, continuing her work. "You seem to have a worthy mind yourself, but you are pitifully ignorant as to how it works."

Hemeth finally remembered what he was doing and where he was, or at least where he was supposed to be. "Are you Janice?" he said, more to himself than to her.

"In the flesh." She laughed at her own joke. "Well, not really in the flesh."

"But you look so ... young," said Hemeth before he could stop himself.

For the first time the woman stopped what she was doing. Janice turned to face him, and Hemeth could see that she was indeed young and exceedingly beautiful. He also noticed that the holes in the wall behind her began to multiply while she was not paying attention to them.

"I suppose it has been a long time, has it not?" said Janice in a voice that seemed to Hemeth both ancient and sad. "One tends to lose track of time in here—sometimes on purpose. I suppose I had better not ask how old I really am. I think it would just depress me."

"You don't know how old you are?"

"I have been at this for some time now. Night and day, I protect this island—and the whole world—from what lies on the other side of the island," she said. "My grandmother, Eve, taught me how to use my mind. I believe she foresaw how my gift might be needed in the future. Since her death, I have kept the Dark Ones contained on the other side of the island while I wait for the prophecy to be fulfilled."

"I have heard mention of a prophecy several times since we arrived, but what is it exactly?"

"The only prophecy that matters to me. Grandmother Eve told me I must protect this island until the light in the eastern sky brings forth one who will bring an end to Adam's torment. When that time comes, mercy will be mixed with justice. So, I have protected this island since the death of Eve."

"You are telling me you have been doing this for more than three hundred years, night and day?"

Janice's eyebrows shot up. "Has it really been that long? I expect it has. I was so young when I began learning from Eve, but now I suppose I have grown old and ugly."

As she spoke, the holes in the wall began to increase in both size and quantity. Hemeth saw gleaming eyes appear through the breaks in the walls. One of the holes had become so large it looked as if the face of a hideous creature could poke its way through.

Seeing the terror in his eyes, Janice spun around, elbowed the creature in the face, and began repairing the wall as quickly as she could. "This is why I never let anyone in," she yelled as she feverishly worked on the wall. "Three hundred years I have kept this place safe, and with the entrance of one young boy everything goes to pieces."

## Chapter IX

"I am sorry," said Hemeth.

"Don't be sorry." Her hands moved so quickly Hemeth could only see a blur. "Do something to help."

"What do you want me to do?"

"What do you see next to you?"

Hemeth looked around and saw construction supplies had appeared to his left. "I see a bunch of mortar and bricks."

"Good. Take them and begin working on the wall below me. I will never be able to get down there in time to fix those holes."

"Yes, ma'am."

"And do not talk to me again until after you have every hole patched. Do you understand?"

"Yes, ma'am."

Hemeth set to work, hardly knowing where to begin. As he moved the construction supplies over to the wall, he found the first few bricks so heavy it took all of his effort to even pick them up. Perspiration streamed down his face and chest until he was soaked in sweat, but he did not quit. Whatever was on the other side of that wall, Hemeth wanted it to stay there. Although he had never worked with bricks and mortar, Hemeth found he had the skill to do the job.

At first, he was not convinced he could work fast enough to repair all the holes that were appearing around him, yet he kept working. Finding new ways to improve his movements with each repetition of the process, he began to work faster and more efficiently. As he carried more of the bricks to the wall, he found the effort, though still hard, had become manageable. He worked as if in a fever, blocking one hole after another. He forgot about Janice and why he had come to search for her in the first place. All his concentration centered on the task at hand. His mind began to see a pattern to how the holes were appearing in the wall. Calculating, he shifted his work to match and overtake the pattern. Soon, he was able to anticipate the holes and correct them as soon as they appeared. He moved with such speed he completely lost track of time. Finally, after what seemed like only an hour, he heard someone behind him speak.

"Stop now, Hemeth."

"No, there is just one more hole to fill," he replied.

"You must stop now!" said the voice sharply. "If you do not, you may never stop, and your talents are need elsewhere."

Hemeth recognized the voice from some corner of his mind and knew it spoke the truth. With the greatest effort he had ever made, he forced his hands to cease their motion. The wall in front of him disappeared, as did the field he was standing on. He found himself back in the room where he had encountered Janice. However, the bench in front of him was empty. Turning around, he found Janice behind him, looking the age she was in the physical world.

"You have redeemed yourself, Hemeth." Her hard features broke into a smile.

"Did we stop the attack from those ... those creatures?" he asked.

"We slowed them down, which is the best we can do."

"What about the wall?"

"Yes, that is how you pictured it, isn't it? A wall keeping the Dark Ones out?"

"Yes. Isn't that what it is?"

"It is certainly a barrier. I have often pictured it that way too, but it is not a wall made of brick and mortar. No, it is a mental projection I have in place surrounding that portion of the island. In recent days the pictures have faded, and I find myself fighting to protect my people here. When you landed, the attacks increased in intensity so much that I could barely stand. I am grateful for your assistance."

"Don't you need to be defending it now?" he asked.

"Part of me *is* defending it, even now. But the attacks have receded significantly. I do not know why, but I am grateful for the break because there is much to discuss and very little time."

"What were those creatures on the other side?"

"They are dark, hideous spirits attracted to the misery and grief of my grandfather, Adam."

"Adam? I don't understand. What does he have to do with them?"

"Centuries ago, before the birth of his last-born son, Zirci, the Created One and our Mother Eve spent much of their time on these islands to allow the Firstborns to spread out and rule the world. My twin brother and I were chosen to serve them. When our Mother Eve died, Adam blamed himself and was filled with regret. A small number of Dark Ones were attracted by his pain and began to hover about him like moths around a flame. I have no idea where they came from. Not everyone, even on this island, could see them. But I could. It was a chilling sight, even though there were only a few in those days and they stayed close to Adam.

"It turned out their arrival was a dark omen of things to come. I know now from the scent I picked up from your Zirci friend that Lois, the dear girl I once knew, still lives, and for that fact I am grateful. But at the time Zirci and his descendants were driven into the Tortured Mists, we all believed they were completely destroyed. That is when something inside Adam just ... broke. Floodgates seemed to burst all around us here on Atalànt as Dark Ones poured in around my grandfather, drawn by his despair. My brother insisted he should remain with Adam to console him, but really he was taking the opportunity to exert more and more influence over him. Worse yet, my brother learned to control the Dark Ones and make them do his bidding."

"Do Adam and your brother know what you are doing?"

"I would think Xavier has some idea. He knows he was always my inferior when it came to our Gift."

"Really? If he has so much influence on the island, why doesn't he have you killed?"

"I suppose he could have, but as I said, he has probably guessed that I am the reason why the Dark Ones are trapped on this island. Where would he be if they left? I think there are a few Elder Born on Atalànt who surmise the truth about me, but they keep it to themselves. No, if he were to make a move against me, he might have to admit to a bigger reason for his action, and it would never do to let everyone know that I have kept his demons at bay for centuries. His ego could not allow that to happen. Instead, he wishes to beat me by sheer force, but he was never fully trained as I was."

"By Eve?"

"Yes. I was her handmaiden and her most trusted helper throughout many of her pregnancies. My father believed my Gift was merely physical. I am sure Gallios has told you I can identify all types of fragrances. That is only a small Gift compared to the mind I was given. Our Mother Eve knew this and forbade me to tell anyone else, even my father. She took it upon herself to teach me how to use this Gift, and she prepared me for the task I would need to accomplish. I think she had a sense of what was coming, because when she became pregnant with Zirci, a light went out of her eyes. Somehow, she knew her days were coming to an end. It was then she told me the prophecy of the Light in the Eastern Sky."

"And now you believe it was fulfilled when we arrived."

"Yes. It is your companion—the One-Who-Should-But-Does-Not-Glow—who will bring mercy to Adam," she said.

"Logan."

"Yes, Logan. You must get him back to the docks where your ship came in. There he must face my brother who rules those Dark Ones. It will not be easy for him. You and the Sethite Firstborn must help him, but as powerful as you both might be, neither of you must cross over to the other side of the island until the danger has passed. I am now sure the Bright Dark One has come onto the island."

"Bright Dark One?"

"He is the most powerful of all the dark spirits, but he is far, far greater than those we contained here. He is to them like we are to ants. I believe the Bright Dark One is attempting to deaden the light that comes from your friend. But even he, with all his immense power, is not completely successful. Some light still remains."

"Why have I never heard of the Bright Dark One?"

"It is because your people do not call him that. When Ono spoke of him at all, he referred to the Bright Dark One as 'the Liberator,' as my father does."

Hemeth realized he had never considered Janice's lineage. From her extreme age he reasoned that she must be very, very early human, and after doing a quick calculation in his head, he suddenly felt uncomfortable.

"Who is your father?" he asked, already knowing the answer.

"Lord Cain."

Hemeth froze in fear.

"You disapprove, I see," said the woman. "Has my father's influence affected his whole line that much?"

"I have only had painful experiences with your people."

"Cain may be my father, but his descendants are not my people. I was never allowed to marry nor have children."

"Why is that?" asked Hemeth. "I thought all of the Elder Born were required to populate the earth."

"With the exception of me, that is true," she said. "I earned the ire of my father the moment I came into the world. You see, I was born several minutes before my twin brother. This displeased my father. He saw it as a weakness on his part to sire twins where a female came first. When Eve requested that I attend her, he was pleased enough to be rid of me. He also convinced Adam that Xavier should be his attendant. However, Xavier was allowed a mate for a time. Later, as it looked like I was going mad, Cain felt vindicated in his earlier decision to forbid me to marry. He has since decreed that I should never leave this island."

"But you are not mad," said Hemeth.

"Are you so sure, Hemeth?" she asked. "You are the only person I have ever allowed to meet me here. Only the smallest part of my consciousness is ever present to everyone else. To the world, I am a simple fool. Having completely lost myself here, I no longer have the capacity to be 'normal,' even if I wanted to be."

"But that is not right," Hemeth protested. "You hold back the darkness for everyone else. You keep the people of Atalànt safe, yet they treat you like an imbecile."

"That is my burden to bear. And in the briefest of moments I almost failed because part of me was still vain enough to be distracted when you reminded me of how old I have become. I had to nearly lose everything for which I have fought all these years to see how little that matters. That is also why you must leave now. While part of me covets your help more than I can say, another part of me knows beyond any doubt you have other important parts to play—things you cannot do if you stay here."

"But how could you know that?" he asked.

"During my centuries-long battle, I have seen glimpses of events yet to come in our world. At least, that is what I think they are, because I do not understand most of them. Some events seem to have something to do with you and your friends."

The old woman suddenly grew pale, and her eyes widened.

"What is it?" asked Hemeth.

"You must leave now," she said with tears in her eyes. "The attacks are starting again in earnest, and I must buy you time to get Logan back to the harbor. Hurry!"

With that she walked away and disappeared in the darkness that began to surround Hemeth. He tried to reach out and move toward her, but unseen hands restrained him. He struggled and pushed, but his limbs felt like lead and his throat felt dry and painful.

"Hemeth, stop it," said a familiar voice. "It is okay, relax."

Hemeth began to relax against the hands that held him down. He realized his eyes were shut tight and tears were rolling down his face. He opened his eyes and found he was lying on a mat in a dark room lit only by a gourdlight. Lamech and Logan were kneeling over him with worried expressions. It was Logan who had spoken to him.

# X

*"Have I not commanded you? Be strong and courageous. Do not be afraid; do not be discouraged, for the* Lord *your God will be with you wherever you go."*

Joshua 1:9 (NIV)

"Finally!" Logan said softly. "Here, drink this." Hemeth took a drink and let the cool water soothe his parched throat.

"There is no reason to whisper, Logan," said Lamech. "Everyone is awake now."

Hemeth glanced around the dimly lit room and saw several other young men on mats like his, sitting up and peering in his direction. Searching his memory, he realized he was back in the sleeping quarters of Gallios's residence and wondered how he got there. His mind snapped into focus and he remembered he had to get Logan back to the harbor.

"We have to leave immediately!" said Hemeth in a cracked

voice as he tried unsuccessfully to rise. His muscles felt stiff.

"Relax, Hemeth." Lamech pushed him back down. "You are in no position to go anywhere."

"Let him sit up, Lamech," said Logan. "Maybe he can drink some more water and eat something. Are you hungry, Hemeth?"

"Yes," said Hemeth, realizing how famished he felt. After sitting up and having some water and a piece of dried meat he felt a bit better.

Lamech noticed that everyone was listening to their conversation. "We had better move outside," he said.

"How did I get here?" asked Hemeth after his friends helped him stumble outside to the courtyard. "The last thing I remember was being in the room with Janice."

"That was three days ago, Hemeth!" said Logan.

"What? How is that possible?"

"We found you seated on the floor in the drawing room facing Janice," said Logan. "You were holding her hand. She might be crazy, Hemeth, but she is one of the Elder Born. You know you have no right to touch her. Gallios was livid."

"But she invited me to speak with her," Hemeth protested.

"So we understand," Lamech cut in. "She said something to that effect the day before yesterday when she awoke, but I am not sure Gallios believed her."

"She awoke that long ago?" he asked.

"Yes," said Lamech. "Although she was acting as crazy as ever, she said she had spoken to you and that she needed your help for a bit longer. Then she ran out of the house."

"How she is able to split her mind like that I will never know," Hemeth murmured.

"What are you talking about?" asked Lamech. "Did something happen like when you were with Tubal-Cain and me back at Adoraim?"

"Yes, but I can tell you that Janice is far, far more powerful than Tubal-Cain. She protects this entire island with the power of her mind." Hemeth described as best he could everything that happened when he entered Janice's consciousness, including the wall, the dark spirits, and all that she had told him. For their part, Lamech and Logan described how they had watched over him and could get him to drink something from time to time, but could never wake him up.

"So even when you were no longer in physical contact with her, the mental bond between you remained unchanged?" Lamech asked.

"Yes. Once we were connected, she was able to sustain it whether we were touching or not."

Lamech whistled. "I have never heard of anyone with that kind of mental strength. Even Enoch could not do such a thing. Janice must have been the person who warned us about the reef as we approached the island."

"Undoubtedly."

"So, what do we do now?" asked Logan.

"That is obvious, isn't it?" said Lamech. "We have to get you to the harbor."

"Really? You believe him? What do you two think I can do to help Adam?"

"Janice said you were the only one to face them," said Hemeth. "She was very specific. Neither Lamech nor I should approach the other part of the island until the threat has passed."

"But I have no clue what to do, and Janice is not exactly sane. I am not sure we should be taking advice from her."

"She is not mad," said Hemeth with more emotion that he had intended.

"I know that you are sure of that," said Logan. "But I am not."

"Then you will just have to put your faith in Hemeth's judgment," said Lamech firmly.

"What?" cried Logan in surprise. "Why are you of all people siding with Hemeth?"

"Look, Logan," said Lamech, "I was not joking with Callos back at the harbor. We have come too far and gone through too much to turn back now. Both Enoch and Janice seem to think you are connected to this whole thing. You—all of us—need to at least try, even if we fail. I know you have no idea what to do, but the Head of Days will tell us in time. Besides, we have been here for three days and nothing has happened. We have barely even seen Gallios since he brought us here. Perhaps it is time to get back to the harbor."

Logan thought for a long time. "Very well, it is almost light now," he said. "We will leave at dawn."

"Good! With that settled, I have something to do before we go," said Lamech, disappearing inside.

"I will get ready to go with you," said Hemeth, trying to stand up.

"No, you won't," said Logan. "You are in no shape to go anywhere right now. I don't like leaving you here with Gallios so angry with you, but if it is as urgent as you say, you will only slow us down. Let's see if we can get an audience with him to tell him what we are doing and see if there is anything we can do to keep you from being punished."

"I suppose you are right, but that is something I am not looking forward to."

There was little time to wait, because dawn was only an hour away. Logan quickly packed several things he would need for their journey while Hemeth remained in the courtyard and had a little more to eat and drink. As he sat alone, Hemeth listened to the waves crashing against the rocks far below the cliff on which Gallios's residence stood. Looking up at the early-morning sky, he wondered how Janice was faring against the onslaught of dark creatures. The memory of their hideous forms frightened him, and he was so lost in thought he did not hear Lamech approach.

"Come on," said Lamech. "Gallios is awake, and we need to tell him we are leaving." They entered the building and found Gallios in the dining room beginning his morning meal.

"I see my Lowborn kin is finally awake," said Gallios as he saw the young men enter.

"Yes, Lord Gallios," said Lamech. "He awoke early this morning."

"Well, boy, what do you have to say for yourself? Why should I not beat you for touching an Elder Born?"

"My lord, I meant no disrespect," Hemeth said firmly. "When I kept her from falling out of the tree several days ago, she told me to speak with her."

"Lamech tells me that, as incredible as it sounds, you—a Lowborn—have the Gift of the Mind."

Hemeth did not answer him for fear he would be punished even more for putting on airs.

"Is that true?" Gallios asked.

"Yes, sir."

"So how am I to know you did not place a thought in her mind?"

"I can assure you that she spoke to me. Not the other way around."

"You mean she spoke to you in your mind?"

"Yes."

"But Janice's Gift is physical, not mental."

Hemeth was silent for a moment, contemplating his answer. He came to a decision. "I am sorry, Lord Gallios, but you are mistaken. Her greatest Gift by far is her mind."

"So you, a Lowborn who only just met Janice, know more about her than I, who have known her since I was a child?"

"Yes."

"I could have you punished even more for such rudeness."

"But you will not."

"And why is that?"

"Because Janice told me that a few people on this island suspect the truth about her, and I believe you are one of them. That is one reason you look after her and protect her. If that is true, I am sure you know the prophecy of the Light in the Eastern Sky has come to pass. Do you really want her centuries-long struggle to be lost on account of your stubbornness?"

Gallios looked down and remained silent for an uncomfortably long time. Finally, he spoke. "What was she like?" he asked, raising his head. His eyes were wet.

Hemeth let out the breath he had been holding. "She is like no other person I have ever met. She is amazing." He recounted all he could remember about his encounter, including Janice's command that he and his friends leave at once for the harbor. When Hemeth finished, Gallios got up from his breakfast and did something that surprised Hemeth: Gallios embraced him.

"Thank you," he said. "My mother, Ono's wife, had little time for me as a child. She was too busy bearing my father as many children as possible. Janice looked after me and raised me. She had an uncanny ability to know what I was thinking and would on occasion speak to me in my mind. I suppose it was so natural for her and we were so close that I do not think she even noticed she did it. I never asked her about it. Instead, I kept it to myself, never telling a soul until now. She started to go mad about the time Adam disappeared from public life. Those of us who were around him during that time saw how the darkness that now hides Adam's estate seemed to emanate from within the residence. It grew and progressed toward our side of the island until it stopped at our doorstep, almost as if an invisible hand prevented its progress.

"Though few would admit it now, many of us were terrified by what it meant. It was then that Janice withdrew from all of us, preferring to be alone. In the months and years that followed, her behavior became increasingly erratic until most everyone decided to keep their distance from her. Even her father would not speak with her. All this time she has been protecting us."

"Lord Gallios," said Lamech, "it is time we left."

"Yes, of course," he said, coming back to the present. "It did not sound like Janice gave you much instruction. Do you know what you have to do?"

"No," said Lamech. "We only know we must bring Logan to Adam's side of the island. We have to trust the Head of Days from there."

"Well, I have never been a big believer in the Head of Days. But perhaps this will help." Gallios took out of his cloak a white stone that was about as large as the palm of his hand. "Janice returned late last night and gave me this stone. Though she spoke a great deal of other nonsense, she was quite clear that I was to give it to *the One-That-Ought-But-Does-Not-Glow*. By that I think she meant you, Logan."

Logan, who had listened quietly to the whole conversation, looked up at the mention of his name. "For me?"

"Apparently so." Gallios handed him the white stone. "There appear to be some strange markings painted on it. Do they mean anything to you?"

From where he stood, Hemeth could see the black slash marks Gallios was referring to and, like Gallios, they meant nothing to him. It was clear, though, that the same could not be said of Logan. The moment he laid eyes on the stone the blood drained from his face.

# XI

*"Teach me your way, Lord; lead me in a straight path because of my oppressors."*

Psalm 27:11 (NIV)

As he jogged along the path toward Tipharah and Atalànt's harbor, Logan considered how "normal" life had seemed in Pellios after he accepted that he would not be returning home. Even the journey since leaving his home among the Tortured Mists had been clear. All he needed to do was focus on his end goal—Atalànt. However, ever since he had set foot on the island, everything seemed to be completely muddled. Strange things kept happening, definite signs of his old life were intruding into his new one, and none of the signs made any sense.

His glow, which everyone told him about but he could never see himself, now appeared to be absent, and that seemed to bother Janice, one of the earliest humans who existed on the planet. Yet at the same time this ancient woman—who did not appear altogether sane—could sing Sunday school songs from the distant future and paint English words on white rocks even though her people had yet to develop a formal written language.

Logan had hoped that when he inspected the rock more closely, he would find that his first impression was wrong and that Janice had painted random marks that only resembled English letters. But instead he saw that the letters L-E-G-I-O-N were painted clearly. Of course, Lamech, Hemeth, and Gallios had wanted to know if the marks were a symbol for something. Logan told them they were a symbol for one hundred fighting men. At least that was what Logan thought "legion" meant, because of course, he had not studied much Roman history by the age of thirteen. There was no use in describing it more than that because the Ancients had no concept of a modern standing army, but one hundred fighting men made sense to them. Hemeth asked if the individual marks were mathematical symbols that equaled one hundred or if the marks somehow designated the term "one hundred fighting men."

*He is a clever one*, Logan thought as he jogged alongside Lamech. As helpful as Hemeth had been over the past several weeks, Logan was glad he had stayed behind with Gallios. Hemeth had little stamina when he was fully fit, and having been weakened by a three-day fast, he would have slowed them down considerably.

Logan and Lamech spoke little during their three-hour journey as they were intent on making it to the harbor as quickly as possible. As they neared their destination, the question of what they were going to do once they got there gnawed at Logan.

"Lamech," Logan panted, "this mission we are on is very unusual for you."

"What do you mean?"

"Well, our plan seems to be to just return to the harbor, cross the bridge to Adam's island, and hope for the best."

"Yes, and?"

"You usually have a more detailed plan and know exactly what you want to do. This task seems rather thin on strategy."

"Perhaps my grandfather's madness is rubbing off on me. Or perhaps I have come to trust the insight of our friend Hemeth."

"Yes, you do seem to trust him far more than most people these days. That is odd to me, particularly since the two of you did not get along too well at first."

"I know what you mean. But if you had been there when he faced off against Tubal-Cain, you would know he is not someone to be trifled with. He may be Lowborn, but he is not easily fooled. Hemeth has a way of seeing through illusions to the heart of matters. If he trusts this Janice, then I think I should too."

"I wish I had your confidence. While I know we are here for a reason—Enoch made that clear enough—I have no idea what I can do that the people here could not do for centuries. I have no Gift of Combat or Gift of the Mind like you and Hemeth. I am just a stranger in a strange land."

"Maybe that is exactly what we need right now, Logan," said Lamech. "Maybe it is not by might or power you are meant to succeed. You asked me about my strategy. Perhaps I have resolved in my mind that the only strategy left to me is to trust God Most High."

"As I said—not much of a strategy."

"I don't know. That is how my grandfather seems to live his entire life. But be assured, I will do everything I can to protect you."

As the two of them descended the low hill into the scenic valley through which they had traveled previously, they found there were ten men barring their way. Each one held an odd cylinder-shaped instrument in his hand. Logan was not sure what the contraptions were or how they operated, but whatever these men wanted, he knew it could not be good.

"It seems the lookout I saw earlier ran ahead and alerted Callos of our arrival," said Lamech.

"You saw someone spying on us?"

"Yes. About an hour ago."

"Why didn't you mention it?"

"You seemed preoccupied."

"Great," said Logan. "What do you suppose those things

are that they are holding?"

"Not sure," Lamech said. "But they look like some kind of weapon. They probably know they cannot beat me by sheer force, so they are trying to even the odds."

"Can you take them?"

"Not without bloodshed, particularly because I don't know what those cylinders are. Removing the threat without killing them becomes much less probable."

"Killing an inhabitant of Atalànt will not go over well with the Firstborn Council."

"I know," Lamech said with surprising confidence. "But if things happen like I hope they will, it might not come to that. Just be ready to run the rest of the way to the bridge on my signal."

Whether or not he wanted to, Logan was going over the bridge to Adam's residence, so he mentally prepared himself for what he had to do. Lamech and Logan proceeded toward the men without slacking their pace, and in response their opponents gripped their weapons more tightly.

"Greetings, Lord Callos," Lamech said as he slowed to a stop a stone's throw away. "Why do you block our path to the harbor?"

"Lamech, son of Methuselah, do not pretend you are heading for the harbor," Callos replied. "Xavier told us you would now seek an audience with the Originator, and that is not allowed by his own decree."

"We seek much more than that, Callos. We come to complete the prophecy our Mother Eve spoke centuries ago, the one you and your companions have sought to discredit. But you cannot stop it. Three nights ago, you saw the light in the eastern sky, which comes to mix mercy with justice," Lamech said firmly, repeating what Hemeth had told him. "We have come to fulfill that prophecy, and if I have to stop every one of you to do it, I will."

The assembled men gasped at Lamech's words. Callos just glared at him. "You forget, Firstborn, we are of the Elder Born. You have no authority here, and you are sorely outnumbered."

"Once again you are only partially correct," said Lamech.

## Chapter XI

"While it is true I have no authority here, I do have allies who know the importance and nobility of our cause. They will fight to prevent you from stopping us."

"And who might they be?" Callos asked with a smile.

"Us," said a voice from behind him.

Callos and his companions spun around to see Captain Lubin standing several dozen cubits away with a sword in his hands. Spread out and positioned behind rocks in an arc were the crew of Lubin's ship, all of whom had arrows nocked on their bowstrings and trained on Callos and his men.

"You see, Callos," said Lamech, "you are not the only one who uses his brain. I saw this spot as we were leaving and knew its strategic importance for an ambush. This morning I sent a signal to have the crew of *Tomorrow's Destiny* meet us here in case you decided to take things into your own hands."

Without another word Callos gripped the cylinder weapon tightly in his hand was about to pull one of the levers on it when Lamech, quick as lightning, nocked an arrow to his bowstring and sent it flying into Callos's right thigh. Callos cried out in pain and the cylinder weapon fell from his hands. "I thought you would have learned from the last time," said Lamech, who already had another arrow ready to shoot.

Callos's men, unaccustomed to violence, took a step back, unsure how to proceed.

"The rest of you should think hard about what you want to do right now."

After a few tense moments, the men slowly lowered their odd-shaped weapons.

"Go now," Lamech whispered to Logan.

# XII

*"Do not turn me over to the desire of my foes, for false witnesses rise up against me, spouting malicious accusations. I remain confident of this: I will see the goodness of the in the land of the living."*

Psalm 27: 12-13 (NIV)

Logan took off past the men and through the valley. Minutes later, between the two hills, he spotted the bridge that connected the two parts of the island. As he crossed the bridge, Logan looked down at the deep fissure the bridge spanned. On the other side of the bridge an imposing wall with a metal door blocked his way. He would have to scale the wall. It took him several minutes, but he reached the top, and what he saw on the other side stunned him into an awed silence.

While he had been able to see the spires from the ship and the other part of the island, the ground below the castle had been hidden by a ridge above it. To say that everything was overgrown would be a complete understatement. Wild vines as thick as Logan's biceps hung like party streamers among the trees. A canopy of prickly flowers bursting with vivid colors covered the forest like a ceiling. In the distance, he could hear animals moving about as if predators were stalking and attacking their prey. Something in this beautiful, violent forest stirred a deep fear within him.

One small path through the dense foliage lay before him, and Logan figured it was the path Xavier kept open for those rare occasions when he met with his cousins on the Elder Born side of the island. Logan estimated the base of the closest spire—the one dedicated to Cain—was only about a hundred meters away. He could see it breaking through and towering above the forest. Knowing that the distance he would need to travel was short did nothing to decrease his dread of traveling it. He had half a mind to turn around and see if indeed Lamech might join him. However, his years of training under Kedar kicked in, and his courage did not depart him.

He jumped down from the wall, took out his sword, and held it in his right hand. Whispering a prayer, he moved forward into the forest. However, the moment he stepped foot in it, dark thoughts descended on his mind like a heavy wet blanket. Doubt and fear seeped in.

Is this wise? You have no idea what you are supposed to do. You ought to know what you are to do before you begin. You are not ready. You are no match for the task before you. Leave these things to those greater than you. Only an arrogant man would think he was important enough to break into Adam's residence. Adam will cast you from his presence. You will die. You will fail!

While these thoughts crowded Logan's mind, the ever-present fear of his physical surroundings gave him a sense of claustrophobia. He found himself unable to focus his thoughts on anything other than his fear. The edges of his vision grew dark, and he felt as if he were being suffocated by terror.

Strangely, the sensation of being suffocated brought back a vivid memory. Decades ago he had felt a similar sensation when he and Lamech, riding Midnight, rode like madmen through the Tortured Mists. The world around them had turned into a watery hell, becoming worse by the second. The injuries Logan had sustained at the hands of the brutal Okrans had taken their toll on his body and mind. He had lost all hope and will to live until Lamech took Midnight's reins and pushed on. When all seemed lost, they shot out into a beautiful grassy field in Pellios. He was barely conscious at the time, but the relief he felt when he awoke was something he would never forget.

That memory gave Logan hope in a way that surprised him. The Head of Days had not let him down then. He would not let him down now. Logan's vision began to clear, and he looked around with new eyes. He realized that despite all the terrors he had allowed to enter his mind, he was actually in a much better position now than last time. He had his sword, and he was older and stronger—trained to survive. Logan believed beyond any doubt he had been brought to the Ancients for a reason—perhaps for such a time as this. If this was the purpose for his life, Logan would not turn back from it. Not now.

With great effort Logan moved forward as fast as he could and found himself stepping out of the forest into a small grassy knoll in the middle of which stood the base of the Cainite tower. For a moment, he was relieved to be out of the forest. Then he saw the face of a lone figure standing in the entryway barring the path to the tower and presumably to Adam.

The man wore a simple tunic and held no weapon. He was very old with a round face and what modern-day people would call Asian features. His dark-gray hair was unkempt and shaggy, as was his long beard. Though clearly old, his limbs looked solid and his cloudy gray eyes betrayed a keen mind. The look of those eyes reminded Logan of the moment of clarity he had seen in Janice several days ago.

"You must be Xavier," Logan said, speaking with as steady a voice as he could manage.

"I am."

"I am Logan of the Zirci."

"I know who you are, but how a Zirci still exists, that is a mystery. I know why you have trespassed on this island, and you are not welcome."

"Then you know my companion, Lamech, Firstborn among the Sethites, seeks an audience with the Created One, as is his right."

"I do not recognize this right, but even if I did, why does the Sethite coward send you, a descendant of the long-dead Zirci?"

"There are some battles he is not meant to fight."

"But you, young one—you are meant to fight them?"

"Yes."

"And I am the one you are to fight?"

"Will you allow me to see the Created One?"

"No."

"Then yes," said Logan. "Today will be the last day you will hold the Created One captive."

"Strong words for one as alone as you."

"I am ... enough."

"Tell me Logan of the Zirci," said Xavier, "who do you think you are serving in coming here with such confidence?"

Logan was at first at a loss for words, startled by the strange change in subject. Finally, he said, "I serve the Head of Days, God Most High. And it will be he who will ultimately defeat you. Not me."

Xavier smiled, but his expression contained no mirth. "'Head of Days,' you call him? The beginning of all things?" asked Xavier with a derisive laugh. "I suppose you are right in a twisted sort of way. But your 'Head of Days' did not create the beginning of things in the way you might think."

"Really now, Xavier, why would I believe you?"

Ignoring the question, Xavier continued. "What would you say if I told you the being you serve is nothing more than a powerful demiurge—a sadistic entity—who is self-righteous and jealous of anyone who dares question him? What if I told you that he was beginning of all our torment?"

"I would say that does not describe the God I serve," said Logan. He was cautious, having expected an attack, not a lecture.

"Are you so sure?" asked Xavier. "You are young. What

could you really know of this being you serve? Have you ever seen him? I am of the Elder Born. I have walked with the Originator and our Mother Eve. I know the story of the Deep Past."

"So do I."

"I am told the story is dying out, even among the Sethites," he said. "What could a young one like you know of the Deep Past?"

"I have been told much," said Logan. He began quoting the second chapter of Genesis, translating it into the Ancient tongue. "'The Lord God formed the man from the dust of the ground and breathed into his nostrils the breath of life, and the man became a living being.'"

A flicker of surprise crossed Xavier's face as he heard the quoted text. Logan wondered if his mysterious glow might have flared for a moment.

"Very well stated. It certainly lends itself to my point."

"How is that?"

"Do you not see that the demiurge in your own story imprisoned us? He breathed our spirits into this flesh. In his depravity, he sentenced us—you, me, and all our descendants—to be encased in these bodies. Though this evil flesh can serve us, it is not who we are. Luminous beings are we."

"You are wrong. The Head of Days created Adam and Eve from the dust of the ground and made them mind, spirit, and body. He did not imprison anyone. He gave them a radiant garden in which to live. How can you, if you have walked with our Father and Mother, not know this?"

"He gave our Father and Mother an illusion, and you still believe in that same illusion because you have been taught it as truth. He tempted them with free will—the knowledge they needed to escape—and then cursed them when they dared accept it."

"Our Father and Mother chose to eat of the fruit from the Tree of the Knowledge of Good and Evil. They set all of this into motion," Logan said, gesturing to the wild growth around him.

"You blind young fool! Our only hope came from one who showed them the way and gave them courage to rebel."

"You are referring to the Bright Dark One!"

"The Liberator," corrected Xavier.

"The Serpent."

"Yes!" cried Xavier. "No other being in the universe had the intelligence to find his way to us or the will to force himself into our existence. He gave our Father and Mother the push they needed to make the right choice. Only later did they foolishly waver and despair. Regrettably, they passed this sentiment along to some of their children. Now the Sethites spit on the Liberator's sacrifice with their barbaric Crushing Festival. They do not honor the Liberator for what it took for him to find his way here."

"Honor him ... for what he did?"

"Do you not know that the Liberator comes from the same place as these beings around us?" said Xavier, pointing to the empty air around him. "Such beings are not of our existence. The Liberator needed to force his way in here. Now these lesser beings are being drawn here ..."

Xavier stopped and cocked his head as if he were listening to something.

"They tell me you cannot see them," said Xavier as he began to laugh. "The Head of Days sends a fool who cannot even see what he is supposed to fight? There are many scores of Dark Ones in the sky above us. Here around you stand a hundred of my chosen servants ready to do as I command."

Logan felt his temper begin to rise, but knew anger would only cloud his judgment. Instead, he decided he needed to regain control of the conversation until he could think of something to do.

"I suppose the Head of Days knows what he is doing," said Logan, "as does your sister."

"Ahhh, I heard you met my dear Janice," he said with a bit more tension in his voice. "She is quite mad. Whatever tale she told you, you would do well not to believe it."

"Oh, I believe her all right. You more than anyone know she is sane," said Logan. "It must be galling to endure defeat day after day, especially with this army of Dark Ones at your command."

"She has no power like mine," said Xavier.

"No," said Logan. "My friend Hemeth saw for himself that

her power is much greater than yours."

Xavier glared at him, and Logan knew he had hit a nerve.

"I don't know where you came from, or if indeed you are from Zirci's diseased line," said Xavier, "but I shall show you power!"

He turned away from Logan and spoke to the air around him. "Come, my servants. It is time we reveal the power of our might!" At that moment, Logan saw his opportunity. Grasping his sword he tried to raise it, only to find he was completely unable to move his arm. His body suddenly felt heavy like he was on a planet with far stronger gravity. Stumbling, he fell to his knees. His body was not the only thing affected. Logan also found it hard to think clearly. It was not like he was drugged, because he was perfectly aware of the things around him. Instead, it seemed like something had sucked all the joy, peace, and pleasure out of the world.

Xavier walked over to Logan and kicked him in the head. Logan fell backward in a heap and dropped his sword. Bending down, Xavier picked up Logan's sword and examined it. "Do you now see the power I possess?" he asked in what sounded like a slightly different voice. "The hundred Dark Ones that surround you now are only a few of the thousands I command."

Logan fixed his eyes on the man before him, but could say nothing. Darkness once again gathered on the edges of his vision. He could not focus, and his mind became a jumbled mess.

"Now you will die, Logan, servant of the Most High, and your God will know that this world belongs to another."

Logan groaned in response. His head ached, and his emotions reeled from a cold emptiness that invaded his mind. All the fears he had mastered while walking through the forest came rushing back to him with a vengeance. He had never felt such despair, not even during the attack by Tubal-Cain. Everything around me is hopeless, he thought. No light ... no way out.

In the midst of his hopelessness, Logan heard the small voice of a woman in his head.

I have done all that I can, Beloved. But the Bright Dark One has directly entered the fray, and I can no longer contain them. You alone hold the key to extinguishing the flaming arrows of the Evil One. Raise your shield, use your sword and—

Logan shuddered as the voice went silent, and his mind tried to interpret what he was experiencing. That must have been Janice, he thought. Her cell phone must have dropped the call. *Cell phone? How can she be on the phone? They have not been invented yet. How do I know that? Where am I?*

Logan opened his eyes and stared at Xavier, who still held the sword in his hands. His malicious smile told Logan the man knew exactly what was happening and that he was clearly enjoying the spectacle. *Oh, I know where I am*, Logan thought. *I am on Atalànt. Janice was speaking into my mind. They can do that here. But she was cut off. Maybe they killed her.*

The importance of his mission came back to him, followed by the fact that he was failing at it miserably. This new line of thought shamed Logan into an even deeper depression. *What is the use? I cannot fight these beings. It does not matter anyway. The world will end in a Flood. These people are all doomed no matter what I do. Everything is pointless.*

At that moment, another voice came into his head, only this time it was not Janice, but a memory from his own past. *Perhaps it is for this reason you were chosen and sent to us, Logan,* Enoch had said when Logan first came to Parvaim. *You must learn to identify what is important and what is not.*

*What do you mean?* Logan heard himself asking Enoch in the memory.

*In serving the Head of Days, there are times when I, a prophet of the Most High, cannot succeed and other times when I cannot fail. But succeeding and failing make no difference. The result of my obedience matters little compared to the act of obeying itself. Do you not think He could devise a better way than to send someone like you or me?*

The memory faded and Logan began to weep.

*Ah, Logan,* said another, almost-remembered voice, "*You brave little boy. It is okay for you to cry, but do not fear; you are not alone.*

*Who was it who said that to me?* Logan thought. A moment

## Chapter XII

later the answer came to him. *It was Lois, the Great Mother of the Zirci. She said it to me shortly after I came to Pellios on that dark morning before the dawn. Why was I out there in the darkness? I remember now. I needed to see something from my world ... the world the future had stolen from me. I remember; I looked for something permanent, something that would remain until the time of my birth. I was remembering the patterns of stars in the night sky, not how Methuselah described them, but in the way my dad, Joshua, had shown them to me.*

Logan's mind fell silent for a moment.

*I remember something else about the stars. Something I read in a book. "Shine like stars in the universe," it said. Was that it? But there are no books here. There is not even a written language, but still I remember this was a book—a very important book.*

Logan's mind once again fell silent. Then, his memory stirred. *Do everything without complaining or arguing, so that you may become blameless and pure, children of God without fault in a crooked and depraved generation in which you shine like stars in the universe as you hold out the word of life.* After reciting this verse to himself, Logan opened his eyes and saw Xavier looking at him. This time, the expression on Xavier's face was not so enthusiastic. *Something else is familiar,* Logan thought. *Janice said, "Extinguish the flaming arrows of the Evil One." I remember that too.*

Using his voice for the first time in what seemed like ages, he spoke aloud, quoting in English from a passage he had learned years ago, "Take up the shield of faith with which you can extinguish all the flaming arrows of the Evil One. Take the helmet of salvation and the sword of the Spirit, which is the Word of God."

Logan's mind became increasingly clear as he focused on every word he spoke. The Scriptures he had memorized came to him like a flood. Without knowing why—as if the words had been given to him—Logan became sure of the things he must declare.

"What is this babble you speak?" demanded Xavier.

Though still on the edge of losing consciousness, Logan

continued. "What ... what I speak is not babble. Somehow you know that, don't you? And it frightens you, as it should."

Xavier stood transfixed at the sight of Logan on the ground.

"You have told me of the Deep Past, Xavier. So, I will give you a message from the Distant Future, one that will have been spoken to those like you." Translating what he had memorized years ago from the book of Isaiah, Logan continued, "Remember this, keep it in mind, take it to heart, you rebels. Remember the former things, those of long ago; I am God, and there is no other; I am God, and there is none like me. I make known the end from the beginning, from ancient times, what is still to come. I say, 'My purpose will stand, and I will do all that I please.' From the east I summon a bird of prey; from a far-off land, a man to fulfill my purpose. What I have said, that I will bring about; what I have planned, that I will do. Listen to me, you stubborn-hearted, you who are now far from my righteousness. I am bringing my righteousness near, it is not far away; and my salvation will not be delayed."

As he spoke, Logan rose up on one knee and then to his feet. Logan knew he would soon pass out from the combination of the blow to his head and his extreme mental exertion. He knew he had to finish quickly.

"Hear now a word from God Most High, concerning you, Xavier." Logan pointed a trembling finger at the old man. "Your doom has now come upon you. Until the day you die, these demons you have commanded will command you. You Dark Ones within, hear me now. I name you Legion, for you are many! In the name of Messiah, who has sealed me until the day of judgment, I bind you until the coming of the Son of the Most High God. Understand this, Legion, the day will come when the Son of the Most High will judge you for all the evil you have wrought."

At that moment, Xavier fell to his knees screaming and thrashing about. Foam came from his mouth and he yelled, "No! You are my servants. You listen to me. No! Stop! I am your Master! No!"

Logan looked away from Xavier and up at the air above him.

## Chapter XII

"You Dark Ones that still swarm around the Created One," said Logan, "I may not see you, but by faith I know you are there. Hear me! Because you have tormented the Created One, the Most High God now commands that you seek out the arid places of the world searching for rest. But hear me, you will never find it. You are banished from Atalànt, never to return."

After speaking to the air and seeing no change, Logan dropped to the ground in exhaustion. He needed to send word to Lamech for help but did not know how that was going to happen. Logan placed his head between his knees, trying to keep from losing consciousness.

He stayed there for several minutes until he felt good enough to try sitting up. In his semiconscious state, he had completely forgotten about Xavier. Raising his head, Logan saw Xavier, only a short distance from him, picking himself off the ground and looking straight at him. The old man looked completely different than he had just a few minutes before. Two haunted eyes glared at Logan with a look of utter hatred, and he could see muscles in the man's face twitching at irregular beats. The old man gave a guttural scream and charged with lightning speed at Logan, who did not have a chance to prepare for the blow. Logan was knocked off the ground and smashed into the trunk of a large tree at the edge of the forest.

The man-who-had-been-Xavier paused to look with disgust at Logan for several moments. Then he turned around slowly, bent over to pick up Logan's sword, and walked toward the prone figure on the ground.

**Click or scan the QR Code to learn about the sign posts in this chapter.**

# XIII

*"Wait for the* Lord*; be strong and take heart and wait for the* Lord*."*

Psalm 27:14 (NIV)

Lamech stood tense and brooding at the edge of the valley. It felt like forever since Logan left, and he could not take his eyes off the other side of the island. He had let the crew of *Tomorrow's Destiny* disperse Callos's men and take their odd-looking weapons from them. Lamech had no interest in them; he only watched and waited for a sign from Logan.

Captain Lubin stood silently next to Lamech. Lamech had told Lubin about his promise to obey Hemeth's warning to remain on this side of the island. Waiting for things to be safe was not Lamech's style, but he had promised. Lubin asked how they would know it was safe.

"Hemeth was not sure," Lamech said. "He only said we

would know."

"You three are a strange bunch," said Lubin. After that, there was nothing more to say, so both just stood and stared at the dark island next to them. It took all of Lamech's discipline not to go looking for Logan.

When Hemeth had first told him about what Logan had to do, Lamech thought it was insane to let Logan go running off by himself. "There are some battles you are not meant to fight," Hemeth had said to him. Two weeks ago, a comment like that coming from Hemeth might have cost the young man dearly, but now Lamech let such things pass. When he was younger, Lamech could not imagine a battle he could not tip to his favor. But after his time with Tubal-Cain, he had come to question whether he would care to fight any battle in the future. Nothing seemed to matter. Now Lamech was beginning to understand what Enoch had often told him: "Stop trying to control everything. Be content with the part you have to play for the Head of Days." At this moment Lamech was trying to be content watching and waiting.

"Lamech, look!" said Lubin. Without warning, something changed. As if snapping into existence, there stood a majestic spire rising high above the island, piercing the sky. Beyond the first tower stood several other spires, each different from the other but still grand in its own unique way.

Lamech, however, paid no attention to the view as he was already off at a full-on run toward the bridge before him. He came to the barrier and bounded over it, immediately spotting the path through the dense forest. He flew through the trees, dodging roots and branches with the skill that comes from growing up in a forest. As he entered the grassy knoll he stopped abruptly, taking in the sight of what looked like a very old yet fit man raising his sword over the prone, unconscious figure of Logan.

Could his old man be the Created One? Lamech asked himself. It does not matter who he is. He will not kill Logan! Lamech grabbed his knife and sent it flying into the man's right shoulder blade. Lamech was startled by the ferocity with which the man roared. Quick as lightning he turned and charged Lamech, raising his sword to strike. Lamech was ready for him and parried the blow, but found the man was far stronger than he had expected. Lamech jumped out of the way to get some distance between himself and the man, but his attacker came at him again, as quickly as before. As strong as the old man was, he seemed to have very little skill with the sword, relying on brute force to win the combat. Lamech parried once again and this time came around with a glancing blow to the man's right shoulder in hopes that it would force the man to drop his sword. It did not work. The man kept coming as if he did not feel the wounds in his back and shoulder.

Could this be Adam, or is it Xavier? Lamech kept parrying blows, but he was growing tired under the man's relentless attacks. He did not wish to, but Lamech knew in order to survive he would have to deal the man a mortal bow. He backed away, allowing the man to feel he had gained the advantage. As soon as the two of them were on the edge of the forest, Lamech feigned then ducked. As he expected, his opponent swung his sword in an arc and lodged it within the thick tree directly behind Lamech. With that momentary distraction, Lamech lunged and thrust his sword into the old man's left side. It went clear through him before Lamech withdrew it.

The man, still looking at him with intense rage, backed up and stumbled. Then, to Lamech's utter surprise, the man turned and ran to the other side of clearing, disappearing into the forest with Lamech's knife still lodged in his right shoulder. After the moment of shock passed, Lamech ran over to Logan. He knew from seeing men in similar shape during numerous battles over the years, it did not look good for Logan. He had a nasty bruise on his head, and based on the broken branches behind him, it looked as if he had been knocked squarely into the trees.

Since Lamech and the others had arrived on Atalànt, much of the island had been in an uproar. Lamech wondered if any of the healers on the island would treat Logan. First, though, he would have to bring him to the others. Sheathing his sword, Lamech bent down and picked up his unconscious friend. Carrying Logan in his arms, he had begun walking toward the path back to the other side of the island when a voice spoke to him, the sound of which was as clear as if a person next to him had spoken. The voice sounded strangely familiar, though Lamech was sure he had never heard it before.

*Lamech, son of Methuselah, Firstborn among the Sethites,* it said. *The young man will die if you go that way. Bring him to me.*

"Who are you, my lord?" Lamech asked aloud.

*I am the Created One and your father, Adam.*

## XIV

*"The LORD said, 'Go out and stand on the mountain in the presence of the LORD, for the LORD is about to pass by.' Then a great and powerful wind tore the mountains apart and shattered the rocks before the LORD, but the LORD was not in the wind. After the wind there was an earthquake, but the LORD was not in the earthquake. After the earthquake came a fire, but the LORD was not in the fire. And after the fire came a gentle whisper. When Elijah heard it, he pulled his cloak over his face and went out and stood at the mouth of the cave."*

1 Kings 19:11-13 (NIV)

LOGAN FELT HIMSELF TRAVELING THROUGH A KALEIDOSCOPE of light and motion. He longed for the moments of darkness, because they were brief respites from the long periods of pain. In those moments, feelings and images flashed back and forth before his eyes like a whirlwind of color and sound. Then silence would again descend on him before the next whirlwind began. During the whirlwinds he became so dizzy that he retched with dry heaves. He lost track of the number of intervals. Logan learned to anticipate the excruciating pain, and his mental strength drained away. His will to live deserted him as he felt himself falling down an endless chasm. But each time he fell, his descent stopped when something reached out to grasp his arm. Despite the pain this caused, each time Logan was pulled up from the depths. He looked up to see what prevented his fall, but his eyes could see only darkness. After what seemed like an eternity, the whirlwinds slowed and then stopped. In their place, memories of pleasant colors, sounds, smells, and flavors came to him in a fashion and speed he could handle. He saw his childhood home. Then he saw the Mediterranean island that had risen from the sea and the doorway through which he had fallen. He remembered the painful time in the Okran camp, his relief at Lamech saving him, and his fear when riding Midnight through the Tortured Mists. In a matter of minutes, he relived his peaceful decades among the Zirci and his harrowing adventure escaping with Hemeth from the artisan camp. Then he remembered all the events of Adoraim City and the voyage to the Island of Atalànt. He relaxed as a quiet peacefulness surrounded and pervaded his mind. He began to feel whole as one does when he has had a deep, healing slumber.

After this long period of peace, Logan noticed a piercing point of light far in the distance. He focused on the point of light as it came closer to him. As he focused on it, he realized there was not one light, but two. Both were extraordinarily bright flaming tongues of fire floating in the air. As Logan concentrated and widened his vision, he began to see two men standing under those flames, and himself in a clearing at the edge of a forest at dusk. He realized the two men were his father, Joshua, and Elijah the prophet. They had not moved since he had seen them in his last vision. Now, however, they were speaking in unison. He could not understand the language they were speaking. The area around him was illuminated as if the dusk were reversing itself. As Logan continued to focus on his father, he felt his ears open up as if he were recovering from a head cold, and now he could understand what his father and Elijah were saying.

"Your sons and daughters will prophesy, your old men will dream dreams, your young men will see visions. Even on my servants, both men and women, I will pour out my Spirit in those days. I will show wonders in the heavens and on earth, blood and fire and billows of smoke. The sun will be turned to darkness and the moon to blood before the coming of the great and dreadful day of the Lord. Everyone who calls on the name of the Lord will be saved; for on Mount Zion and in Jerusalem there will be deliverance as the Lord has said, even among the survivors whom the Lord calls."

Joshua and Elijah finished speaking. For several heartbeats, they stared in silence at the flaming tongues of fire above each other. Finally, Joshua spoke. "What has happened to us, Eliyahu?"

"We have been anointed for special work by the Spirit of the Living God."

"It reminds me of Pentecost when the Spirit was poured out on Jesus's apostles."

"You will have to tell me more of this, Joshua, now that we can properly understand each other. Strange, though, you now speak a dialect of Hebrew that is much older than mine."

Joshua cocked his head in a way that Logan remembered indicated he was concentrating very hard. "Yes, Eliyahu, you are right. I know that somehow. Why is that, I wonder?"

"As I said, we both have been anointed for a special purpose."

"And what is that, Eliyahu?"

"When I met with our Lord during my travels here, he told me that we—you and I—must bear witness for God Most High and against his Beast and False Prophet."

"But why do I speak an older dialect than you?"

"You have come in the power and spirit of Moses, just as someone else came in the power and spirit of me."

"But why me? Why not Moses himself?"

"You already know that answer, my friend. It is appointed once for man to die, and Moses has already passed. One day he will enter the Promised Land, but that time has not yet come.

Joshua still had his head cocked to the side. "You are correct. The dreams I have been having for these past many weeks make sense now. Only—"

"Joshua!" Elijah interrupted, pointing to the space directly above Logan's head. "Do you see that? There is a third tongue of fire floating in the air above nothing."

Logan looked above himself to find one of the glowing tongues of fire brilliantly shining inches above his head. It was the reason the darkness around him had seemed to lighten a few moments earlier. Returning his attention to the men, Logan found his father looking directly at him. Logan's heart skipped a beat.

"I do see it, Eliyahu." Joshua looked very intently at Logan. "But I think there is indeed someone standing beneath it, and it is so hard to see who it might be."

"Could it be a messenger from God Most High?"

"I am not sure. It looks like a young man." Joshua ran over and stood directly in front of Logan, staring at him.

"Wait a minute," said Joshua with utter shock on his face. "This cannot be."

"What is it, Joshua?"

"He looks older, but there is no doubt. He is my son!"

At that moment, everything went dark for Logan.

## XV

*"The Lord will indeed give what is good, and our land will yield its harvest. Righteousness goes before him and prepares the way for his steps."*

Psalm 85:12-13 (NIV)

"Dad!" Logan yelled as he sat straight up. Tears filled his eyes. Lamech and Hemeth, who had been in a deep discussion, stopped what they were doing and ran over to Logan's side.

"It's only a dream," said Lamech. "You are safe now."

"What happened? Where is my dad?" asked Logan frantically.

Logan's friends looked at each other.

"Tell us something," Hemeth said slowly. "How are you feeling?"

"I feel like someone used my head to play basketball," Logan responded in English.

"Logan!" said Lamech with frustration, "You cannot speak to us the way you do with Enoch. We don't understand you." Logan looked at his two friends as recognition slowly crept upon him, and the loss of his father caused his heart to sink. He closed his eyes. The shock of seeing his father in his dream faded, and he remembered where and when he was.

"My head hurts," replied Logan in the Ancient tongue. "I saw my father in a vision, and this time he saw me."

"Your father?" asked Hemeth.

"Yes. It is a very long story I do not begin to understand. I am sorry. It is a very difficult thing to explain."

"When you are better, I would like to hear more about it," replied Hemeth.

"Yes, yes," said Lamech impatiently. "But how are you feeling?"

"My head hurts, but I think I will be okay. I suppose that deranged maniac did not kill us, then?"

"It seems Xavier was about to kill you, but Lamech stepped in and stopped him," said Hemeth.

"I have never seen anything like it," said Lamech. "For an old man, he was very strong. He could take a beating and still stand."

"Well, not anymore," added Hemeth. "The men of the island found his body several hundred cubits away in the woods, or at least what was left of it after the wild animals were done with him."

"But I got my knife back!" said Lamech with a smile.

"Well, I would hate for you to lose your knife on my account," said Logan. He sat up straighter and took a look around.

What he saw shocked him. It was the nicest place he had slept in since he had come into the Ancient world decades ago, and there was something vaguely familiar about the room. It was shaped like a large rectangle, and a beautiful rug covered half the floor. The head of his bed was against the wall on one of the short sides, and an open door was opposite him at the far end of the room. There were several windows on the long wall to his left and a large, empty fireplace was on the wall to his right.

## Chapter XV

Logan noticed he was in what approximated a modern bed. Typically, the Ancients slept either in hammocks or on sheepskins. Taking a closer look at the walls, he could see they were painted. While it was common to have painted walls within permanent structures in the Ancient world, these colors were very different from the colors he normally encountered. Then it dawned on him. The colors were similar to the color of his room as a child. In fact, the shape of the room was very similar, and the bed was placed in about the same position as his childhood bed.

Logan was so lost in thought he did not notice that Lamech had been talking to him. "Logan, are you sure you are feeling well? I don't think you are hearing me."

"Do not worry, I am feeling better," he said. "It is just this room ... Where am I, and how long was I unconscious?"

"You are always so demanding when you wake up after I have saved your life," Lamech said with a grin.

"You have been asleep for two weeks," said Hemeth, ignoring Lamech. "But you were moved here about a week ago."

"I was moved here?"

"Yes," said Lamech. "After the fight, the Created One wanted me to bring you to him in the Cainite tower. It was he who healed you. The others on the island helped, of course, but it was mostly Adam's doing. He said your injuries were severe and he needed you to stay mostly unconscious to heal. He only brought you out of it enough to eat and relieve yourself. During those times, we tried to talk to you, but you were in a daze."

"Adam did not want to keep you in the Cainite tower too long," said Hemeth. "He knew his Cainite sons were not pleased that you, a Zirci, were in the tower dedicated to their patriarch. Adam had you moved to his residence and was very specific about how he wanted this room arranged. He made the color used for the walls himself and had Lamech and me paint it."

"Then he had the artisans on the island make this thing for you." Lamech kicked the wood frame of the bed. "I think he chose his residence because he never finished constructing the Zirci spire and it would be rather uncomfortable. The main residence is a kind of neutral ground among the sons of Adam. I think it also helped him to have you close by so he need not climb so many stairs to check on you. The Created One may still be strong, but I imagine he does not navigate stairs well—though he would never allow us to see him try."

"He may appear healthy, but I am glad we made it here before he dies this year," said Logan without thinking.

Lamech and Hemeth exchanged glances.

"How did you know about that, Logan?" asked Lamech. "We only just learned that Adam sent for his sons and daughters because he believes his days are quickly coming to an end."

"It is one of those things you just know about, isn't it Logan?" Hemeth added.

"Yes, unfortunately, it is exactly one of those things." The thought of Adam's impending death brought other thoughts to Logan's mind. "What happened with Janice? Is she all right?"

Hemeth looked down. "No, she is dead. Gallios's men found her body in her small residence near the coast."

"I am sorry, Hemeth," said Logan as memories of the grief he felt during his fight with Xavier came back to him. "I should have done something to save her."

Hemeth looked up. "It is not your fault, Logan. You—we all—did what we came to do. She knew her job was done once you arrived. It was her time."

"How do you know that?" asked Logan.

"She told me."

The three young men were silent for several heartbeats. As Logan looked at his friends he saw something new on Lamech's arms.

"And what are those, Lamech?" Logan asked, pointing at each arm.

"This," Lamech said, "is the fine mark that Gallios gave me shortly after we knew you were going to survive."

"I am pleased for you, my friend. You deserve such a great honor and such a fine mark on your arm. Did you come up with the pattern yourself to represent your descendants?"

"Not completely. Hemeth helped with its design."

"Very nice," said Logan with a big smile. "And now, tell me, what is this on your other arm?"

"It was a gift the Created One bestowed on me yesterday when I was officially presented to him as a Firstborn. I was the first Firstborn presented to him in more than a century. Perhaps he gave it to me to commemorate the occasion, but to be honest, I do not know exactly why. He just said he wanted me to have this to remember him by. When the Created One gives you a gift, you do not question. You just accept."

"Here, let me see it more clearly."

Lamech bent over slightly to allow Logan to better view the unique gift. Strapped to Lamech's right bicep were two flattened spheres connected together. They were jet black and on the surface were etched with beautiful, ornate markings. The spheres looked like they were made out of a hard stone like granite. How Adam could have crafted such artwork was a mystery.

"What do the markings mean?"

"No one knows, not even Gallios," Lamech replied. "I think they are just artistic designs."

"You are very fortunate, Lamech," said Hemeth. "Gallios tells me that Adam has never before given such a unique gift like this to a Firstborn of any of his sons."

Lamech nodded.

From behind them, they heard someone else speak. "But Lamech was not the only one presented to Adam."

The three friends turned their attention to the open door at the far end of the room and found Captain Lubin standing in the doorway.

"Yes," said Lamech. "The good captain, here, Firstborn of the Adoraim, was also presented yesterday."

"At least I got that for all my trouble," said Lubin. "Particularly after my ship sank over a week ago as we tried to repair the damage it sustained from having to bring you three here."

"I am so sorry, Captain," said Logan.

"Do not feel too bad for him, Logan," said Lamech. "Adam agreed to replace it with a new and larger ship."

"And I think Adam will have a hand in designing it for him

as well," added Hemeth.

"Well, there is that," said Lubin as a wide grin broke out across his face. "How are you, Logan of the Zirci?"

Logan smiled. It was good to have friends. "I am still alive, thanks to all of you," he said. "And mostly thanks to the Head of Days."

"Head of Days, the Liberator, Molech," said Lubin, listing a variety of deities. "As captain, I thank them all and make my sacrifices to them too. You can never be too sure who is going to show up."

A wistful smile came to Logan's face. *I can*, he thought.

"Besides coming to check on you, Logan," Lubin continued, "I came to tell you that the first ship has been spotted, but it is still at least a day's journey away."

"Are those in response to Adam's message you told me about?" asked Logan.

"Yes," said Lamech. "Apparently, before your encounter with Xavier, word was sent to the mainland instructing the Firstborns to come to Atalànt. Since most of them were probably still in or near Adoraim for the Firstborn Council it was easy to round them all up quickly."

"The Council sent word back that they would leave at once," said Hemeth. "Now it appears they are not far from the island."

"I am glad you woke up today so that you can meet with the Created One before they arrive," said Lamech. "Now that the Created One has met with Lubin and me, I am sure the other lines would insist their Firstborns be presented to Adam before you, particularly the Cainites."

"Yes, I suppose you are right," said Logan. Strangely, the thought of meeting Adam filled Logan with unease. Obviously, Adam had seen Logan numerous times while he was unconscious. In fact, Adam must even have used some of Logan's memories to recreate the room in which he found himself. Still, being awake and meeting the First Man—the one who walked with God in the cool of the day in Eden—would make anyone uncomfortable.

"When will I be presented?" asked Logan.

"We were instructed to bring you the day after you awoke.

So that would be tomorrow morning," said Lamech. "Assuming you are up for it."

"I will be."

Logan spent the rest of the day taking time to walk around the residence. The bruise on his head had almost healed, and though the muscles in the rest of his body felt weak, he was pleased to get out and see the magnificent structure properly. During his battle, Logan had had little time to notice the beauty of the architecture. Even if he had had the chance to look, the dense trees and foliage would have prevented him from seeing much of anything. He remembered looking at the spires he could see from Lubin's ship as they entered the harbor. Though they were architectural wonders, the spires seemed to have become rather dilapidated.

As he walked about, he was astonished by the amount of change that had occurred in just two weeks. The forest around the residence had been removed, including all the trees and foliage he had been forced to walk through to get from the bridge to the Cainite spire. Fountains overgrown with plants and shrubs had been cleared out and were now running again. He walked past a few of the other spires and marveled at how much they had already been repaired. Representatives of all the sons of Adam who lived on the island had worked night and day since Adam's side of the island had been opened to them. Each clan had set about repairing their family tower as well as collaborating on renovating Adam's main residence.

"Each tower was built to house twenty to thirty men who would act as representatives from each clan that would come to visit Atalànt," Hemeth informed Logan as they walked past the Ono spire. "But of course, Adam closed himself off from everyone shortly after they were built."

When Logan and his friends walked past the Sethite tower, Logan could not help but notice it was still in dismal shape. Since Lamech was the only Sethite on the island and he was busy looking after Logan, there had been no one to work on the Sethite tower. The same was true of the Zirci tower, only it was in much worse shape. Because it had not been complete when that half of

Atalànt had gone fallow, it had fared worse than the other towers. Logan thought of his family in Pellios. Kedar had told him years ago about how he had worked with his father as they laid the cornerstone and began building the tower. It would be sad to tell Kedar and Lois about the state of this monument to their clan.

By the end of the day, Logan was exhausted and ready to sleep. Lubin walked them back to Adam's residence and said his farewell before joining his crew at the inn near the harbor. Lamech and Hemeth slept on their sheepskins in Logan's room. By the time Logan's head hit the pillow, he was already asleep.

The next morning came quickly. As usual, Lamech rose with the sun and woke the other two. "Time to get ready!"

Hemeth took a new tunic and trousers from his bag and gave them to Logan. "Gallios had these made for you for the occasion." Logan looked at them admiringly. He had never had such fine clothes. Clearly they were very expensive, made of the finest fabric. As with most tunics in the Ancient world, there were no sleeves, so that the bands on the arms could be displayed prominently.

"It is time to go," said Lamech, pointing out the window to the position of the sun in the sky. "We must not be late."

As they walked out of the room and headed toward the main hallway, Lubin came running up to them. Logan considered Lubin one of the most calm men he had ever seen in the face of adversity, even when the Leviathan had attacked. Now, however, he seemed visibly shaken.

"Lubin," Lamech said. "What is it?"

"The ship we saw yesterday ...," Lubin began. "It flies the flag of a Firstborn, but it did not come from Adoraim."

"What do you mean?" asked Logan.

"The ship flies the flag of Cain himself," said Lubin. "It is he who approaches the island."

"How could he have known to come now?" asked Hemeth. "Nod is much further from here than Adoraim. There is no way he could have received his summons yet."

"I know, that is what is so puzzling about it," replied Lubin. "He will make it to the harbor in several hours."

## Chapter XV

"I don't care who it is," said Lamech. "We are going to see the Created One, and we will sort out how to deal with him later." The four men kept walking along the hallway to a spacious room. At the end of the room stood two huge wooden doors, and in front of those doors stood a man Logan was not pleased to see: Callos.

"What is he doing here?" asked Logan in surprise.

"As the next-eldest on the island after Xavier, Callos is in charge of looking after Adam," said Lamech. "He has continually discouraged Adam from visiting you, and his constant presence is also why we stayed in your room the entire time. After we defeated Xavier, Callos apologized for trying to stop us and claims he was only acting under orders from his cousin."

"Then why is he allowed to serve Adam now?" asked Logan.

"The same reason you are wearing that fancy tunic: tradition. Callos is the eldest, so he gets the position," said Lamech.

"Great," Logan responded sarcastically as they walked up to Callos.

"I see you are feeling better, Logan of the Zirci," said Callos with a smile.

"Yes, I am fine enough," said Logan.

"I am so glad to hear that. After an uncomfortable pause, Callos continued. "I was wondering, though, how did you disperse the Great Spirits?"

"It was not me, but the Head of Days who dispersed the Dark Ones," Logan replied.

"Such humility," Callos said sweetly. "I suppose you consider yourself a hero? Unfortunately for all of us, you have tampered with forces you know nothing about and have caused great damage by releasing such creatures into the world. The next few weeks were to be a great celebration with all the Firstborns where Xavier would show them the mysteries of the cosmos. You see, by controlling them here on Atalànt, Xavier gained deep and hidden knowledge."

"Perhaps some things are better left unknown," said Logan.

"What a quaint notion. Fortunately, not everything was lost. My cousin Xavier passed along some of his secret knowledge to others. It is a quality of knowledge no human—not even the Originator—could know."

"Not all knowledge is beneficial for man."

Callos gave them a bitter smile. "On that, I think, we disagree. One last thing—I am sure your friend Captain Lubin did not miss the fact that Lord Cain will be arriving shortly."

"He informed us," Lamech said, reinserting himself into the conversation.

"Since Lord Cain is the eldest of all the sons of Adam, it is his right to see his father immediately upon arrival in our harbor. I am afraid I will have to ask you to postpone your audience with the Originator until Cain has a chance to meet with him first."

Logan saw Lamech's hand form a fist. "There is nothing preventing you from making such a request, Lord Callos," said Lamech, barely able to contain his contempt for the man.

"But you will not abide by it," Callos said, finishing Lamech's sentence.

"We will not," said Lamech.

"Very well, then," said Callos. "It is unwise to ignore tradition or to cross Lord Cain. Do not say I did not warn you, my young friends."

"You can keep your advice," said Logan sharply. "And as Gallios said when we first arrived, we are not your friends."

"Too true," replied Callos. With that he walked away from them down the corridor.

When he was gone, Lamech turned to Logan. "It is time, my friend, to meet your father." Logan looked at his three friends. "Thank you." Then, turning toward the doors, he opened them and walked in.

## XVI

*"From one man he made all the nations, that they should inhabit the whole earth; and he marked out their appointed times in history and the boundaries of their lands. God did this so that they would seek him and perhaps reach out for him and find him, though he is not far from any one of us."*
Acts 17:26-27 (NIV)

THE ROOM INTO WHICH LOGAN WALKED was in the shape of a large half circle. In some ways, it reminded Logan of the Council Chamber he had seen in Adoraim, only this room was cut in half and the focal point was not the middle of the room but the far wall, where a smaller semicircle was outlined. In that semicircle stood an empty, throne-like chair that seemed slightly off center, as if another chair was supposed to be beside it.

Twelve distinct seating sections emanated from twelve seats. Like the Council Chamber in Adoraim, each section became progressively larger toward the back of the room. Logan guessed that when Adam held court in years past those twelve seats were occupied by his twelve surviving sons. Behind them would sit their kin in order of generation.

There was a sizable skylight above, and large openings around the perimeter functioned as windows, allowing light to pour in. Logan guessed that the door behind the throne led to Adam's chambers. The door through which Logan had entered was the only one the sons of Adam were allowed to use. Unlike the Council Chamber in Adoraim, all of Adam's children would be forced to enter together.

"So, you have come at last," said a gravelly voice. Logan saw a very frail, old man walk in from the door behind the throne. He shuffled around to the massive chair and sat down. The man had light-brown skin and long hair that was white as salt. What startled Logan the most were his eyes. One was blue and the other brown. The man wore a sleeveless tunic like ordinary men, but he bore only one mark on his arm.

"Father?" said Logan.

"It is I, the Man, Adam," the old man replied. "You may approach."

Logan walked silently up one of the aisles.

"I am Logan, last son of the Zirci," Logan began. "And I—"

"I know who you are, Logan son of Joshua," Adam interrupted. "You do not remember, but I have seen you before—many times."

"Thank you for healing me, Father," said Logan, startled to hear his dad's name for the first time in decades.

Adam ignored Logan's gratitude. "There may well be Zirci blood in your veins, but we both know you are not of this place."

Logan was unsure what he should say or how much he should speak. "No," he confirmed.

"Logan," said Adam, not unkindly, "Under normal circumstances, I would not grant you an audience nor allow you to speak freely."

"Yes, father."

"But we both know these are not normal circumstances, do

we not?"

"Yes, Father."

"There is so little time left, my son. You may speak freely."

"Thank you, sir."

"So," Adam continued, "are you from the End of All Days?"

"I do not know that, Father. But I do come from a very distant future, yes."

"The question then is—why are you here?"

"I don't know exactly," said Logan. "But I was told that I must meet you at all costs."

"Really? That is what you were told?"

"Yes, Father."

"And who told you this?"

"Enoch, son of Jared, prophet of the Most High God and Firstborn among the Sethites."

"Prophet of the Most High, indeed!" cried Adam. "Enoch is a harbinger of trouble! Did you know that I rejected him, never granted him an audience with me?"

"Yes, Father."

"Did he tell you why?"

"No."

"Of course not! Why would the prophet of the Most High want such a thing to be remembered? Do you wish to know why?"

"If I may be allowed to know, yes."

"Very well. I will tell you. As you surely know, Enoch has a Gift like those of the Elder Born," said Adam. "In the year before his first son's birth, Enoch's mother died in a tragic accident. Jared grieved deeply for the passing of his wife. In his despair, Jared fell in love with a Cainite woman. I know something of being lonely, Logan. Enoch was angry and tried to use his Gift to force his father not to marry a daughter of Cain, but it is forbidden to use one's Gift in such a fashion—to manipulate others."

Logan wondered at how out of touch Adam had become. Did he not know that Enos forbade intermarriage with Cainites or that Tubal-Cain used his Gift to abuse others?

Adam continued. "Being young and foolish, Enoch was ignorant of how to use his Gift properly, so he was discovered. He was almost put to death for his interference, but because of me his life was spared. As a punishment, though, I refused to bless him. I also stopped any further meetings with Firstborns."

"That was when you sought solitude for your grief?"

"Yes."

"But, that was not why you retreated here, was it Father?"

"No."

"It was because of Zirci," said Logan. "Wasn't it?"

"Yes," said Adam said slowly, as if it pained him to even speak of such things. "Around that same time, my last son, Zirci, and his people were driven into the Tortured Mists by the Cainites. It was then I lost all hope. My youngest son was dead. Like Abel he was taken from me by Cain and I did not stop it. Only this time I could have no more sons to replace him."

"Your wife, our Mother, Eve, had died," said Logan, filling in the gaps. Logan was surprised to see a flicker of fierce anger cross Adam's dual-colored eyes, but all he replied was "Yes."

Although terrified at continuing, Logan felt he must press on. "Why does no one speak of our Mother Eve?"

"Because when I left the world of men, I commanded, under punishment of a curse, that no one speak of her death."

"Why? How did she die?"

"I do not wish to speak of it."

"But now, no one speaks of her at all."

"It is better that way."

"I am told that memories in this Ancient time are long. Yet, nothing remains about my Mother Eve for the Latter Born to remember. They doubt her very existence, and you have retreated so far from view that many doubt whether you even exist," said Logan.

Anger flashed across Adam's face, and this time it did not disappear. "Do you not think I am aware of this?"

"If you are aware, why do you allow it to continue?"

"Do not question me thus, boy!" Adam rose from his throne. "I did not ask you to come here. I wanted nothing from you."

"If you wanted nothing from me, why did you save me?" said Logan, trying his best to sound brave. "You could have just

## Chapter XVI

let me die, but you didn't."

Adam glared at Logan for a long time. Though terrified, Logan returned his gaze. Through that glare, Logan could see a pained expression on the old man's face. Then it disappeared as if a mask that had slipped down was put back in place.

"I saved you because you intrigued me, Logan, son of Joshua," said Adam. "And curiosity is a luxury for me. Until you came, there was precious little for me to be curious about. But you ... you are something new. You glow with a very peculiar light—a kind of light I thought had gone out of the universe. But now you show up on my island and it clings to you. You use it to push away the Dark Ones. I suppose that is why the Serpent dampened it for a time. But even he cannot hide a candle under a bushel for long. I tried to glean from your mind where and when you came from, but I was ... prevented from doing so. I only learned a few things about you."

"Like my father's name and how my bedroom looked as a child," said Logan.

"In truth, only little things like that were revealed to me," said Adam. "So I had to wait until you awoke to learn more. You are alive to stand before me now because you intrigue me, but curiosity has its limits."

"My Father," said Logan, "this has been a long journey for me—I have not always understood it. In fact, I am not sure I understand it now; but for thirty years I have been on a journey to come to this island and meet you, apparently to free you."

"Yes, you freed me," said Adam. He continued, "But perhaps you would not have been so merciful if you truly knew me."

"Why did you allow the Dark Ones in?" asked Logan.

"Answers to some questions are better left buried. They cause only pain. Let us end our meeting here."

"No, Father," said Logan with more force than he had intended. "Tell me."

"You presume too much, my son."

Logan remained silent.

"Very well," replied Adam, relenting. "Long ago a

messenger of God Most High, a Cherubim, gave me one warning, one command, and one prophecy, all of which concerned the future. The warning was that the world would be destroyed if the stench of sin rose up to reach God Most High. The command, then, was to make preparations that would allow humanity to continue if the world had to be cleansed. And the prophecy was that the future would bear witness against me for the sin I had committed.

"I have never told anyone about the warning or the command—you are the first. But I did prepare as I was commanded. But, more than that, I wanted to keep my world from ever being destroyed, so I forced laws upon my sons and their children to make sure their ways remained pure. The world would not be destroyed if I could stop it. But as my children increased on the planet, I saw I could not control them. Then my son Zirci and his people were destroyed by the Cainites, and I saw that all my efforts were without benefit. And so, as I said before, I retreated here with the Dark Ones. Only it is worse than you know. While the Dark Ones are followers of the Serpent, they had no power to find their way into this existence ... not without a beacon."

Logan's eyes widened as comprehension dawned upon him. "*You* were that beacon drawing them here."

"Yes," said Adam. "For the last two centuries, I have cared nothing for the world outside my residence. My pain became the beacon that drew the Dark Ones into this world's existence from ... somewhere else. I knew what I was doing, but I did not care what happened to me or this world. No one can truly understand the evil I have unleashed upon Creation. Then I saw you come to the island. Despite the work of the Serpent, I saw the light about you and ... you became a beacon for me. For the first time in centuries I tried to fight them, and although I was able to distract them, I had grown weak. It was not until you drove them away that I was free of them."

Tears formed in Logan's eyes. "I am pleased to serve you, Father. But, you said you never told anyone about the first two messages from the Cherubim. What about the third?"

Adam looked down with a bitter smile. "I am connected to

this world in a way no one can understand. When the door first opened in the Sacred Cave, I could *feel* it. Even here on Atalànt amongst the Dark Ones, I sensed it open. I have no way to describe to you how, but I knew it was a rip in time. I knew the prophecy was coming true. When rumors reached us of a metallic creature that killed people who came close, I became convinced you would not be far behind. So I told Xavier and the Dark Ones about the prophecy."

Adam stopped and considered his words carefully. "And I told them that should anyone ever come through that door, they should be prevented from coming here, because I had no wish to see you. It is for this reason you were taken from Parvaim by the Cainites and held captive by the Okrans."

Logan reeled in shock as he listened to Adam's words. "You ordered that? Do you know how Tubal-Cain used his Gift to harm me? Do you know what the Okrans did to me?"

"Yes," whispered Adam. "Lamech told me when we met."

"Did Lamech tell you what Tubal-Cain did to him or how the Cainites tried to kill us when he helped Hemeth escape the disgusting experiment in their camp?"

"Yes."

"Did he tell you how we were purposely sent through dangerous waters to be attacked by a Leviathan? And that we did all this so that we could come here to meet with *you* and ultimately free *you*?" Logan said, almost shouting.

"Yes."

Both remained quiet and Logan's heart beat wildly for several seconds. Finally, Adam spoke.

"When something is personal, forgiveness and mercy are not so easy to grant, are they Logan, son of Joshua?" he asked, looking down. "I heard the bold words you shouted at Xavier. You exacted a judgment upon him, as if you were sent for that purpose." Adam paused. "Will you exact judgment upon me?"

Logan prayed silently, trying to calm his anger. How could the man he was sent to rescue want to hurt him so much? As if in reply, a passage Logan had memorized came to him. It was something Jesus of Nazareth himself had quoted regarding what he was to do in the world:

> *The Spirit of the* Lord *is upon me,*
> *because he has anointed me to proclaim good*
> *news to the poor. He has sent me to proclaim*
> *freedom for the prisoners and recovery of*
> *sight for the blind, to set the oppressed free,*
> *to proclaim the year of the* Lord's *favor.*

Logan remembered how after Jesus had said these things about himself, the people of his own town wanted to throw him off a cliff. At that moment, Logan knew the answer to Adam's question and how he would respond.

"No, my Father," said Logan. "I am not your judge. You seem to have exacted enough judgement upon yourself. I am here to mix mercy with justice."

Once again there was silence in the room.

"But you have never answered my question, Father," Logan said. "How did Mother Eve die?"

The Created One looked down, unable to speak.

"Why do you fear to speak of your helpmate?" Logan asked.

Adam raised his head, and the look in his eyes pierced Logan's heart.

"I was not meant to be alone, Logan, but because of *my* weakness, my mate is dead, and she died so young," he said in words saturated with emotion. "In the beginning, at the time she needed me most, I failed her. In the garden, I knew what to do ... I knew what was right but I did not stop her. I failed in all that I was supposed to do. Later, even with all my knowledge ... with all my Gifts, I could not save her, and so she died bearing my last son, Zirci."

Logan's eyes widened in surprise. He had spent decades among the Zirci and they had never mentioned that Eve had died bearing their patriarch. They had always been vague about exactly when Eve had died. Adam's shame ran deep in the hearts of men.

"For years, I raged against God Most High," Adam continued. "I asked myself, 'How could he take her away from me? How could he threaten to destroy my world if it displeased him? How dare the future condemn me! What right did he have, what right did anyone have, to condemn me? This is my world!'"

Adam paused. "But I could not escape my own sense of justice. Deep down I knew ... I know ... all that has transpired is my fault. God Most High had every right to condemn me, and so would all of my children if they knew. That thought terrifies me. I wanted to bury it, so I commanded that the symbol of my greatest failure never be spoken of again, lest a curse befall the one who spoke of it. I would force the memory of Eve's death, even her life, out of the minds of men. So, Logan, son of Joshua, do you still think I am worthy of mercy?"

"No, my Father, you are not," said Logan. "But it would not be mercy if you were."

Adam began to weep.

Logan said, "Father, you told me you could not look into my mind as I slept. Something prevented you from seeing much of the world from which I came. If it is possible, would you now like to see that world through my memories? I was very young when I left that world, but I saw more of it than most people twice my age. Some of what you see will not be easy, because there is much pain in store for your offspring, but at least you will know the plan God has for saving this world. But you must promise me you will never speak to anyone of what you see. It is a gift for you only."

"I will accept, my son," said Adam. "And I promise to keep your confidences. In addition, I offer you a gift as well, one that only two men have ever received from me. One of those two died at the hands of the other."

"You mean Cain and Abel?"

"Yes."

"What gift is that?"

"I will let you see into *my* mind, into *my* past," said Adam. "It is the greatest gift I can give. While you do not have the capacity that my son Cain has, you will still see much, and I think there are things you must know if you are to prepare this world for its future. However, I must tell you this: if you accept this gift, I will know everything you know. Nothing will be hidden from me."

Logan gulped. Having a man who did not seem to be completely sane running around in your head was bad enough, but to have him know everything about you was even worse. "How do I know I can trust you?" he asked.

"I swear to you by the name of God Most High," said Adam. "You will not be harmed, and I will not tell a soul what I learn from you."

Then the Created One opened his mouth and breathed a sound that seemed to come from deep within him. Logan could never be sure if his ears actually heard physical vibrations, but he knew beyond any doubt that something deep within his own soul stirred in response.

"I accept," said Logan.

"Kneel, Logan, son of Joshua."

Logan knelt, and Adam placed his hand on Logan's head as if he were giving Logan a traditional blessing. After one terrifying moment, everything went blank.

# XVII

*"So God created man in his own image, in the image of God created he him; male and female created he them."*

Genesis 1:27 (KJV)

Logan felt as if he had been completely unmade, though some part of him was observing this sensation, so he knew he must still exist. The next moment, Logan took a deep breath of fresh, cool air. His lungs filled with anticipation. A rushing wind blew around and through him. He felt it flow through the very Earth itself and rumble round the solar system and through the galaxies beyond. Logan stilled his mind and heart to listen closely. He detected a central melody in the sound of the wind, to which all of Creation seemed to respond in harmony. The melody reminded Logan of the sound Adam made to seal his promise. But this sound was richer, more melodious, and full of beauty and love. Logan knew he was seeing what it was like not to be born, but created.

The picture shifted and he stood in a garden, if something that sublime could be called by such a simple term. The trees stood tall and strong, with beautiful fruit on every branch. A warm breeze blew all around him. Animals of every imaginable shape, color, and size came in and out of sight, and the sound of running water indicated a stream nearby. Looking up, Logan saw a picturesque mountain range soaring high on one side of the garden. It was a place so full of life and smells and sounds and colors that even in his greatest dreams Logan could never have fully imagined a scene like this. Then again, that was not completely true. There was something oddly familiar about the garden, but he could not put his finger on it.

Looking to the right he saw a woman. Though naked, there was no shame, for the glory of the LORD shone about her. Something about her ... *Was it in her face? Was it in her expression?* Logan could not say, but something about her made it clear she was a great woman—a queen, full of compassion and love and strength. There was no doubt in Logan's mind that the Mother of All stood before him.

He wished he could stand there forever, as he felt an abiding presence that gave him peace and contentment such as he had never felt in all his life. Unfortunately, this did not last long, for a worm of doubt entered his mind in the form of a question. It was a simple question.

*Is this enough?*

It was followed by another question.

*Do you not want to know more?*

Then another.

*Don't you deserve more?*

Then he heard himself answer, "No! It is enough."

The voice asked again. *Is it?*

Logan looked at his hands and saw the answer. The core of an unknown fruit lay there with its juice running down his hands, staining them red as blood.

The scene about him changed again. Now he was running for his life. Something immense and mighty was behind him, chasing him out of the garden. While Logan could not see the creature, he could hear it. Its voice boomed a warning, a command, and a prophecy. Then the creature grew quiet, and the silence frightened Logan even more than the voice. The next moment the mighty creature did something unexpected. It began to sing, and Logan knew then this creature must be the Cherubim, about which he had heard so much.

From what Logan remembered about Lois's explanation of the Cherubim's Song, he expected it to be a soulful, sad dirge, the sound of which would break his heart as it did Adam's—but it did not. Instead, the song reminded him of the first spring morning after a long New England winter. It was a song brimming with hope and redemption. He stopped running and turned around. What he saw shocked him more than anything in his life.

Before him stood an enormous creature holding a massive sword that flashed back and forth. The creature had four heads and eyes all over its body. One of its heads was that of a bull, another an eagle, a third a lion, and the last one was that of a man. All four faces were singing the glorious hymn in beautiful harmony with each other. All the eyes of all the faces stared intently at Logan; however, the expressions on those faces were not of contempt as Logan had expected. Instead, the eyes that beheld him were filled with wonder.

Logan had been so preoccupied by the Cherubim he did not notice at first that Adam stood next to him with an expression of amazement on his face. The memory from Adam's mind that Logan had obviously been experiencing had ended.

This was something new.

"You hear the Cherubim's Song?" asked Adam with tears in his eyes. Clearly the song was still painful to him.

"Yes, Father," said Logan.

"And it is pleasing to you?"

"Yes, Father. I could go on listening to it forever and ever," Logan said without a second thought. Then another voice interrupted their conversation. It came from the face of the man on the angel before them. It had stopped singing while the others continued their melody.

"Why, oh Man, do you wonder that the young one hears a different song?" the angel said in his booming voice with his sword still flashing in his hands. "He comes from a time when the great mystery has been revealed, an era between the already and the not yet. Surely you have just seen this in his memories of things yet to come."

"Yes, Great One, I have," replied Adam, bowing.

"You have been shown mercy to know the mystery that will be hidden for ages to come. To see the world as it will be. No doubt, it was a severe mercy you were given, but mercy nevertheless."

"Indeed, Great One."

"Time grows short, Created One. Prepare the way!"

"I shall."

The next moment, the Cherubim disappeared, as did the garden and everything else. Logan and Adam looked at each other.

"He is right; time is short," said Adam sadly. "I will make you ready."

Adam reached out, and when he touched Logan's head everything went black.

The next thing Logan remembered was hearing Adam speak to him as if he were a great distance away, but he could not make out the words. He opened his eyes to see that Adam was holding him up to keep his head from hitting the floor. The Created One was looking down at him, and in Adam's face Logan saw a new countenance. Adam's expression reminded Logan of his father comforting him as a child and telling him to get back on his bike after he had fallen while learning to ride. One lone tear rolled down Adam's face. It hung for a moment on his chin before splashing onto Logan's tunic.

Then Adam rose stiffly, which allowed Logan to rise as well. The old man shuffled over to the window and looked out to the spires beyond. "We are almost finished," he said.

It took a moment for Logan to realize Adam had spoken to

him in English.

"You speak English? How is that possible?"

Adam said, "I told you, Logan, whatever you knew, I would know. That includes your language. While it is a crude illustration, think of it like a tablet downloading something from the Internet."

"You understand what the Internet is ... was ... I mean, will be?" Logan wondered how in the world the most ancient of all men could understand something like the Internet.

"Of course," said Adam with an impish grin. For the moment, he seemed to have recovered from the somber mood he had been in when Logan first walked into the room. "I did not just learn facts from your mind; I learned their context as well. That is why I can understand things like computers and the Internet. I only wish you had been a bit older than thirteen when you came through the door. I would love to have learned much more about the world. But you are right; you did see more of the world than most thirteen-year-olds."

Logan stood in complete shock.

"What strikes me as the most ironic—and that is a great word, 'ironic'—we don't really have a word for that concept yet in our language," said Adam. "Anyway, what I find most ironic is that your greatest minds have everything backwards!"

"What?"

"Your great minds think humanity descended from the apes," Adam exclaimed incredulously. "Even you believed this for a time."

"Yes, I did."

Adam's mood seemed to change. Sadness returned to his eyes and he said, "And I am a myth to the people of your time."

"Yes, that is true too."

"It is ironic, because my helpmate, Eve, and I were to be the very beginning of something that would indeed have become more and more beautiful; but our choices changed all that. The Serpent has cleverly clouded the greatest minds of your time, making them believe our species evolves, when in reality it can only devolve.

"Your Holy Scriptures say that 'sin entered the world

through one man, and death through sin, and in this way death came to all people, because all sinned.' This is what I have done for the world."

"I cannot deny that," said Logan. "But I also know that 'the gift is not like the trespass. For if the many died by the trespass of the one man, how much more did God's grace and the gift that came by the grace of the one man, Jesus Christ, overflow to the many!'"

Smiling, Adam shielded his eyes from the brightness Logan knew must be coming from him.

"The angel was right," said Adam. "I have been shown a severe mercy, because I know in very real ways the destruction I have wrought on my children."

"You also know, Father," said Logan, "that through the Messiah we have redemption through his blood, the forgiveness of sins, in accordance with the riches of God's grace that he lavished on us. With all wisdom and understanding, he made known to us the mystery of his will according to his good pleasure, which he purposed in Christ, to be put into effect when the times reach their fulfillment—to bring unity to all things in heaven and on earth under Christ." Logan smiled. "Must I quote the entire New Testament to you?"

"No, Logan, son of Joshua," he said. "I have had enough of self-pity for one lifetime. There is nothing I can do to change what I have done. But there are a few things I can do for you and my children whom I will leave behind when I die, which I understand from your mind will be very soon."

"I am sorry you had to learn of your death in that way," said Logan.

"I did not need your ancient book of Genesis to tell me my days were ending. That I knew already," said Adam. "But come now; listen to what I have to tell you. First, you must inform Enoch, prophet of the Most High, that he must find a way for us to meet. I believe there is something I must teach him."

"Yes, Father. But why can't you just order him to come to you?"

"With the arrival of Cain on the island, many things will

become much more complicated, and I do not wish to cause any more grief than necessary to Enoch by publicly meeting with him. But Enoch is a crafty fellow; he will find a way."

"Yes, sir."

"Second, I give you a warning, my dear Logan. It appears you have a long life yet to live here in our Ancient world, and I believe you have more parts to play in the drama that will unfold when I am gone. You and I are not so very different. You must guard your ego."

Logan was caught off guard by Adam's comment. "What do you mean?"

"I established Atalànt so that everyone would know for all generations the greatness of my mind," said Adam. "It was to be a permanent testimony, but I know now there will be a time of what I will call 'Many Waters,' when it will all be washed away—every last bit of it. The only thing to remain will be vague myths of an island under the sea. All of my accomplishments will be erased from the pages of history. The only thing I will be remembered for is foolishly eating a fruit at the wrong time and in the wrong way."

"I don't understand," said Logan. "What does that have to do with me?"

"Don't you know?" asked Adam. "You know Scripture profoundly well. In fact, you have memorized large parts of it. But there is more than one reason why you searched and studied the Scriptures so much during your time in Pellios, wasn't there?"

"I suppose so," Logan said, looking down. "I was so very young when I came here. I knew very little of the Bible, so I searched it for any hint of what I might do."

"And did you find anything, Logan?"

"You know the answer to that question already."

"Yes, I do. You found nothing."

"Was it so bad to look for that?"

"No," said Adam, "not yet."

"I mean, if God Most High brought me here for a reason, how could nothing be recorded about me anywhere in Scripture?"

"If and when you find your answer to that question, Logan," said Adam, "you will have become a far greater man than I."

The two men regarded each other in silence for a moment.

"It is time you left me," said Adam.

"But there is so much more I wanted to ask," said Logan with tears in his eyes.

"I have told you everything you need to know for now, and I have given you great gifts, some you do not yet understand."

"But Father ..."

"I know how to give good gifts to my son," said Adam forcefully. "If you asked for bread, would I give you a snake or stone?"

"No, Father," said Logan, recognizing a similar passage from the Gospels.

"That is where you are wrong!" answered Adam. "I would indeed give you a snake and stone, but only because you need them. But now, my firstborn son approaches, and it would not be good for you to be here when he arrives."

"Yes, my Father," said Logan sadly.

Adam opened his arms in the same gesture Logan's own father had used when he put him to bed as a child. The two embraced and tears filled their eyes. Logan stepped back and bowed low. Then he turned and walked toward the door. Before he reached it, Adam spoke.

"Logan."

Logan turned toward Adam, who once again had an impish grin upon his face.

"In your mind, I saw a silly question about me that intrigued the foolish people of your time," Adam said. Then he raised the bottom hem of his tunic to reveal his midriff. Logan laughed to himself and nodded farewell to the Created One. In that moment, Logan promised himself he would keep the secret of whether or not Adam had a belly button to his last day on earth.

**Click or scan the QR Code to learn about the sign posts in this chapter.**

# XVIII

*"And the* Lord *said unto Cain, Why art thou wroth? and why is thy countenance fallen? If thou doest well, shalt thou not be accepted?"*

Genesis 4:6-7a (KJV)

As Logan exited the chamber into the large foyer, he found Lamech and Hemeth pacing back and forth. Hemeth caught sight of him first and ran over to him. "So, you are finally done? How did it go?"

"Never mind that now, Hemeth," Lamech interrupted. Turning to Logan he continued, "You were in there a long time, and according to Lubin, Cain has landed and is coming straight here. We have to get going now!"

"Oh," said Logan, still lost in thought from his meeting with Adam. "Yes, let's go."

Lamech quickly pointed them toward one of the hallways

leading from the foyer, but before they reached it, Logan heard a powerful voice behind him.

"You!"

Logan and the others stopped. They turned and saw a sizeable group of people emerge from an entrance on the opposite side of the foyer. Callos was in front, limping along because the injury he had sustained from Lamech had yet to heal. Walking next to him was a very old man dressed in fine, flowing garments. Though hunched and using an ornate staff to walk, the old man remained an imposing figure with a large and sturdy frame. His long white hair fell down the length of his back, and his weathered face held dark, piercing eyes. An ancient mark of the Line of Cain was tattooed into the olive skin of his right arm. Clearly, this was Lord Cain, and his gaze was fixed on Logan. From behind Cain several warriors fanned out to surround him. Logan noticed that the lead warrior had the marking of a Firstborn.

"That is Geber, Tubal-Cain's grandson," Hemeth whispered to his friends. "He often came to the artisan camp and was the leader of those who pursued us."

At this, Lamech stepped forward and put his hand on his sword.

"I care nothing for you, Sethite," Cain said dismissively to Lamech. "It is the spawn of Zirci to whom I speak. I have learned from Callos that because of your activity here on the island, two of my children are dead!"

Logan swallowed hard and his pulse raced.

"You should not be here!" continued Cain.

"Yet here I stand, Lord Cain," Logan said simply.

Cain opened his mouth to speak, but stopped and looked toward the door to Adam's chamber. His eyes narrowed as he returned his gaze to Logan. "The Originator beckons me to join him. Know this, Logan of the Zirci, you and I are not yet finished."

Cain nodded to Callos, who quickly opened the door to allow him into Adam's chamber. Closing the door after Cain, Callos spoke with a diplomatic air, "My friends, I am afraid I was correct when I told you Lord Cain would not be pleased if you chose to seek an audience with the Originator before him. You chose to dishonor the wrong person."

"I guess Lord Cain will have to learn to live with disappointment," said Lamech derisively.

Geber stepped to the front of the group. "So, this is the Sethite Firstborn with the Gift of Combat? And you are responsible for stealing my prize artisan and for the death of my men in forests outside Adoraim City?"

Lamech simply nodded.

"It is a shame we did not have the opportunity to meet earlier outside of Adoraim. You would not have found it so easy to harm me, Lamech."

From behind Lamech, Logan could hear Hemeth whisper, "It is reported that Geber has a Gift of Combat as well."

"Hiding behind your protectors again, Hemeth?" said Geber, switching his attention to him. "It seems you have done that your entire life, or so I heard from your brother." Logan saw Hemeth stiffen as Hedred stepped out from the group of people behind Geber and glared at him. "Hedred here has told me all about you and how you disapprove of my line's kindness to your people."

Hemeth was further startled when his sister, Sara, also stepped into view just behind Hedred. Despite the tense situation, she smiled reassuringly at him, which seemed to calm Hemeth a bit. Then she turned her attention to Logan and smiled again, as if to communicate how pleased she was that he had succeeded in meeting the Created One. The last time Logan had seen Sara, she had acted strangely, with a wide-eyed, frightening look about her as she spoke what sounded like nonsense. Now, however, Logan noticed how beautiful she was and how she naturally possessed a dignified, almost regal, countenance. She was unlike any Lowborn he had encountered during his travels so far.

"He is under my protection, Geber. You will not touch him!" said Lamech with bravado that Logan believed was a bit manufactured, given his friend's recent trauma.

"I see," said Geber. "So, if I chose to take him now you would fight us all?"

"I will—" began Lamech.

"There you are, Hemeth!" said someone entering the foyer from the door through which Logan and his friends had been planning to exit. It was Gallios, followed by the same group of sons who had come with him when the *Tomorrow's Destiny* first limped its way into Atalànt's harbor.

"Oh, is that you, Callos?" asked Gallios coyly. "I see you have brought our Cainite guests directly from their ship. Strange! I would have thought you would have allowed them to freshen up from their long journey before meeting the Created One."

"Great timing as always, Gallios," Callos responded dryly. "You seem to enjoy visiting this side of the island lately."

"Yes, well, Lamech sent word that Logan here would be meeting with the Created One this morning. I thought I would just come and collect him and Lamech along with my kinsman Hemeth. I am here to escort them to my residence. Is there a problem with that, Callos?"

Callos remained silent and glared at him.

"There is no problem, Lord Gallios," said Geber respectfully. "I am Geber, Firstborn of the Cainites. I am sure I can continue my discussion with Lamech in the future."

"It is good to make your acquaintance, Geber," said Gallios. "I notice you have two of my kin among you now. They are welcome to come with me to my residence as well."

"No, Lord Gallios. They will remain with me."

"As you wish. We had better be going now."

"Yes, I suppose you should," replied Geber, keeping his eye on Lamech. "Until we meet again."

Logan noticed Hemeth smile at his sister one more time before he turned to leave. Lamech was the last to exit the room, backing out slowly. Once away from Callos and the Cainites, Logan started toward his room, but Gallios stopped him.

"No, Logan. You do not need to go that way. I had one of my descendants fetch your belongings. He is waiting outside. Since you are the only Zirci and Lamech the only Sethite on the island, it seemed unwise for you to remain here with a ship full of Cainite warriors in the harbor. You will need to stay with me at my residence for now."

"Yes, sir," said Logan as he followed the group out of the residence.

As they walked, Hemeth turned to Logan and said, "So, tell us what you and Adam spoke about."

"Hemeth," said Gallios firmly but without the negative tone he had used with Hemeth weeks earlier, "that is a very rude thing to ask your friend. What passed between those two will remain between them unless he chooses to discuss it."

"Yes, sir," said Hemeth, chastened. Then he quickly added, "But do you want to discuss anything, Logan?"

"No," replied Logan.

The group talked freely about other subjects, however, as they enjoyed the walk to Gallios's residence. A number of Gallios's descendants joined in, having become friends with Hemeth over the past few weeks. Logan marveled at how different this trip was from their first one after arriving on the island. Gallios had become much more relaxed and easy to speak with, and he seemed pleased with, even proud of, Hemeth.

"Thank you for your hospitality, Lord Gallios," said Lamech. "Logan and I will surely join with your descendants in the daily work in the gardens. I would guess that representatives of my line will be arriving in a few weeks. Then Logan and I can move to where they are staying."

"That is a good plan, Lamech," Gallios said. "Soon members of my line will be arriving as well, and they will need a place to stay. The population of the island will swell as people from everywhere come for this special occasion, however depressing it is. In the meantime, Hemeth and I will continue designing Janice's tomb."

Logan felt deep remorse as he remembered the last words of Janice and how they were cut off mid-sentence. Hemeth noticed this and placed his hand on Logan's shoulder.

"We will be sure to honor her sacrifice," Hemeth said. "Gallios and I will design a magnificent marker for her tomb. I can tell you it will be something of beauty and grandeur to demonstrate her importance to this island and to all of humanity."

"I am pleased to hear that," said Logan.

"I have made a decision, one that I do not take lightly,"

Gallios said solemnly.

"What is that, Lord Gallios?" asked Lamech.

"Over the last several weeks I have gotten to know your friend Hemeth as we have talked about Janice and begun designing her tomb. He has a remarkable Gift unheard of among the Lowborn. I have not seen such a powerful and artistic mind in many generations. Such a thing should not be wasted constructing roads on the mainland. Thus, I have decided to make him my student, and he has agreed."

"I know he is not directly related to you, so will his clan have a problem with that?"

"If his family was willing to give him to the Cainite brutes to learn churios, they should have no problem allowing one of their own line to train and raise him."

"That is great!" said Logan.

"Yes, he will live with me and learn from me, as if he were my own son," Gallios said, turning to Hemeth. "Am I correct that the two Ono with Geber were your brother and sister?"

"Yes, sir."

"That is even better. Having members of your own family here on Atalànt will make it even easier to make the arrangements."

"I am not so sure, sir," said Hemeth. "My brother Hedred hates me and may cause trouble."

"We shall see."

"What is the first thing Hemeth will do?" asked Logan. "Will you continue to train him in churios?"

"No, not at first. He must learn something more practical," replied Gallios. "I have already introduced him to the main architect and builder of Captain Lubin's new ship. Hemeth will be learning about ship design and construction."

"Really?" said Logan.

"Yes, I think he will be very good at it. Starting the day after tomorrow Hemeth will move to the harbor with Captain Lubin and his crew to begin his training. You and Lamech may visit him if you wish, as long as you keep to yourselves and take some of my descendants along to escort you. With a ship full of Cainite warriors in the harbor it is wise to take precautions."

"You will have no argument from me," said Logan.

"Good." Gallios smiled. "Now, let's pick up our pace. I have planned a banquet as soon as we get back. It is in your honor, Logan, and I am getting hungry!"

# XIX

*"Be still before the* LORD *and wait patiently for him; do not fret when people succeed in their ways, when they carry out their wicked schemes."*

Psalm 37:7 (NIV)

THE NEXT TWO WEEKS WERE VERY GOOD ONES FOR LOGAN. For the first five days after he arrived at Gallios's residence, he was required to rest to ensure he was fully recovered from his injuries. Though Logan did not wish to admit it, he was glad for this extra time alone. It gave him the opportunity to not only finish healing, but also to ponder all that he had experienced in the last several months. When Gallios felt confident that Logan was strong enough, he sent him with Lamech to work in the orchards. Logan was pleased to get outside and work again, although he had to take everything he did slowly. It would be months before he would be at full strength again. For his part, Gallios was impressed with Lamech, informing him that none of the Ono Firstborns, particularly the younger ones, would ever have consented to work in the orchards.

Logan and Lamech saw nothing of Hemeth during the first two weeks, since he was busy working with Lubin's crew constructing the hull of the new ship. But they heard news of him from those who traveled to the other side of the island on business for Gallios. Hemeth enjoyed being among Lubin's crew and spending time with first mate Huppim. Construction of the new ship had, however, slowed due to the fact the Created One had sent word to the lead designer that he wanted to make a few modifications to the ship's design. Although it would take a little backtracking, once the designs were implemented the ship would be better for it. When Logan heard this, he wondered if some of the modifications Adam was requiring came from things extrapolated from memories he had seen during their shared experience.

Almost two weeks after Logan's meeting with Adam, it was reported to Gallios that Adoraim and Zior ships transporting Firstborn delegations from all the sons of Adam had been spotted and would soon arrive. Men and women from all parts of the known world began descending upon Atalànt. The night Lamech heard the news, he asked Gallios to allow himself and Logan to travel to the other side of the island to await Seth, Enos, and the other Sethite Firstborns. Gallios gave his permission with a reminder to stay away from the Cainite delegations.

The next morning Logan and Lamech set out for the harbor in the company of several of Gallios's descendants who had business there as well. After a pleasant and uneventful journey, they thanked their fellow travelers and went off to find Hemeth. By the time they found him, he was sitting with Huppim and the rest of Lubin's crew eating their midday meal. He looked completely at home, and Logan was sure he had never seen him so happy.

"Hello, Hemeth!" Lamech said as he and Logan approached. The crew raised their heads in Lamech's direction and gave him a wave.

"Greetings, Lamech, Logan," Hemeth called in response. "Come join us for a meal!"

"I think we will," said Lamech. As Logan and Lamech ate with the crew, Hemeth explained all that he was doing and how everything would work and fit together.

"At first, Captain Lubin was not pleased that the construction of his ship slowed down because of modifications Adam insisted on," said Hemeth, "but now he sees how much sturdier and faster his new ship will be."

"Where is the good captain?" asked Lamech.

"He went over to inspect Adoraim's spire on Adam's portion of the island," Huppim said, speaking for the first time. "He intends to give his elders a complete list of things they will need to repair it and bring it back to pristine shape from its dilapidated state. The captain should be returning shortly, I would guess."

"I did the same thing with the Sethite spire several weeks ago while I watched over Logan during his recovery," Lamech said. "It was not a pretty sight. I thought about going over there today, but I think it would be unwise to venture off by myself. It would be too easy to run into trouble with the Cainites."

Huppim frowned and fixed his eyes on something over Lamech's left shoulder. "You may not be looking for trouble, but it might be coming to look for you."

Logan and Lamech turned to see Geber, Sara, and Hedred approaching them, flanked by two Cainite warriors. Logan noted with interest that Sara walked to Geber's right with Hedred walking behind.

"Please do not cause any trouble, Lamech," Huppim said quickly. "While I do not care for them personally, our line has good relations with the Cainites. It would not be good to draw their ire."

"Have no fear, Huppim," said Lamech. "I do not think they are here to fight. They would have brought more warriors if that were the case."

"What do you suppose they want?" asked Hemeth.

"I do not know, but let's find out." Lamech put down his meal and rose to his feet, as did those around him. Opening his hands to show he was not reaching for a weapon, he walked toward the newcomers. Geber made the same gesture in response as he approached.

"Greetings, Lamech, Firstborn of the Sethites," said Geber. "I thought perhaps we might see you here before now."

"There has been nothing on this side of the island to draw my interest until now," replied Lamech.

Geber smiled at the slight, but otherwise ignored it. "The Firstborns will soon arrive and we shall see how events with Adam's passing will transpire."

"Yes, and I am sure you will be pleased to meet up with your grandfather and the rest of the Firstborn Cainites to plan more trouble for the world."

Geber smiled again. "You are so much like your Sethite fathers. It is a pity you cannot see all the good we bring to the world. But it does not matter now. When the rest of the Cainite ships arrive, I will no longer be a Firstborn."

Logan and Hemeth looked at each other in confusion. Lamech was clearly confused as well. "What are you referring to, Geber?"

"I have learned from a very reliable source that whatever trick your friend Hemeth here did to Lord Tubal-Cain, it has cost him the title of Firstborn ... at least for now. My grandfather has a rather complicated lineage, and if he ceases to be a Firstborn, so do I. In fact, I do not believe he will even show up here for the festivities."

"Does Lord Cain know of this?"

"Not yet, but he soon will."

"Why would you tell us this?" asked Lamech skeptically.

"Undoubtedly, you think that we Cainites are liars not to be trusted," Geber said slyly. "Perhaps I just wanted to show you we are not all like that."

Lamech and the others remained silent, unsure how to respond.

"I also wanted Sara and Hedred to be able to visit their brother," continued Geber. "It has been a long time since they have had a chance to see him." The expression of surprise that flashed across Hedred's face told Logan that this reason for the visit was news to him. While Hedred stood there, unsure what to do, Sara took the opportunity to run over to Hemeth and give him a bear hug. With tears in her eyes, she held him for several moments.

"You see," said Geber with a smile, "Cainites are reasonable people."

"Hmm," Lamech managed to say.

"In fact," Geber continued, "we recently received a message from Lord Gallios asking Hedred if Hemeth could remain on Atalànt to become his student. It sounds as if he might make him his son. How very kind of the old man." Another wave of surprise flashed across Hedred's face, telling Logan this revelation was also new to him.

"What do you say about such an arrangement, Hedred?" asked Geber. "Even though you are Lowborn, you are Hemeth's eldest brother, and your word would carry the most weight when the Ono deliberate the boy's future. Should Hemeth be allowed to stay on Atalànt and be raised by Lord Gallios?"

Hemeth's eyes grew wide in surety of what would be coming next from his eldest brother.

"No!" cried Hedred. "That boy should not be rewarded for what he did! He is a worthless excuse for a man in my line! No, I will never agree to such an arrangement!"

Geber opened his mouth to say something, but Sara spoke first. "I will stay with you, Geber, if Hemeth is allowed to remain with Lord Gallios."

Geber closed his mouth with a slight smile. "What did you say, my dear?"

"I willingly agree to stay with you and not return to the Ono lands if Hemeth is allowed to stay here on Atalànt."

"No!" Hemeth could no longer contain himself. "You cannot do that!"

"Shut up, brother!" Hedred said sharply. "Learn your place!"

Geber gave Hedred a sharp look. "My apologies, sir," Hedred said sheepishly.

Returning his attention to Sara, Geber said, "Are you sure, my dear?"

"Yes."

Geber said to Hedred, "If your sister is to remain with me, I suppose I would agree to allow you to remain as well. Or would you prefer to return to your village in the Ono lands, Hedred?"

Now Logan knew the reason for the unexpected visit. It had been designed in typical Cainite fashion for Geber to achieve his end, which was to keep Sara with him. Not only was she beautiful and intelligent, but she was a seer—something Logan was sure Geber had discovered and was looking to exploit.

Watching the expression on Hedred's face was almost comical. Logan could almost see how the man's small brain was grappling with the alternatives, trying to determine if he hated Hemeth enough to sentence himself to the ordinary life of an Ono Lowborn, or if it was worth giving Hemeth what he wanted if that meant Hedred could seek his fortune among the Cainites. Finally, Hedred's spite lost to his selfishness.

"Very well, sir."

"Well, I am glad to hear that," said Geber. Turning to Lamech, he continued, "It appears our business with you is concluded. You have nothing to fear from us while you wait for your elders to arrive. Unless you decide to start something, we will not trouble you."

Geber began walking away, but then turned around. "Oh, but I do have one note of caution for you, Hemeth," he said with a grin. "I would try to avoid Tubal-Cain's sister, Naamah. She has always been very fond of her brother, and she is said to have a legendary temper. I doubt she will be pleased to meet you when she arrives."

With that Geber nodded to Sara and retreated.

Sara, taking that as her cue to leave, kissed Hemeth on the forehead and told him not to be concerned. "I will always protect you, my brother," she said quietly so that only Hemeth and Logan heard. Then she turned and was gone. The look of contentment that Logan had seen earlier on Hemeth's face was now replaced with lines of worry. Logan placed his hand on the young man's

# Chapter XIX

shoulder and saw there were tears in his eyes.

## XX

*"As a jewel of gold in a swine's snout, so is a fair woman which is without discretion."*

Proverbs 11:22 (KJV)

Logan and Lamech spent the rest of the day with Hemeth and the crew of *Tomorrow's Destiny* and slept in their quarters that night. Logan did his best to encourage Hemeth, but Logan knew his friend would always feel an aching sadness for his sister whose life would now be forever changed. Hemeth told him that, unlike Hedred, Sara had never wanted to venture far from the Ono lands. Although she had natural elegance and was as clever as the day was long, she preferred the simple things of life. Living among the Cainites, life would be anything but simple.

The next morning a large Zior ship flying the flags of Seth and Enos entered the harbor. Because Seth and Enos were the two eldest Sethite Firstborns, their delegations were quite large.

Lamech and Logan watched from above as the two Firstborns and their mates exited the ship first and waited for an elevating box to raise them up the side of the cliff.

Lamech and Logan knelt before them in greeting. "Welcome to Atalànt, my fathers," Lamech said.

Seth placed his hand upon their heads, one after the other. "Thank you, Lamech. Rise now, my son. Rise as well, Logan of the Zirci," he said.

"Yes, sir," they both said as they stood up.

"I wish to hear of your journey here and all that has gone on since we last met. However, I must first move with haste to see my father. Tell me this, though. Did you meet the Created One, and did he bless you?"

"Yes, sir. He also gave me this," said Lamech, pointing to the armband with two flattened orbs on it.

"Very interesting." Seth looked closely at the gift.

"Do you have any idea what the markings on the stones mean?" asked Lamech.

"I am afraid not, my son. But, I will inquire about them when I meet with Adam."

"Thank you, sir."

"And what of you, Logan of the Zirci?" asked Seth. "Have you succeeded in meeting with my father?"

"We did meet, sir, but not without trouble. However, all was accomplished, I believe."

"I believe I see the results of that trouble in the new scars upon your body and some bruises that have not completely healed," replied Seth with concern. "Still, I am pleased you succeeded in your goal. We will discuss this more later, but now I must go. Enos will talk with you now about these subjects."

"Yes, sir."

Together with his wife and some attendants, Seth proceeded toward Adam's side of the island. Enos suggested they walk in the same direction to evaluate the state of the Sethite spire.

"As you probably saw as you approached the island, the Sethite tower is in great need of repair," said Lamech as they walked toward the tower.

"We did indeed." Enos shook his head in frustration. "It did not look good."

"I have determined the supplies required to repair it and ordered them from local merchants. We need only to send men over to collect them and begin the work."

"Good man, Lamech. That is thinking like a leader."

Lamech smiled at the compliment.

"Now please," continued Enos, "tell me of your adventures on this famed island."

Lamech began the tale, starting just after he and his companions left the harbor of Adoraim City in haste. He explained all about his self-destructive tendencies during the storm and how Hemeth had drugged him to keep him safe. Enos's frown deepened as he heard about how Captain Lubin had chained him up in the hold during most of the trip.

"He held one of our Firstborns bound for two weeks?" Enos said with indignation.

"I am sorry, sir," said Logan after being given permission to speak. "That was my idea. Lamech was not thinking straight, and we could not take any chances that he might do something to himself during the trip."

"I see." Enos eyed Logan closely. "So, you will resort to very extreme measures if needed, Logan of the Zirci?"

"Yes, sir. Enoch told me that I had to ensure we all made it to Atalànt. I saw it as the only way, so I persuaded Captain Lubin to do it."

"Hmm. You have grown much more determined since you first showed up with Enoch years ago," Enos said. "Continue now, Lamech."

Lamech told him all about their battle with the Leviathan and how together he and Logan had saved the ship. Enos beamed with pride. "Now that is a Sethite!" he said triumphantly. "But tell me, how did you know you were going the wrong way?"

Lamech looked to Logan for help with this question. Logan confided in Enos about the map he had in his possession and how he determined they were seriously off course.

"Again you surprise me with your mysterious gifts, Logan

of the Zirci. Perhaps this is why Enoch is so fond of you."

By this time, the group had reached the Sethite spire. They had spotted several Cainite warriors milling about along the way, but as Geber had promised, none of them had approached. Tears came to Enos's eyes when he looked up at the spire he had helped build and saw the state of disrepair into which it had fallen. However, he did not tarry but quickly sent some of his attendants to fetch the supplies Lamech had ordered. Meanwhile, the rest of the Sethites began doing what they could to make the place livable.

"Father Enos," said Lamech, "it is a good thing, in a way, that we approached from the east, because Atalànt has no defenses on that side of the island and we were not expected. If we had approached in a normal fashion, the inhabitants might have attacked us. Why was no message sent to Atalànt as we were promised?"

"No message? That is concerning indeed, Lamech," replied Enos in surprise. "We were delayed in sending the carrier pigeon because of the storm, but I personally sent it on its way several days after your departure. It should have made it before you arrived. I fear there has been foul play. As you know, the Okrans are excellent falconers. They could have dispatched one of their birds of prey to intercept it. The fact that you survived is nothing short of a miracle. The Head of Days has blessed you and the young captain who brought you here. But now, tell me about what occurred to unshroud the Created One's residence and also about your meetings with the Created One."

The next hour was spent reliving the challenges the friends encountered once they spotted the island and how Janice urged them to change course. They described how Hemeth communicated with her after meeting her, how she had protected the island from the Dark Ones, and how she told Hemeth what Logan had to do.

"Did you ever meet Janice?" asked Lamech.

"Yes, several times, but I never knew her well," replied Enos. "I did not know she had such a powerful Gift."

Together Logan and Lamech described how Logan had

banished the Dark Ones from Atalànt and had almost been killed by Xavier, but recovered under Adam's healing touch. Lamech allowed Enos to inspect the odd stone armband Adam had given him.

"That is a beautiful design on the two stones, but I confess it is a mystery to me. I hope my father will persuade Adam to tell us what, if anything, it means," said Enos. "Now, Logan, what of your meeting with our father Adam?"

"I believe it was a success," said Logan.

"My impertinent Firstborn descendant Enoch informed me I should not inquire about the meeting, because what was spoken between you two must remain private," said Enos with a rueful smile. "I suppose that is true?"

"Yes, sir," Logan said.

"Then at least tell me this," said Enos with a grin. "What did he look like?"

Logan and Lamech exchanged confused looks. Both knew Enos had met the Created One several times over the course of his life, and Logan wondered why he would ask such an odd question.

"Well, for one thing," Logan said, "he had one blue eye and one brown, which I found rather disturbing."

Enos laughed. "I see! Even now near the end of his life he must be in the midst of another change."

"What do you mean?" asked Lamech.

"His appearance ... it has altered many different times over the last 930 years. I do not think he can tell exactly when it will take place. It just does."

"You mean his skin ... his facial features ... all change?" Logan asked.

"That is correct," replied Enos. "If you had seen him when you were a child, you may not recognize him now that you are a man. However, he remains in essence himself. I have always believed that the Head of Days chose to make him the embodiment of unity in diversity. It was a Gift—one that he could not pass on to his children."

"Why has no one ever told us this?" asked Lamech.

"There are matters the sons of Adam do not discuss,"

answered Enos. "For some Adam's changing appearance is frightening, and for others it is a sacred matter. Either way, it is not spoken of lightly."

Just then some of Enos's attendants returned with the supplies for repairing the Sethite spire. "I suppose it is time we now made this place look the way it was intended!" said Lamech, looking at everything being brought in.

"I agree," replied Enos.

For the rest of the day, Lamech and Logan worked with the other Sethites under the direction of Enos to begin the much-needed repairs. The following day many more ships arrived carrying delegations of Firstborns. A dozen Zior and Adoraim ships filled the harbor. Because of the need to transport so many nobles to the island before Adam's passing, the restrictions on who could know the location of Atalànt had been lifted.

Logan was pleased to see the flags of Enoch and Methuselah hoisted above one of the incoming ships. He spotted the flag of Enoch's father, Jared, on the same ship. Logan wondered how interesting that voyage must have been with all of them aboard. With so many Firstborn delegations arriving, it took a while for all the people to be transported up the cliff face. When Enoch and Methuselah finally stepped off the elevating box, Logan and Lamech were the first to greet them. Tears streamed down Methuselah's face as he embraced Lamech and found him once again in his right mind. Logan and Lamech led them to the Sethite spire and once again related all their adventures since leaving Enoch and Methuselah in Adoraim City.

"So," said Enoch after hearing everything, "during all this time Janice was protecting us. The Head of Days is truly amazing. And I am glad you succeeded in reaching the Created One before the rest of us made it here. It would have been very difficult otherwise."

"Oh, that reminds me," said Logan, "Adam specifically instructed me to tell you to find a way for you to meet with him. He believes he has something important to teach you."

"Really?" said Enoch in surprise. "After all this time, he wants to meet me. He must have really changed."

"Do you think you will be able to find a way into Adam's presence without others finding out?"

Enoch smiled broadly. "I think together with Seth and Enos, I will be able to manage it."

"I hope so. It seemed important to him."

"Interesting," Enoch said.

One of the Sethites working high up on the spire shouted to Enoch and the others below. "There is a man running toward us, and I do not recognize him!"

"Is he armed?" Lamech called back.

"It does not appear so, and he is coming alone."

Lamech unsheathed his sword in preparation for trouble. Other Sethites stopped their work and came over to help if needed. A moment later Huppim, first mate of *Tomorrow's Destiny*, came running into view.

Logan felt himself relax after seeing who it was.

"Do not be concerned," Lamech called to those around him. "This is Huppim, a friend!"

"Is something wrong?" asked Logan.

"Yes," Huppim replied. "Naamah, Tubal-Cain's sister, just arrived and immediately asked where she could find Hemeth. Everyone here on the island knows who he is now, and they told her he was with us at the construction site of the new vessel. She has been making a huge commotion by yelling curses at him, and at the rest of us for allowing him to work alongside us. Captain Lubin went up to intervene, but he cannot get her to stop. After the events in Adoraim City, he is not much liked by the Cainite Firstborns. As I told you before, we cannot afford to have the Cainites against us any more than they already are. The Ono delegations have not yet arrived and few, if any, of Gallios's descendants are in town, so we need you to come now and take Hemeth to Gallios's residence before something more happens."

Lamech looked to his father for permission to leave.

"Go, my son. It appears you are needed," Methuselah said resolutely, but not without a tinge of sadness. "It appears our reunion will have to continue later."

"Thank you, Father," said Lamech as he took off with

Huppim to help Hemeth.

"Logan," said Enoch before Logan could say anything, "I am sure you wish to go as well. And you may. But be careful. We will find our way to Gallios's residence to meet up with you in a few days."

"Yes, sir."

"And Logan," he continued, "do not underestimate the spite of a Cainite woman!"

"Yes, sir!" Logan ran after Lamech. It took him only a few minutes to make his way to the bridge to the Elder Born side of the island. He heard the yelling even before he reached the other side. A woman's voice was calling down every imaginable oath on Hemeth from the whole pantheon of gods the Cainites worshipped. A small group of people stood near her on the top of the cliff, including Captain Lubin. Several of them were trying to persuade her to stop, but she stubbornly refused and was becoming increasingly agitated. The Cainite warriors guarding her were pushing away anyone they thought was coming too close.

Logan spotted Geber off to the side watching the spectacle with an amused expression. When Geber saw Logan, he gave a short nod as if to say, "I told you so." Logan frowned at him and continued.

Proceeding quickly to the elevating box, Logan found that Lamech and Huppim had already begun their rapid descent. Lamech caught Logan's eye and signaled him to wait for their return. Not knowing what to do in the meantime, Logan stood watching the spectacle until he noticed another woman staring at him. A trickle of fear went down his back when Logan realized it was Jared's Cainite wife, Milali. Logan watched as Milali made her way over to Naamah and after a few unsuccessful attempts, was able to get the furious woman's attention. She pointed toward Logan.

*Uh-oh*, Logan thought as he saw what was coming. Looking down, he saw Lamech and Huppim had made it to the ground, and Hemeth was running over to board the box with them for the return trip up the cliff face. Running over to the men who were cranking the pulley, Logan offered to assist them in bringing his friends up faster.

"No thank you, Logan of the Zirci. We will be fine," said one of the men. Nodding to something behind Logan he continued, "Besides, it looks like you will have to concentrate on other matters."

Logan spun around to see Naamah marching toward him with her Cainite warriors in tow. He swallowed hard and walked toward her in the belief that if he could not avoid the confrontation, at least he might divert her attention for a few moments to buy his friends some time to get to the top. As he approached he looked over at Geber, who still wore the smirk on face and now had his hand on his sword.

"You!" Naamah shouted when she was still far off. The vehemence of her voice sounded remarkably similar to Lord Cain when he had first encountered Logan.

"You must be Lady Naamah," said Logan in as pleasant a tone as possible.

"You know very well who I am," said Naamah as she came within a few arm's lengths of Logan. "It is because of you and your friend that my brother has been disgraced!"

"Your brother attacked my friends and used his Gifts against us," said Logan. "How is any of this our fault?"

"Tubal-Cain is a great man who created opportunities for Lowborns of different lines to make more of themselves than they ever would have in their own lines. Now you and your friends have destroyed all that because our elders have stopped his enterprises."

"Well, that is a relief." Logan was irritated by the woman's haughty tone. "I would not want him manipulating anyone else!"

"How dare you, you diseased piece of Zirci filth!" she yelled. "You and your friends bring nothing but bad luck and trouble to our lands. Lord Cain was right to destroy your kind. You have no right to stand upon the shores of Atalànt!"

"Yet here I am, and your brother is not," Logan said smugly. Just then Logan's eye caught a glimpse of something reflecting in her left hand. He realized too slowly that she had some kind of weapon concealed in the sleeve of her robe which had dropped into her hand. As he instinctively raised his arm to try and deflect the strike, he felt himself being shoved roughly onto the ground. With the wind knocked out of him, it took a moment for him to realize it was not one of Naamah's guards who had shoved him, but Lamech, who was now standing over him glaring at Naamah and her guards with his hand upon his sheathed sword as if challenging them to attack. Naamah was holding her left wrist, which was clearly in pain from being grabbed by Lamech.

"You dare strike a member of the Cainite Highborn family!" cried one of the Naamah's warriors, drawing his sword. Logan noticed that Geber too had drawn his sword.

"When she wishes to kill a friend of mine who is under my protection," said Lamech in a matter-of-fact tone, "yes!"

"It looks to me as if he was the aggressor, Lady Naamah," Geber called as approached.

Hemeth came up from behind and picked up a dagger that was lying on the ground. After inspecting its intricate design for a moment, he cleared his throat loudly, attempting to get Lamech's attention and receive permission to address the Firstborns.

"What is it, Hemeth?" asked Lamech.

"This weapon has a design on the handle that Geber's family is particularly fond of, if I remember correctly. In fact, Geber showed me his dagger once at the artisan camp, and it had this same pattern of precious gems along the edge here."

"Perhaps you stole it," said Geber, smiling. "After all, you have shown yourself to be very untrustworthy."

"Let us take this matter directly to the Created One," interjected Logan, not wanting the situation to escalate. "He will judge between us."

"Lamech and I can settle this little problem, Logan of the Zirci." Geber fixed his eyes on Lamech and continued, "There is no need to bring the Originator into this dispute." At these words, Lamech's fist tightened around the handle of his sword and Logan could see he was doing all he could to resist the temptation to fight.

Logan spoke quickly. "I am afraid I must insist that we bring this matter to the Created One. It would be a great insult to have his children fight each other after being invited to his island."

"You were not invited here, Zirci!" said Geber, turning to him.

"Perhaps not. But I was granted a rare audience with the Created One, and he did welcome me here. I would not wish to disparage his hospitality. Would you, Geber?"

Geber's eyes narrowed. He knew he had been outmaneuvered. "I suppose it would be best not to disturb the Originator. I am sure this was all a misunderstanding."

"And Cainite women are famed for their tempers," Lamech interjected. "For the sake of Adam and his desire for peace, let us call this matter closed."

"For now," said Geber in resignation, "I agree."

"What?" cried Naamah, who had begun to recover from her initial shock at having the dagger knocked from her hand. "You are going to let me go unavenged, Geber?"

"For now," Geber said in resignation, "there is nothing to avenge."

Naamah unleashed a tongue-lashing upon Geber that rivaled the one she had given Hemeth earlier. Logan and Lamech looked at each other and seized the opportunity to leave the area, but not before Geber gave them a slight nod to indicate this situation was far from over. Hemeth, taking his cue, threw the dagger into the ground and followed his two friends away from the argumentative Cainite woman.

Logan saw Enoch watching them from under a tree in the distance. Lamech also caught sight of him and headed in that direction, with Logan and Hemeth following.

When they reached him, Lamech said, "Hello, Enoch. Did you not care to intervene?"

"Me?" asked Enoch. "Do you think my words would have done anything but provoke them?"

"No, Grandfather," said Lamech. "Now that I think of it, you would have made things worse."

Enoch smiled broadly. "Besides, you two did well on your own. It looks as if you two are learning something about how to defuse situations without fighting. There is hope for you yet."

"It was your father's wife, Milali, who pointed me out to Naamah," said Logan.

"That is not surprising. She will cause us trouble anytime she can."

Just then Captain Lubin and Huppim walked up.

"I wish I could have distracted her," said Lubin. "But she would not be consoled."

"Greetings, Captain Lubin, Firstborn of the Adoraim," said Enoch formally. Then he added, "Do not trouble yourself. I would not expect a Cainite woman to be so easily consoled."

"Greetings, Enoch, Firstborn of the Sethites," replied Lubin in equally formal terms. Turning to Lamech and the others he continued, "You had all better leave here quickly, before Lady Naamah starts up again with you."

"Agreed," said Enoch. "I think it is a good idea if you three return to Gallios's residence until everything quiets down here. I will come in a few days to speak with Gallios."

"Unfortunately, I do not think you will be able to work on the ship with Captain Lubin's crew for a while, Hemeth," said Logan.

"That is fine with me," said Hemeth in relief. "Anything to stay away from that woman is good with me!"

"And now," said Enoch, turning to Lubin, "I think the captain and I need to return to the Sethite spire to settle our accounts, seeing that you all made it here safely."

"That would be very good," replied Lubin.

"Then I wish you well until we meet again, Grandfather," said Lamech. Turning to Logan and the others he continued, "Let's go, and quickly!"

# XXI

*"The L*ORD *watches over the foreigner and sustains the fatherless and the widow, but he frustrates the ways of the wicked."*
                                        Psalm 146:9 (NIV)

Logan straightened his tunic as he walked down the hallway toward the great room of Gallios's residence. It had been more than a week since his return after the encounter with Lady Naamah. Thankfully, it had been a quiet period of time, although his right arm was still tender from the new mark he had recently received. Looking down he could not help but feel proud of both the designs on his right bicep. The first one was, of course, the Zirci design Kedar had marked him with several years ago. It had caused him so much trouble, as people of all lines feared his mere presence might spread the Zirci ailment of sterility to them. Even with Adam's recent public pronouncement to all his sons that Logan was free of any such ailment, Logan knew it would be a long time before people stopped making the now-familiar hand motion to ward off bad spirits every time they saw him. Even with all the trouble he had experienced because of it, he was proud to wear the Zirci mark. They had, after all, protected and taught him for so many years. They were a noble people, even if the rest of the world did not know they still existed.

His eyes then focused on the new mark designed for him by Gallios to indicate the new position he would enjoy after one of the two ceremonies he would be attending today. He was now dressed in his best tunic and headed toward Gallios's great room. Looking at the new mark, Logan saw the artistic skill for which Gallios was famous. He had created a design that identified Logan as part of Methuselah's branch of the Sethite Line, but with subtle hints of the Zirci pattern in the background. Gallios had thought it would be fitting for Hemeth to be the one to tattoo the mark on Logan's arm. "Besides," Gallios had said, "it would be good practice for him." Despite some trepidation at Hemeth's lack of experience, Logan acquiesced to Gallios's request. While Hemeth had been a bit less gentle than Logan had hoped, which resulted in a fair amount of bruising, Logan found his friend had done a superb job on the design.

Before Logan's official adoption took place, another ceremony would occur; this one having to do with Hemeth. In it, Gallios would commit to take responsibility for Hemeth, including his education, and to raise him as his own son. While Hemeth would not be completely adopted into Gallios's branch, the result was almost the same. To make this declaration official, Hemeth's brother, Hedred, would need to be present and agree to the arrangements on behalf of his immediate family. Along with him, several other Ono individuals were needed to act as neutral observers. Finding such people would not be a problem. In the days since Logan, Lamech, and Hemeth had returned to Gallios's residence, Ono delegations had begun arriving on the island. It was agreed that some of the less important members of the older Firstborn delegation would be housed at Gallios's residence because they were unable to fit into the Ono spire. The younger ones, however, refused to send any members to Gallios's residence after they learned of his desire to adopt Hemeth. Instead they chose to have their overflow delegation members camp near the harbor.

From those Onos who were housed at Gallios's residence Logan learned more about what had happened to Tubal-Cain after they left Adoraim City on the *Tomorrow's Destiny*. In fact, the whole island was ripe with gossip about Tubal-Cain and his recent reversal of fortune. Instead of sailing for Atalànt, he had disappeared from Adoraim City shortly after he awoke. Many of those who came from the Firstborn Council thought his departure was due to embarrassment. Logan, however, was not so sure. It seemed to him that Tubal-Cain would not be suppressed so easily.

He also learned that while Lady Naamah had remained part of the official Cainite delegation, her status in the family was greatly diminished due to the reduced status of her brother. This, of course, was the genesis of her unhinged behavior at the harbor several days earlier. In place of Tubal-Cain was his half brother, Jubal. While Jubal was technically not born first, he represented his Firstborn brother, Jabal, who was a herdsman with no interest in being leader. Apparently, Tubal-Cain and Jubal hated each other, and this was just the most recent political development between the two sides of the family. Keeping all of these intrigues straight was not easy, and Logan sighed to himself as he thought about the machinations of the Cainite Line.

From the people coming and going at Gallios's residence, Logan also learned more about what Adam had been doing since Logan's audience with him. Day after day, meetings occurred between Adam and various groups of people to whom the Created One made known his decrees. First, he met with each of his twelve sons individually, discussing issues and problems they were facing as they ruled their people. Then he convened a collective meeting with all Firstborns. There, he was able to resolve trade and territory disputes that had plagued the Firstborn Council for hundreds of years.

Among Adam's more controversial actions was when he pronounced that Logan was a descendant of Zirci but was free of the Zirci disease. However, he agreed to the Cainite demand that

Logan not be allowed to sire offspring, lest the disease return. Then Adam declared to all his sons that Logan should be left in peace.

Adam also met with the leaders of the Elder Born on Atalànt. Much to the chagrin of Callos, Adam instituted a new government structure for the island, changing from the rule of the eldest to a council form of government in which a rotating group of men would determine and administer the laws. Gallios was one of the members chosen to serve on the inaugural council.

The most intriguing of all the meetings was the one Adam conducted with his daughters and granddaughters, many of whom either came as part of the official delegations or lived on Atalànt. Since all of the women involved in this meeting stubbornly refused to reveal anything about what they had discussed, Logan was sure it would become the subject of much conjecture among the men for centuries to come.

When Adam was not meeting with his descendants, he was alone in his workshop, busy with projects about which only he knew. According to Methuselah, the days of long meetings with people and the even longer nights working on his projects were taking a severe toll on his body.

All these subjects swirled in the Logan's mind as he made his way into the great room, which was the largest in the residence. Unlike modern-day structures which tend to place such rooms near the middle of the house, Ancient architectural practices tended to place them to one side of the main portion of the house. The great room seemed to be little used, as this was the first-time Logan had ever been in it. Like every other room Logan had seen in Gallios's residence, the great room possessed a beautiful and artistic flare all its own. The walls of the large, rectangular chamber were painted with amazing geometric shapes in myriad colors, and the many alcoves in the walls contained sculptures of equal complexity. As in the rest of the house, the windows contained ornate stained-glass patterns. Several doors led to other parts of the residence. In the front of the room was a raised dais on which Gallios now stood, talking with Enoch and Methuselah. The two had arrived a couple of days after the altercation with Naamah to thank Gallios for the service he had rendered to Lamech and Logan. Gallios caught sight of Logan and motioned for him to join them. Logan bowed slightly in respect and walked up to the group.

"Good to see you, Logan." Gallios was obviously in good humor. "I see the mark Hemeth made on your arm has started to heal."

"Yes, sir."

"You are a bit early, so the others are not here yet."

"I wanted to make sure I could find the room," said Logan. "It is still not easy to find my way around in your beautiful but complex residence."

Gallios chuckled. "That was the idea when I built it!"

"Logan," said Methuselah, "at long last you will be joining my family. I am pleased."

"Thank you, Father," said Logan, though the words sounded strange in his mouth.

Enoch placed his hand on Logan's shoulder. "You are a very different man from the young boy who came to us decades ago."

"Yes, sir."

"Tomorrow we will return to the Sethite spire, where you and Lamech will meet with Seth and all his Firstborn sons to give an official account of your travels and recent events. Enos has worked very hard to make sure the spire will be ready for our meeting."

"Yes, sir," Logan replied. The door on the other side of room opened, and Captain Lubin and Huppim entered.

"Captain Lubin," said Logan in surprise. "I did not know you would be able to take time away from the construction to come!"

"Enoch invited us to the ceremonies, and as strange as you three are, we have been through a lot together. It seemed appropriate to honor you and Hemeth."

"Hemeth will be pleased you have come," said Logan.

"He is pleased indeed!" said Lamech as he and Hemeth entered the room through the same door through which Logan had entered. "We could hear you down the hall."

Hemeth was positively beaming. He looked to Gallios for permission to speak, which Gallios granted with a nod.

"Good to see you too, Captain, Huppim!" Hemeth warmly greeted the two men. "Thank you for coming, both of you."

"It is our pleasure," replied Lubin.

"I understand your future is now connected with this island as well," said Enoch.

"Now how did you hear about that already?" asked Lubin.

Enoch smiled. "I am a prophet of the Head of Days, after all."

"What is he talking about?" asked Hemeth.

"In my patriarch's audience with Adam, he discussed the strife that has already begun to surface within our line now that the treachery of my grandfather and uncle has been exposed, although both of them still refuse to admit they switched my map. Unfortunately, there are still many factions within the Adoraim that support them and do not care one way or another about their guilt. It is unlikely they will receive anything but a small reprimand for their deeds. However, as recompense to me, Adam has made my ship the head of the small fleet of trading vessels between island and mainland. My home port will now be here in Atalànt. My job will be to facilitate trade between the island and all lines on the mainland." Lubin paused and took something out of the bag he had brought with him. He unrolled a brand-new map, artistically drawn with bright, vibrant colors. "I also have a new map drawn by Adam himself to replace the old one."

"Are you allowed to show us this?" asked Logan.

"Seeing that you already know your way here," said Lubin with a smirk, "I do not think it matters. Besides, the secret has pretty much been let out to all the Firstborns and their delegations now."

"This is beautifully drawn by the Created One!" said Gallios, taking a closer look at the map. "You are greatly honored, my young captain."

"Thank you, Lord Gallios."

Just then, some members of the Ono delegation staying at

## Chapter XXI

Gallios's residence entered on the far side of the room.

"Ah, it looks like my family members who agreed to witness Hemeth's ceremony have arrived," said Gallios. "Come, Captain Lubin, I will introduce you and your first mate. I have begun to make some trade agreements with them, and we may need a sturdy ship to transport some important goods between us." With that, Gallios, Lubin, and Huppim left to speak with the Ono.

"Now all we have to do is wait for your brother to show up," said Lamech. Hemeth's face darkened at the mention of his brother.

"I am sure he will be late," said Hemeth dourly. "He will take his time just to spite me."

"We cannot control the actions of others, Hemeth," said Enoch evenly. "But I am sure he will show soon enough."

"He had better not be too late!" said Lamech. "From what I hear, he and his subclan will be handsomely rewarded for their consent to this arrangement." Hemeth had told Lamech and Logan the entire story of what happened after their meeting with Geber. As promised—and to the chagrin of the younger Ono Firstborns—Hedred made no objection to the arrangement Gallios had proposed. Still, the ceremony would be the culmination of days of wrangling over details of the exchange between Gallios and the subclan to which Hemeth belonged. The elders of his subclan agreed to relinquish all claim upon Hemeth in exchange for a prodigious amount of gold and onyx. It was also agreed that his family would not seek retribution on Hemeth for fleeing the artisan camp, which they considered a "dishonorable act." This would hold true as long as he remained on Atalànt. Since Hemeth had no desire to ever return to the mainland, he readily agreed to the arrangement.

"It is quite a big commitment to remain here on Atalànt for the rest of your life," said Enoch while they waited. "Are you sure it is wise to agree to such a thing?"

"Yes, why would I not?" asked Hemeth.

"What my father means is," Methuselah interjected, "this is a small island and you are still very young. You may one day want to leave the island, but by agreeing to this arrangement you may be killed without any right of revenge if anyone finds you off Atalànt."

"Unfortunately, sir," said Hemeth, "I really do not have much choice. My brother is quite adamant that I never be allowed on the mainland again."

"That is unfortunate," replied Methuselah.

At this Enoch grunted. "Given how angry some of the younger Firstborns are at Hemeth, it was not easy, even for Gallios, to negotiate the arrangement. I sense there is a fracture developing in the Ono Line between the young and the old. I fear what this split might mean for the future of the Ono as the younger Firstborns grow bolder. For now, the elder Firstborns remain strong, and they are not pleased with how their progeny are carrying on with the Cainites—particular Ono himself. Hemeth was fortunate that they supported him in this matter."

"It does not hurt that Geber supported this arrangement and manipulated the situation to his advantage," sighed Hemeth.

Enoch frowned and looked across the room to the members of the Ono delegation with whom Gallios was speaking. "That is not something we want to talk about much. While the elder Ono Firstborns undoubtedly know something of the arrangement, they are never pleased to hear about anything benefiting the Cainites."

"I know, sir," said Hemeth. "But I cannot stop thinking about how much trouble my sister will now experience because of me."

Enoch placed a hand on Hemeth's shoulder. "Your sister seems to be a very capable woman. She made a very difficult decision that will no doubt have consequences, but she did it for you. Do not waste the chance you have been given, Hemeth. Besides, the Head of Days may yet redeem even this situation."

Hemeth smiled sadly. "That is little comfort."

"It will have to be enough," said Lamech, nodding toward a door on the other side of the room. "It looks like your brother and the others have arrived."

Logan saw Geber, Hedred, and two Firstborn Onos had entered the room. Behind them came several Cainite and Ono attendants. He could feel the tension in the room rise. Hemeth turned pale when he saw his brother, and at the same time Lamech clenched his fist when he saw Geber. Fortunately, the fist remained at his side. Logan was surprised to see the Ono Firstborns in person. Unlike Hedred, they were not required to attend. Instead, they could have sent representatives in their place. They were the same two Firstborns who had come to the Sethite compound in Adoraim City during the Firstborn Council. If Logan remembered correctly, the father was Yarad and his son was Chul.

"It does not look like Sara is with them," Hemeth said dejectedly.

"Do not let them see you distraught, Hemeth," said Lamech with quiet intensity. "That is exactly what Geber wants you to feel and why he did not bring her. Do not give them that satisfaction."

Hemeth nodded, put on a mask of determination, and walked over to stand next to Gallios. Logan and the others took their places off to the side to watch the ceremony. Gallios, with Hemeth at his side, walked over to greet the guests.

"Greetings, Yarad," said Gallios. "I welcome you and your son to my home. Lord Geber, you too are welcome, though I wonder why a noble in the Line of Cain would wish to attend such a ceremony."

"Why, Lord Gallios, it is my pleasure to be here," Geber said pleasantly, looking about as if he did not have a care in the world. "Hedred and his sister have agreed to serve my house, so what affects them affects me. It seemed wise to come with them. Besides, who would not want to see your house? Your work is famous throughout Nod. I am sure Hemeth told you how my grandfather so loved your work that he set up artisan camps to replicate it. But compared to the quality of what you have created here, it was perhaps a foolish venture to even try." As Geber said the last sentence, he shot a piercing glance Hemeth.

"Thank you, Lord Geber," said Gallios warmly despite the awkward moment. "You flatter me."

"Yes, yes, Gallios," interrupted Yarad impatiently. "We understand the pleasantries, but let us get on with the unpleasant task before us."

Ignoring him, Gallios turned to Hedred. "Welcome to you, too, Hedred. I am glad you have decided to agree to this proposal."

"Yes, sir." Hedred bowed his head slightly. Then, like Geber, he looked toward Hemeth. However, unlike the Cainite, he allowed his look of utter contempt to remain as he continued, "He is my brother, after all."

"Will your sister not be joining us?" asked Gallios innocently.

"She could not make it," interjected Geber with a quick look toward Hemeth. "She had other things to attend to."

"I see."

"Now, Gallios," interrupted Yarad, "I assume our payment is ready for delivery?" Gallios frowned and looked over to the eldest of the neutral Ono delegation members, who nodded in reply.

"We have accounted for everything that was agreed to," said the man. "It is packed out back and ready for transport. My sons and I will bring it to your clan's campsite by the spires. We only need to hear the oaths by each side."

"Very well," Yarad said. "Let us begin."

With very specific wording, Gallios promised to take over responsibility for Hemeth, his actions, and his education. He then went on to enumerate all the goods he pledged to exchange on Hemeth's behalf. After this, Hemeth formally accepted Gallios's offer and agreed to remain on the island of Atalànt, lest he be subject to a sentence of death should he be found on the mainland. Yarad then formally agreed to the arrangement in front of the witnesses as a member of the Ono nobility. After Yarad's oath, an awkwardly long silence ensued. The entire time, Geber remained on the side, watching with a look of mild interest.

"It is now your turn, Hedred," Gallios prompted.

"I know, Lord Gallios," Hedred said, his facial muscles taut with apparent rage. "But if I am correct, I am allowed to say something before my oath."

"You are," replied Gallios tentatively.

"Then I wish to say this," Hedred said, turning to Hemeth and gaining a modicum of control. "You, brother, may have escaped the disgrace you have placed upon our family, but do not think I shall ever forgive or forget what you have done. Beware, brother, if we ever meet again. Escape may not be so easy."

After this chilling statement, Hedred quickly gave an oath releasing Hemeth from the family and from the disgrace he had brought upon them. Then, after receiving permission from Geber, Hedred walked out of the room without another word. Geber smiled as if nothing awkward had occurred.

Logan and Lamech clapped Hemeth on the shoulder, as much to break the tension in the room as to commend him.

"Congratulations, Hemeth," said Enoch and Methuselah.

"Now, Hemeth," said Gallios with a smile, "your education begins in earnest!"

Logan heard Geber clear his throat to gain everyone's attention. "With that ceremony completed," Geber said gallantly, "I would like to officially invite you all—Ono, Adoraim, and Sethite alike—to a tournament that Lord Cain and our line will hold the day after tomorrow. Too often our lines have conflicts with each other. Perhaps we can show our father, Adam, that we can all peacefully compete."

"What kind of tournament will this be?" asked Gallios.

"It will be a tournament of all kinds of combat." Geber shifted his attention to Lamech. "It would be good for all lines to send their best representatives."

"I am sure the Ono Line will want to take part," said Yarad. "We are not afraid to demonstrate our prowess in battle."

"That is good," said Geber. "And Captain Lubin, what about the Adoraim? Do you think they will join us?"

"I do not know," said Lubin. "Our combat prowess is demonstrated best upon the seas, but I will inform them of your invitation."

"Thank you, Captain. And the Sethite Line?"

"We shall discuss this with our elders," said Enoch. "We thank you for your invitation."

"Very well," said Geber pleasantly. "I believe we should take our leave now."

"Yes, Geber, let us leave," Yarad said. Turning to the Ono

representatives, he continued, "Have the gold and onyx brought to us in the front and we will accompany it back."

With that, Geber and the Ono Firstborns left with their attendants. Once they were gone, Logan found he could breathe easier. It was not pleasant having to be courteous to a man who several weeks ago was chasing him through a forest outside Adoraim City. Noticing that Lamech's right fist was still clenched, Logan knew it took Lamech even more self-control not to seek retribution on Geber.

Logan took a deep breath and smiled. It was now his turn. He would officially be adopted into Methuselah's family, and he would finish his training under Methuselah and become his son by right.

"Are you ready, Logan?" asked Enoch.

"Yes, I am."

"Then come and kneel before Methuselah." Logan obeyed. Gallios and Hemeth moved off to one side, while Logan knelt on the dais. Methuselah placed his right hand on Logan's head in the traditional blessing gesture. Enoch came between the two of them and placed one hand on each.

"Methuselah, my son, Firstborn among the Sethites," said Enoch, "do you accept the burden and responsibly of bringing up Logan, last of the Zirci, into the Line of Seth?"

"Yes, Father, I do."

"Do you swear before God Most High to protect him as father, to train him as teacher, and to guide him as mentor?"

"I swear, my father!"

Enoch smiled. "Logan, do you now accept Methuselah's protection as father, his training as a teacher, and his guidance as a mentor?"

"I do, sir."

"Then I, Enoch, Firstborn among the Sethites and prophet of the Most High God, bind my son Methuselah to you, Logan, as father, teacher, and mentor—and I bind you to him. Welcome, Logan son of Methuselah, to the Line of Seth. Whatever happens in the future, these things will never change!"

Tears filled Logan's eyes as he knelt in the presence of

Enoch, Methuselah, and Lamech. It was true that Logan, through Noah—who was not yet even born—was already a member of the Line of Seth; but to be honored by these three patriarchs of the Old Testament was something his emotions could not quite grasp. *Could these men comprehend how their names would survive until the end of time?* he wondered. Then he smiled to himself. *Enoch could.*

"Rise, my son," said Methuselah.

"Yes, sir," Logan said as he rose.

The next afternoon, Logan found himself standing outside the Sethite spire with Methuselah, waiting to meet with Seth's Firstborn descendants. He and his new family members had said farewell to Hemeth and Gallios early that morning and returned to Tipharah. As he waited to be invited in, Logan peppered his adoptive father with questions.

"Lamech told me he would be here shortly, but where is Enoch? I have not seen him since we returned to Tipharah."

"I do not know. Enoch was very mysterious about where he was going," replied Methuselah. "There is nothing new about that. But if I had to guess, I think he was going to try and find a way to speak with Adam."

"I still do not know how he will manage it," said Logan. "I have heard that Adam has stopped his audiences with everyone and now remains in his workshop by himself."

"Were you not the one who told Enoch that the Created One wished to see him?"

"Yes, of course. But that does not mean he can actually do it. Not without causing problems. There are so many noble warriors from all the different lines, many of whom were not granted an audience with Adam, but felt they should have been. This is not a big island. If Enoch's covert visit is discovered by any of the other lines, there will be trouble. This place is like a pile of tinder waiting to catch flame."

"Do not concern yourself with Enoch being discovered, my son," said Methuselah with a chuckle. "My father has a knack for discretion when it suits him. How do you suppose he traveled for years throughout the territories of the all the different lines of

Adam, even those who did not want him around?"

"I see your point," said Logan.

"I just hope he will get back soon, because we are going to start with the Sethite Firstborns any time. He does not win friends, even among our kin, by his constant absences and tardiness. But you are quite right about how much trouble could be caused if a fight breaks out between the lines. That is why I suppose Adam chose to give the responsibility for his funeral arrangements to the new Elder Born council of Atalànt rather than having the Firstborns run it. He knows the Elder Born do not want their island destroyed in the midst of fights between the lines."

"That sounds like a good idea," said Logan. "But I heard that Lord Cain was very upset that his line would not be responsible for the ceremony."

"I have heard the same thing," said Methuselah. "I think that might be one of the reasons why he has organized the tournament of combat today."

"He wants to control some aspect of this situation and have a way to show off his line."

"I think so."

"Other lines have responded by organizing their own festivals," said Logan. "I heard the Ono will have an art festival and several other lines will have ones involving music."

"Yes." Methuselah chuckled. "It seems there is competition among the competitions!"

Logan smiled as he considered his next question. It was as good a time as any to ask something he had wanted to find out since he had heard about the tournament of combat the day before.

"So, will you allow Lamech to complete?"

Methuselah sighed. "This is very hard for me, Logan. You are aware, are you not, that Lamech is the only one in the history of the Line of Seth who has ever been granted the Gift of Combat?"

"Lamech has never mentioned that to me, but yes, I have heard that."

"This makes him very important to the dignity of our line and to the standing of the Sethites among the other lines. I know my father cares nothing about such things, but as Firstborn among the Sethites, I feel I cannot ignore them. And I know for Lamech such a tournament is also very important. No matter what I say to his brothers and cousins, Lamech has lost much respect among them because he earned his second mark so late in life. Either they fear he is mad or they doubt he really has the Gift of Combat. This tournament might well be good for his future."

"So, what is the problem?"

"Logan, I am also a healer. While I have had to go to battle in the past, and I will probably have to again in the future, it is not something I desire. Lamech is different. He relishes his ability to fight and destroy. He holds it in check, but it is there. I do not wish to promote that excitement in his mind and in his spirit, because I do not wish to lose him to it."

"What will you do?"

"Many males his age have already earned their third mark and are recognized fully as men," replied Methuselah sadly. "I am sure Lamech would be among them if Enoch had not slowed down his progress. So, I have decided to let him choose for himself."

Enos appeared at the entrance to the Sethite spire and nodded to Methuselah.

"It is time to begin, Methuselah," Enos said, motioning them inside. "Where are your father and your son?"

"I am afraid I cannot tell you for sure about either of them at the moment, but—"

"I am right here, Father," said Lamech, coming around the corner of the structure. "I needed to be prepared for the tournament, which should be taking place this evening."

"So, you have decided to take part?" asked Enos, not without some pride in voice.

"Yes, sir," said Lamech eagerly.

"And you are in support of his decision?" Enos asked Methuselah.

"Yes, I suppose I am."

"Very well," said Enos. "Come, let us meet the other Firstborns. They are already assembled."

The four men entered the spire and moved along to the

central chamber. This meeting, Logan knew, would have long since taken place if the chambers had been ready earlier. Still, Logan was impressed with the speed and quality of the repairs completed under Enos's supervision. The interior was designed with strong lines and painted with rich, deep colors. The previously sagging beams had been replaced with new, strong timbers. They climbed up the staircase until they came to a large, circular room. When Logan walked in, he found four men sitting on simple mats speaking quietly with one another. One was Seth himself, and next to him were his grandson Kenan and great-grandson Mahalalel. Next to Mahalalel was Jared.

Looking up, Logan was impressed by the fresco that stretched half the length of the ceiling. Even in its unfinished state Logan could see it was a very accurate depiction of the night sky as seen from the Sethite lands. The Sethites were known as stargazers, and what Logan saw proved that description to be correct.

"Do you like my painting, Logan?" asked Enos quietly.

"Yes, sir. Very much."

"Wait until it is complete!"

From the other side of the room, Seth spoke. "Come, Enos, bring the newest member of our Firstborn Council and the newest member of our line in so that we may begin."

"Yes, Father," said Enos.

"May I ask where my son is?" said Jared when he noticed that Enoch was not with them. "Methuselah, do you know?"

"I am afraid not," said Methuselah. "But I am sure he will be along soon."

"My son has become a disgrace to this council, Father Seth," said Jared. "I am ashamed of him. He almost caused a major conflict between us and the Cainites before the Firstborn Council. Perhaps he should be excluded from this meeting altogether and replaced by his brother for not taking his responsibilities seriously."

"I too am frustrated with his lack of respect," said Mahalalel. "This cannot continue."

"My sons," said Seth courteously but firmly, "I am aware of

## CHAPTER XXI

the errands Enoch must undertake, and I can assure you he means no disrespect. He will be along presently. Now, let us begin."

Enos took his seat with the others while Lamech and Logan stood in front of the assembled men. Each told his part of the story from the time they left the harbor of Adoraim up to the previous morning. Both of them were intentionally vague in some areas, knowing that much of what was said would probably be reported to the Cainites through Jared. After they finished, each of the Sethite Firstborns made comments and asked questions.

"These are strange times, are they not?" said Enos to Seth.

"Yes, my son."

"All this time, Janice was using a powerful Gift no one knew she had to keep the island safe?" asked Kenan.

"It appears so," replied Lamech.

"And the boy you took from the artisan camp," interjected Jared, "he could communicate with her? He told you all this?"

"That would be Hemeth," clarified Lamech. "And yes, he did. But we did not take him; we rescued him."

"How do we know this Lowborn Ono boy is telling the truth about Janice?" asked Jared. "After all, if he is the only one who could speak with her, how do we know what actually happened?"

"You do not know the strength of this 'Lowborn Ono,' Jared," said Lamech. "You were not there when Tubal-Cain attacked me. In fact, none of you came to my aid. But Hemeth did. He fought that Cainite monster and beat him. If he says he spoke with Janice, then there is no doubt that he did."

"You are young, Lamech" said Jared. "Perhaps this clever Lowborn is making a fool of you."

"Sir," said Logan tentatively, "Janice actually spoke with me once too."

"She did?" Jared turned his attention to Logan. "You did not mention that in your story."

"It did not seem important."

"What did she tell you?"

"She told me it was up to me and that I would need to extinguish the fiery arrows of the Evil One."

"And you knew who she meant by that?"

"Yes."

"And I suppose you think she meant the Liberator."

"The Serpent," corrected Seth.

"Yes—the Serpent," Jared said.

"Yes."

"Did you see the Serpent?" asked Mahalalel.

"No."

"Yet you believe it was there?"

"Yes. It and many other beings were there." Logan shuddered, remembering how he had felt that day. "Hemeth saw the creatures and said they were hideous."

"Assuming, once again, that Hemeth is telling the truth," Jared said.

"And you defeated these creatures by saying a few words?" asked Mahalalel.

"Not completely. But you can see the effects of what happened. The shadow covering this part of the island was lifted."

"It is very strange," Kenan interjected. "The Created One refuses to speak of the matter. It is thought that perhaps he removed the shadow because he knew his time on earth was coming to an end."

This was a time Logan wished he could make the glow around him grow in intensity just by willing it, so he could show them what happened when the Head of Days chose to work through him. However, as always, he had no idea what the glow even looked like, let alone how to make it grow in intensity.

"Are you doubting their words?" asked Methuselah in defense of his sons.

"No, of course not. We are just trying to make sense of the things they are telling us," said Mahalalel.

"How about making sense of why Xavier tried to kill Logan?" Lamech said with more of an edge than he intended.

"Lamech," said Enos, "I agree with your frustration, but these are questions your fathers are undoubtedly being asked by our own people. We must have answers that make sense."

"I have another important issue," Jared said."You told us you were chained in the bottom of the Adoraim ship for two weeks. Unfortunately, the news of this humiliation has already spread among the people."

"And did you also hear about how Logan and I defeated a Leviathan?" asked Lamech.

"Yes, I have heard something of that as well, but how am I to explain that the newest member of our line felt it was appropriate to chain up a Firstborn Sethite for two weeks and that you did nothing to even try to escape? You are supposed to have the Gift of Combat, after all."

"It was for his own safety," Logan protested.

"And perhaps we should be concerned about his sanity as well," said Jared.

"Enough, Jared," said Seth firmly.

There was a moment of tense silence.

"He is right about one thing," Lamech said finally. "I did not try to escape—but only because there was no place for me to go. I was bound more than just physically! I was bound in hopelessness. But I can tell you that Logan helped me find my way out, and now I am readier than ever to be Firstborn. Perhaps that was my real test of manhood, even greater than rescuing Logan from the Okrans."

How gallant of you, Lamech," said Jared. "But there are still questions of your sanity circulating not only among our people, but among other lines as well."

"You can tell your people and your Cainite wife that I was the first Firstborn in hundreds of years to be granted an audience with the Created One, and he approved me as a Firstborn. If that is not good enough for Milali, then I do not really care!"

"Do not bring my wife into this, Lamech!" bellowed Jared.

"Enough," said Seth firmly. "Bickering will get us nowhere. It is clear to me and to Adam that Lamech is very much in his right mind. That is what you can tell your clans—and for now that will have to be good enough."

Clearly that was the end of the discussion, and all Seth's descendants nodded in agreement.

"There is one other thing that might be helpful," Enos said, addressing his father.

"What is that?"

"Lamech has decided to join the tournament today," Enos said with a smile. "I thought it was time he showed the other Lines what a Gift he has!"

"Is this the case, Lamech?"

"Yes sir, it is."

Seth gave the group a rare smile.

"Very well. Let us adjourn and leave these matters for now and see how you do today!"

**Click or scan the QR Code to learn about the sign posts in this chapter.**

# XXII

*"Contend, Lord, with those who contend with me; fight against those who fight against me."*

Psalm 35:1 (NIV)

Lamech stood in the midst of the Sethite delegation and looked around at the competitors from the other Lines, half of whom he had already vanquished in hand-to-hand combat during the afternoon. The other half had lost to Geber, whom he would be fighting shortly. Lamech wished he could have entered into the archery and swordsmanship competitions as well, but unfortunately the rules were clear that competitors could only choose one type of combat. In between bouts, he had gone over to the archery competition to watch Logan shoot. Logan had made it past the first round but was eliminated in the second. This was a respectable performance, and he had done about as well as Lamech had expected he would.

Lamech found it unfortunate that the artistic and musical expositions were taking place closer to Gallios's residence and thus too far away to visit in between his bouts, but he was sure Hemeth was enjoying himself immensely.

Lamech scanned the crowd, and his eyes narrowed when he caught sight of Geber standing on the other side of the field of competition talking with several people from one of the Cainite delegations. Behind Geber Lord Cain sat regally on soft cushions upon a raised dais talking with his wife and some of his children. The dais was uniquely positioned to see all the different matches. However, the field directly in front of Lord Cain would be where Lamech would soon fight Geber, and where Lamech planned to deliver a harsh blow to the Cainites' egos.

He looked around for Enoch, who had still not appeared since after the Sethite Firstborn meeting. Methuselah had left to find him before Lamech's final bout. Now Lamech saw Logan approaching, and from the look on his face his friend was frustrated with his performance in the sword competition.

"I thought I would make it at least into the third round," Logan grumbled without even greeting Lamech.

"You did well enough." Lamech smiled. "You have nothing to feel bad about. In fact, I think Kedar would be proud."

"Hmmm," was all Logan said before someone caught his attention. He left Lamech alone without another word and did something Lamech had never seen before. He made a beeline toward a young woman. Lamech did not recognize her, but apparently Logan did. He followed Logan to see what was going on.

"Sula?" Logan said as he walked up to her.

"You remember me after all these years?" the young woman said as she looked him over. "I am honored the famous last son of the Zirci has kept me in his mind all these years."

"Of course I remember you." Logan blushed. Pointing to his left arm he said, "And now I am a son of Methuselah, a Sethite like you!"

Lamech rolled his eyes. "She is not a Sethite!" he told Logan. "Don't you know anything? Look at her clothes and her hair. She is of the Line of Zior."

Lamech chuckled as Logan looked at her again in confusion. Obviously, Lamech would have to help his friend learn how to tell the difference between females of the various Lines. Lamech realized he should not have been surprised by Logan's confusion, considering females did not have markings like the men, and the only females Logan had been around for any length of time were from the Zirci. Lamech had grown up noticing how the females of each Line dressed and held themselves. Like learning how to speak, he just learned to tell the differences. Logan, however, never had that luxury.

"You must be Lamech, the famous Firstborn Seth with the Gift of Combat," Sula said, shifting her gaze to Lamech.

"I am," he said, bowing slightly.

"Is it true you defeated a Leviathan single-handedly?"

"No, not single-handedly." Lamech reached over and put his arm on Logan's shoulder. "My brother here had a great deal to do with it."

Sula smiled at Lamech sweetly. "I think we will hear much more about you two in the future," she said, returning her attention to Logan. "Indeed, Lamech is right. I am of Zior, and I happened to be in Parvaim all those years ago to see the Crushing Festival. You do remember the Crushing Festival, don't you?"

"Yes, yes, of course I do," said Logan, blushing again.

"It was such a shame those two poor people died who were bitten by the serpent. It is good you killed it when you did, Lamech, otherwise more people might have been hurt."

Lamech smiled bitterly and nodded. "The death of the boy and the young warrior has always troubled my father. To this day, he cannot understand why they did not respond to his treatment."

"Let us talk of more pleasant things, then," she said.

"I must be going soon," said Lamech feeling slightly uncomfortable under her gaze.

"Yes, of course," she said. "I have watched all your matches. You really are quite amazing, Lamech."

"Thank you."

"Oh, before you go, may I see the artwork on your arm? I

hear Gallios drew it for you, and his work is always exquisite."

Lamech reluctantly showed her his arm. She gently felt his arm, at which point he thought he saw a look for anger flicker across Logan's face. "Logan also has a unique mark made by Gallios," said Lamech.

"Yes, I see." Sula cast a quick glance at Logan's marking. "But it is still hard to see with all the bruising. Yours has healed nicely, though."

"Thank you, Sula." Lamech moved his arm away from her touch. "I am glad you like it."

"Yes, well, it is time for me to get back to my people. I do hope we will see each other again."

"Uh, yes. I do too," Logan fumbled.

Sula smiled and walked into the crowd of people.

"You really like her, huh?" said Lamech once she was gone.

"Well, sort of, I guess," replied Logan.

"You know that she is not for you, right Logan?"

"Really, why is that? What is wrong with finding a girl attractive?" asked Logan, although he knew where the conversation was going.

"You remember what Enoch said back at Adoraim," said Lamech. "And you also know what Adam decreed—you are not to have offspring."

"Just because I find a girl attractive does not mean I will have offspring with her." Logan blushed slightly.

"The way you were looking at her," said Lamech, "I would say that is exactly what it means."

"What? I think you like her too and just do not want competition."

Lamech stopped and looked at him for a moment in irritation. "After all we have been through, you are going to say something ridiculous like that to me?"

"I am sorry ... I guess," said Logan in a tone that sounded only half sincere.

"It is time I got back on the field. My bout with Geber is about to begin."

The two walked back to the side of the sparring field.

# Chapter XXII

Lamech removed his tunic and began to warm up. He saw Geber doing the same across the field. The rules were fairly simple: the match would be a combat of physical force and endurance; no weapons could be used. A neutral observer had been assigned to ensure no interference from others occurred. The observer assigned to this match was an Elder Born from the Line of Susi. The goal of the match was not to kill or incapacitate the opponent, but to force him to submit. Lamech's agility and speed had made his last bouts very quick affairs. Several of his previous opponents also had the Gift of Combat, but none of them could match his ability. This bout, Lamech knew, would not be nearly so easy.

When the neutral observer signaled, Lamech marched toward the center of the field to meet his opponent. The crowd grew silent as each spectator eagerly waited to see who would win the epic match. Lamech had watched as many of Geber's fights as he could manage to see the moves Geber preferred and how he began each fight. He determined that Geber liked to attack first with a quick blow to immediately push his opponent off balance. Lamech took this into account as he calculated the means by which he could dominate Geber.

As the two reach the middle and faced each other, Geber nodded to him and waited for Lamech to nod back, which would indicate the official start of the match. Keeping his eyes on Geber, Lamech began to nod in return, but even before Lamech finished the movement, Geber struck with the speed of a viper. Even having anticipated this move, Lamech was barely able to parry the blow with his left arm. Still, he was able to connect his fist with Geber's right side. This jab, however, barely phased his opponent, only making him stumble slightly. A split second later, Geber was back on the offensive with a savage kick that glanced Lamech's side. Quickly recovering, Lamech tried two separate attacks using moves he had not tried that day, neither of which he landed with any force. Both men moved with lightning speed, using techniques that would have been effective on lesser opponents and quite devastating if either of them had landed a solid blow on the other. Geber was definitely a match for Lamech, and he was incredibly fast. *Perhaps even faster than me*, Lamech thought during a brief pause as each sized the other up. As a result, Geber had landed more glancing blows than Lamech. However, Lamech also noticed that Geber did not possess the tactical mind to quickly size up his enemy, at least not to the extent Lamech did. Geber rarely varied his attacks and moved quickly in complex but predictable patterns. Lamech knew, however, that neither of them could keep up their current pace, and he needed to make a move that would give him the advantage. The next time Geber came at him with a blow from the left, Lamech feigned and ducked, tackling Geber to the ground. Grappling on the ground, the two men tore at each other like forces of nature struggling for supremacy. With heart pounding and muscles straining, Lamech finally was able to slip out of Geber's grasp and get a hold on Geber's upper body from behind. With a mighty heave that took all his strength, he threw Geber with as much force as possible. His opponent landed hard on the ground with the wind knocked out of him. Taking advantage of Geber's moment of weakness, Lamech pounced on Geber and put him in a hold he was sure he would not be able to escape from. As he was placing pressure on Geber to force him to submit, he heard someone shout, "Enough! Stop fighting, already."

Then someone pulled him off of Geber. Disoriented, Lamech tried to strike the man, but he was too tired and only swung at air. Lamech finally realized it was the match observer speaking to him.

"Why did you stop me?" asked Lamech incredulously.

"Look around you, Sethite," the man barked. "No one is even watching any more. Something has happened!"

Still kneeling, Lamech look about, and the man was right. Everyone had turned and moved toward the pavilion where Lord Cain had been seated. People were scurrying around with worried looks.

"What happened?"

"It is Lord Cain," said the match observer. "He cried out and dropped to the floor. The healers are trying to help him now."

Lamech strained to see what was happening. Then, remembering Geber, he turned around to see if he was still lying on the ground. When he did, he received a heavy blow to the gut. Doubling over, Lamech fell to the ground.

"What are you doing, Lord Geber?" shouted the match observer. "The match is over!"

Ignoring him, Geber bent down and spoke into Lamech's ear. "This is not over, Sethite. I don't know that is happening, but we will meet again!" The match observer pulled Geber away from Lamech and continued to shout at him. Lamech coughed and pushed himself back up to his knees. Fortunately, because Geber was as tired as he was, his punch, while painful, had not been delivered with enough force to cause injury. Lamech steadied himself as he got to his feet and turned back to where he had left Logan standing. To his surprise, he saw a small group of people crowded around someone on the ground.

"Lamech!" he heard someone cry. It was Enoch, who had left the group and was running toward him. "I saw Geber hit you after the match ended. Are you injured?"

"No, Grandfather," replied Lamech, limping his way toward Enoch. "What is going on? What has happened to Lord Cain?"

"Lord Cain?" asked Enoch incredulously. "I could not care less what is happening to him. It is Logan I am concerned about."

"Why? What happened to him?"

"We do not know exactly." As they reached the huddle of people, those around Logan moved to allow Lamech to see the unconscious body of Logan hanging limp in the arms of Methuselah.

# XXIII

*"And all the days that Adam lived were nine hundred and thirty years: and he died."*

Genesis 5:5 (KJV)

ONE MOMENT LOGAN WAS WATCHING the bout between Lamech and Geber, constantly praying that Lamech would prevail, and the next moment he felt so dizzy that his head began to swim. Wondering if he had become light-headed from overexertion, he reached out for Methuselah's arm to steady himself. However, no one was there to catch his fall, and he hit the ground hard. In a moment his head cleared and he could think again. He found he was no longer standing on the sparring field. Instead, he was in a lush garden, the same one he had been in when he connected with Adam. He looked up and once again saw the sheer mountain range on one side. To his right, about a stone's throw away, stood an old man whom Logan immediately recognized. Not Adam, but

Cain!

"You!" said Cain, glaring at him and speaking in the same harsh tone he had used during their first encounter. Before the old man could say more, a voice boomed from behind the trees.

*"Cursed is the ground because of you; through painful toil you will eat food from it all the days of your life. It will produce thorns and thistles for you, and you will eat the plants of the field. By the sweat of your brow you will eat your food until you return to the ground, since from it you were taken; for dust you are and to dust you will return!"*

Out of the trees ran two people, one a handsome young man and the other a beautiful young woman whom Logan recognized as Eve from his last time in the garden. The pair ran as fast as they could, past Logan and Cain and disappearing into a thicket. Logan saw that Cain had ignored the two runners and was keeping his focus on Logan. Behind them, from where the man and woman had fled, Logan heard a massive crash. Turning, he found the magnificent Cherubim he had seen before, standing above a half dozen crushed and shredded trees. The eyes of each of its four heads stared with ferocious intensity, and in its hand the flaming sword flashed back and forth.

To his surprise, Logan heard Cain's voice. "Why have you brought me here, creature?" he shouted angrily. Logan wondered whether Cain was immensely brave or incredibly stupid. The magnificent being looked at Cain for barely a moment before dismissing him as utterly inconsequential.

Then Logan heard the head of the man on the creature speak. "Time grows short, Created One. Have you prepared the way?"

"I have, Great One," said the voice of Adam. Turning to his right, Logan saw Adam step between himself and Cain. It was not the young version who had just run past them into the thicket. It was Adam as Logan had seen him only a short time before.

"My tasks are complete," whispered Adam with tears

rolling down his cheeks. "It is now for those of the future to walk the path before them." All eyes of the Cherubim looked fiercely upon Adam as if to discern whether he was telling the truth.

"So be it!" boomed the creature.

The other three faces of the creature began to move. Each one—the eagle, the bull, and the lion—began to sing the beautiful hymn Logan had heard before, with each voice singing in harmony with the others. The human head of the creature remained silent, its gaze never wavering from the figure of Adam.

Finally, with a bow that was ever so slight, the Cherubim said, "Now, oh Man, you shall pass!" When Logan looked toward Adam again, he was gazing up toward the sky. Over Adam's shoulder, he caught a glimpse of Cain's brooding expression, but Logan ignored him because in that moment Adam spoke his final words.

Turning his gaze on Logan, Adam gasped, "Logan, Logan, keep seeking! And remember!" With that, the Created One disappeared from view along with Lord Cain and the entire scene around him. The only thing that remained was the Cherubim, who stood looking at Logan.

"Be wise, young one," it said. "Many pitfalls await you before we have a chance to meet again."

A moment later the whole scene faded to black, and Logan found himself being supported in the arms of Methuselah, who had a very concerned look on his face.

"What happened to you, Logan?" Methuselah asked. "You were out, and I could sense nothing from you!"

"He has returned to the dust from which he came," Logan said as tears flowed down his face.

Enoch, who was standing behind Methuselah, heard him and nodded.

"I do not know what you are saying, Logan. You must speak in a way that I can understand," replied Methuselah. Realizing he had once again accidently switched to English, Logan responded in the Ancient tongue.

"It is Adam. He's dead."

# XXIV

*"I will do unto them after their way, and according to their deserts will I judge them; and they shall know that I am the Lord."*

Ezekiel 7:27b (KJV)

The funeral took place the following day. The somber mood on the island was in stark contrast to the previous few days. After all the revelry and frivolity the descendants of Adam had engaged in since arriving on Atalànt, the real reason for their journey suddenly became inescapable. They had to face the fact that their father had died and was not coming back.

Following Adam's wishes, his body was wrapped tightly in strips of cloth that had been anointed with oil and spices. He was placed on a long pallet carried by one representative from all the twelve Lines from the surviving sons of Adam. They took him in a long and winding path through Tipharah so that everyone would have a chance to bid farewell as he passed by. At the end of this long procession the pallet was brought down to a lower set of cliffs on the far side of Tipharah. Twelve elevating boxes had been built for this specific day and set on the side of the cliff, like those near the harbor. This remote portion of the island had a long shoreline but no harbor, because the sea in this area was rough and full of dangerous submerged rock formations. Adam's body was lowered down the side of the cliff, carried across the beach, and set into a small but ornate boat at the edge of the sea. Flammable materials had been placed in the bottom of the boat. More was placed all around Adam's body. The craft was pushed out far enough so that the current would take it. Each of the twelve Lines had chosen an archer to shoot a flaming arrow onto the boat in order to set it ablaze once it was far enough from the island. Lamech was the archer chosen by Seth, and according to Adam's instructions Logan was to be a thirteenth archer to represent the now-extinct Line of Zirci. As the sun set, the twelve direct sons of Adam stood on the shoreline behind the thirteen archers. Each archer in turn shot his arrow. Logan was last and despite the great pressure, his arrow, like all the others, hit its mark. In a short time, the boat was engulfed in flames. A tear rolled down Logan's face as he bore witness to the precise moment Adam's final curse descended on him. The body of the only created man in all space and time was returning to the dust from which it had been formed.

 Nobody moved until after the flames had burned out and the vessel had sunk into the depths of the ocean. Finally, the silence broke as people began shuffling away from the shoreline and back toward the elevating boxes. Logan stood in stunned silence as he, Lamech, and Seth were raised to the top of the cliff. Looking up, Logan could see that the crowd of onlookers had not left, but remained peering over the cliff toward the ocean below. When they reached the top of the cliff, Logan stood for a long time with Lamech and the rest of the delegations on the cliff side looking out toward the sea.

 Eventually, the time came to leave. Turning around, Logan was startled to see Cain staring at him as he had in the garden in their shared vision. It sent shivers down his spine. Before Logan

## Chapter XXIV

could say anything, Seth made his way over to Logan and Lamech, who was standing next to him with his bow still in his hand. Seth gave them a sad smile and placed his hands upon both of them.

"Thank you. You both shot well."

"Thank you, sir," they replied. As others crowded around them, Seth smiled and nodded, leaving them with tears in his eyes.

"Stay here, Logan," Lamech said. "I have to talk with a few people, but then we can walk back together to eat."

"Sure," said Logan, although he was not very hungry. "I will remain here."

Logan looked over the water to the spot where Adam's craft had sunk beneath the waves. When he turned around to look for Lamech, he saw Cain staring at him again, and this time Logan's head began to pound between his temples. He heard a voice intrude into his thoughts.

*My father connected with you in a very deep way,* the voice said. *That is why you were there at his end, wasn't it?* As he heard these words, the crowd around Logan seemed to move in slow motion and then stop altogether. He could not move his head to look for Seth or Enoch. He felt as if he could only look at Lord Cain. Then he realized, unlike Tubal-Cain, this Cain did not need to touch him to force himself into Logan's mind. Logan closed his eyes in a futile attempt to break the connection. When he opened them again, he saw that everyone around him had disappeared.

*Oh no! What is happening now?*

Logan was no longer standing on the cliff side by the sea, and he was not in the garden. Instead he stood alone in an immense structure, hundreds of stories tall and with thousands upon thousands of plain brown doors running down either side of a long hallway. Logan blinked in surprise. It was a place he had never seen before, but it reminded him of a modern building in the future.

From behind, he felt a rough hand grab hold of his left arm in a viselike grip. He was not surprised to find that it was Cain who held his arm. Logan was spun around so that he faced the door to his right. It was a plain door that looked just like all the others.

"What is this place?" he asked weakly.

"It is your mind, of course," said Cain, looking curiously about him. "I need to check on something that should still be here."

"What are you looking for, Lord Cain?" Logan tried not to scream under the pressure Cain was placing on his arm.

"My father said you were cured, but he could never cure Zirci himself. I think he lied. Look at all these doors. How could he *know* you are cured if he did not know where to look?"

"I ... I don't know," was all Logan could say. He tried to think of some passage of Scripture, anything that might help him block out Cain's thoughts, but nothing came.

Cain stopped as if noticing something for the first time. He cocked his head to one side and a look of disgust crossed his face.

"He did much more than read your mind, didn't he?" Cain spun Logan around to look into his eyes. "He actually bonded with you, and in a way that no living man save me has been allowed."

"He shared with me his creation and his fall," Logan said weakly.

"You are nothing but a degenerate Lowborn! Why would my father do that?"

Logan remained silent, though he felt his arm might explode from the sheer force of Cain's grip.

"Tell me!" Cain screamed. Logan's legs began to buckle. Still, he said nothing. Cain looked again at the door hesitantly. "This is the door I want, but it and this whole place looks strange—not as it should. This makes no sense. Tell me, what is going on?"

"It is a building, Lord Cain," said Logan, too weak and tired to resist anymore.

"Yes, but the building your mind represents looks like nothing I have seen or dreamed of."

Since Cain had entered his mind, Logan guessed they were seeing things as Logan's modern mind would naturally represent them.

"That is indeed a building, Lord Cain, just not as you understand or build them now," Logan said in barely a whisper.

"As we understand them?" Cain looked at him strangely. "Who are you? What are you? And where do you come from, since I destroyed the diseased Zirci?"

In response, Logan simply slumped down, too weak to answer.

Seeing Logan's state, Cain returned his attention to the door before them. He moved his hand toward the handle, but hesitated.

"Are you afraid, Lord Cain?" whispered Logan with his eyes barely open. "Does your sin crouch at yet another doorway?"

It was hard to imagine Cain's features taking on any more disdain than they had already, but somehow he managed it. "How do you know such things?" he bellowed. The next thing Logan knew, he was being thrown across the hallway, and his body smashed hard into the door directly across from the one they had been looking at. He hit so hard that the door frame was mangled by the impact.

As painful it was being thrown against the opposite door, Logan immediately began to feel better having his arm released from Cain's grip. As his vision cleared, he looked up to see Cain open the door, and what came out shocked them both. A mammoth serpent slithered its way out with surprising speed and turned to look at both of them.

"It s-s-seems your true father is now the Princ-s-s-e of Lies-s-s," said the Serpent in a voice strangely reminiscent of Adam, though with an odd lisp. "This-s-s is how he firs-s-st appeared to me. I have taken on his-s-s form. Does-s-s it pleas-s-se you, my s-s-son?

"Father?" said Cain in shock. "How can you be here? You are dead!"

"What you s-s-see before you is-s-s but a remnant left behind, a memory I hoped would never s-s-surface; but you have entered Logan's-s-s mind in s-s-search of that part in the Zirci's-s-s Line you alone know, becaus-s-se you corrupted it. When you came to Atalànt s-s-so long ago, it was-s-s not to cons-s-sole me at your mother's-s-s death, was-s-s it? No! Your mother died in childbirth, and you came to exact vengeanc-s-s-e upon your baby brother by cursing him and his-s-s descendants-s-s. I never figured out where you hid your s-s-secret—the disease you passed on to Zirci's-s-s offspring. But now you have revealed it and in doing s-s-so, you have doomed your own offs-s-spring.

"You are dead, Father, you have no power over me," said Cain, now in a rage after recovering from his shock. "Now this last Zirci will die!"

"You will never lay a hand on Logan, for you both bonded deeply with me when I was-s-s alive. Now you two are inextricably linked, and I curs-s-se you, my s-s-son. If this-s-s boy is-s-s harmed, you will be too. If he dies-s-s, s-s-so will you! The mark on his left arm will be my s-s-sign of this protection."

Just then Logan screamed in pain at a burning sensation that made his arm feel as if it were on fire. A unique design reminiscent of Adam's own mark begin to burn itself into the exact place where Cain had held him.

Cain scowled. "A mere memory from a dead man cannot harm me!" He swung round and kicked Logan. Logan went down hard. A second later Cain himself fell to the ground in a fit of coughing.

The Serpent looked squarely into Logan's eyes. "The memory of a great man can do much more than you imagine. Now, Logan, look about you and remember; all future depends-s-s upon it."

Though frightened and not wanting to look away from the Serpent, Logan did as he was told and scanned the hallways, trying to take everything in. However, every door on every floor looked exactly the same. He turned back to Cain and the Serpent, but no one was there, and that was when everything went black.

On the shore, Logan stumbled, falling to the rocky ground. Lamech was at his side in a moment. "Are you okay?" he asked.

"No! Lord Cain was in my head and ... and now my arm ... it hurts terribly," said Logan, clutching his left bicep in the same place he had felt Cain holding him. A ring had burned itself into Logan's arm, and in the middle of it was the symbol that represented Adam.

"What is that?" Lamech exclaimed.

"Look!" Logan replied, ignoring the question. Logan pointed to where Cain had collapsed on the shore.

Cain's firstborn son, Chanokh, was kneeling next to his father and placing his hand upon his head. As a healer, Chanokh probed his father's brain to discover what ailed him. Then he turned toward Logan and shouted, "What have you done to him?"

"What has Logan done to Lord Cain?" Lamech yelled back incredulously.

"Silence, Sethite! I am speaking to the diseased Zirci mongrel."

Hearing this exchange, Geber and several others stopped their conversations and gathered behind their patriarch, glaring at Logan. Seth stepped between the group of Cainite Firstborns and Logan and Lamech.

"You know very well that Adam declared him free of any disease. Besides, this young man is no longer a Zirci only; he is also a Sethite and a son of a Firstborn. You will do well to remember that, my nephew." As Seth spoke, Enoch, Methuselah, and several others came and stood next to their patriarch.

"Does your Zirci pet not know that if our father dies, he will be cursed? Does Lord Cain not still have the sign of protection given to him that no may kill him?" Chanokh said. "Now we will make this Zirci pay with his life!"

"No!" said a weak voice from behind him. Cain was rising to his feet with the help of a few others. "There will be no fighting today."

Cain's son looked at him in astonishment, but did not disagree. "Yes, Father. It will be as you wish."

"We have stayed on Atalànt long enough. Our father, Adam, is dead and gone," said Cain in a somber voice while looking directly at Logan. "We have nothing left in common with these Sethites, so we will leave for our lands first thing in the morning and be rid of these stargazers."

After hearing Cain's words, the shocked Cainite Firstborns as well as the Firstborns from other lines began to move away. The Cainites supported their patriarch as they headed toward their spire to prepare for their departure from Atalànt.

For a moment, Logan took in the surreal scene about him. Glancing toward Lamech, he saw his friend staring fiercely at Geber, whose eyes narrowed when he noticed Lamech. Then, after a long moment Geber turned to join his family. Standing behind the Cainite, Logan could also see Hemeth's two siblings and the contrast between brother and sister could not be starker. To one side stood the beautiful and graceful image of Sara, while on the other stood the massive and scowling figure of Hedred. Tears were in Sara's eyes as she took one last look upon Hemeth. However, before she turned around to leave with Geber, Logan was surprised to see her gaze shift for a moment to Enoch, who noticing this, seemed equally surprised at her attention. He nodded politely in her direction. Sara smiled sadly at the prophet and then nodded slightly in return. Logan found the brief exchange rather odd because the two had never before met. However, he thought little of it as reminded himself that everything having to do with Hemeth's sister was slightly odd.

When the final Cainite had left, Logan let out a deep breath and rubbed his left arm, which still stung. Seth turned and looked curiously at him.

"What is this, my son?" Seth pointed to Logan's arm. "And why did my brother back down from a fight? He has never done that before."

"My father Seth," said Methuselah, coming up to them, "Logan has been through a very difficult time. May we please answer these questions after I have had a chance to look him over to see if he is well?"

"Yes, of course, Methuselah. You are right. Look after your new son now, but let us meet shortly at the spire. We must all hear what has transpired and what it means!"

Methuselah and Lamech accompanied Logan back to the Sethite spire, where Methuselah examined Logan and confirmed he was healthy, though very weak. Shortly after this, Logan met with the Sethite Firstborns and told them about his encounter with Cain and all he had learned about the origin of the Zirci's condition. He explained the whole story, even though he knew that much of what he said would get back to the Cainites through

Jared.

"Though I doubt anyone outside the Sethite Line will believe me, it is clear that Cain did something to Zirci when he was only a baby," Logan said, finishing his story. "But it apparently took several generations to affect his offspring."

"Cain is a very powerful man with many Gifts, second only to Adam himself," said Enos. "If he had the opportunity to be alone with Zirci, there is no telling what he could have done to him without anybody ever knowing."

"Deep down I think Adam always suspected Cain's involvement," Logan surmised. "But, I do not think he ever accused him outright."

Seth, who had been silent during Logan's story, finally spoke up. "You have done well today, Logan." Turning to Methuselah he said, "Continue to look after your son. We will meet again shortly."

With these words, the short meeting ended. Enos took charge of preparations for the delegations to depart from Atalànt; while Enoch and Methuselah worked with Logan to see what more they could learn about his encounter with Cain.

"Are you able to see into my mind and find the door Cain was interested in and what was behind it?" Logan asked Enoch.

"I am afraid not, Logan," said Enoch. "My power over the mind is of a different sort than the Cainites. I can make people see things that are not there and put thoughts into the minds of men, but I do not create images that represent reality like the ones you and Hemeth have experienced."

"Was there anything you could find, Methuselah?" asked Logan. "Was there something that might explain how Cain sterilized the Zirci Line?"

"I could only determine that he did no lasting damage to you. There was no indication of how Cain set into motion the disease the Zirci suffered from," Methuselah said. "If I had been there with you and Cain, I could probably figure it out, but the human brain is just too vast to know how he did it."

"Adam said it was of paramount importance that I remember where I was in the hall of doorways," said Logan. "But what use is it if we cannot get to that doorway again?"

"I do not know," said Methuselah. "Perhaps we will figure it out, but for now I am just glad you are well." As they were speaking Jared, Kenan, and several other Firstborns came down from the spire with Seth.

Enoch said, "You must wait for us outside. Methuselah, Lamech, and I must meet again with our fathers. Enos is preparing for our departure, and there is much our family council must discuss."

"You will be safe here near the Sethite residence and spire," said Methuselah. "This may be a long meeting, but it would be unwise for you to leave unaccompanied."

"Yes, Father." Logan was still not used to calling Methuselah that. "I will stay right here. Though, because Adam has given me this mark upon my arm and has connected Cain's well-being to mine, I suspect that I am safer than ever before in my life."

Logan walked outside to find other Sethites busily preparing for the departure of the delegations over the next several days. Logan did as much as he could to help his Sethite brothers, but in time the activity died down as the men finished their work and went to visit other parts of the island one last time. Logan wanted to walk over to see how Lubin's work on the ship was going, but it had grown dark and he had promised to stay close by, so instead he remained to tend the fire.

As the campfire grew into a greater blaze, it cast more light in the area around him. Logan looked up and saw a young boy standing several meters away. He looked familiar, though he could not place him. The boy stood there watching him with a not particularly pleased expression on his face.

"Hello, young one," Logan called to the boy. "Come sit down by the fire."

The boy said nothing.

"Logan, who are you talking to?" asked Enoch from behind him. Logan turned to see Enoch, Methuselah, and Lamech standing several meters behind him. Several other Sethite Firstborns were heading off into different directions.

"This little boy here by the fire." Logan turned back around,

## Chapter XXIV

but found no one there.

"Logan," said Lamech, "there are no children on the island."

"Well, there was one standing here just a moment ago," replied Logan as he pointed to the other side of the fire.

Enoch walked around the fire to where Logan had pointed. As he did so, Logan could see the prophet's expression turn to one of concern. "Whoever it was, he is gone now," said Enoch. "Let us sit down now, Logan. We must discuss the future and what you will do for the next years to come."

Methuselah described for Logan what the Sethites had planned for him. "You will return with me tomorrow and for several months join me as I build my city. However, Enoch has in his head that you must learn more about navigating the sea. So he has arranged for you to become part of Captain Lubin's crew, at least for part of the year. Construction of his vessel will be complete within six months, and his first voyage will be to the port of Zior. There you will meet him next spring, and for six to nine months out of every year you will learn from him about sailing the sea. The rest of the time you will spend with me earning your last mark of manhood."

"Really, Father," said Lamech, "what does a Sethite, adopted or otherwise, need to know about sailing upon the seas?"

"You never know when that information might be useful," Logan replied.

"Better you than me. Once I get back to the mainland I want nothing more to do with sailing," said Lamech.

"So Lamech will return with us as well?" asked Logan.

"Yes," said Methuselah. "But his main job will be to lead the local Sethite forces in defending my city and our ancestral lands. In several years, once he has received his final mark, he will choose a mate and begin scouting out land for his own city."

Logan shot a glance at Lamech, who ignored him. Logan wondered how Bete might fit into these plans.

"There is much to do before we leave," said Enoch. "May I have a few words with your new son alone?"

"My father is asking permission to speak to my sons," Methuselah said dryly. "There is a first time for everything."

Enoch simply smiled and said nothing, and Methuselah and Lamech left the two alone.

"You know, Logan, that the world has forever changed with the death of the Created One," said Enoch. "I think you know that better than anyone."

"Yes, sir. I have thought a lot about that, and about how much has changed since I arrived here decades ago."

"There is no doubt in my mind that the Head of Days worked all these things together for your good. When you came to us, you were defenseless and I wondered how I would ever protect you. Now Cain himself protects you with his own life because of Adam's curse on him. The Cainites will not touch you—at least as long as Cain lives."

"And this," Logan said, pointing to Adam's mark on his left arm, which still stung. "Why do you suppose Adam marked me?"

"I do not presume to understand the mind of the Created One. But when a Cherubim tells you something, you do it. I suppose the mark will protect you as well, as long as the memory of Adam persists in this world."

"I have learned that memories can be very powerful," Logan said. "It reminds me of what Adam told Cain: 'The memory of a great man can do much more than you can imagine.' Though I wonder ..."

"Yes, Logan?"

"I wonder if Adam meant by that statement the memories that a man possesses, or the memories others have about him?"

"As I told you, Logan," Enoch said, putting his hand on Logan's shoulder, "I do not presume to understand the mind of the Created One."

"Perhaps there *is* something you can tell me."

"What is that?"

"When the Cainites turned to leave after Cain attacked me, Hemeth's sister looked in your direction and smiled, almost as if she knew you. I thought you had never met her?"

"I have not," said Enoch thoughtfully. "I confess that I do not know why Sara looked at me as she did. When it happened, however, a memory of my own came to me. Several times in my life I have had the feeling of reliving a particular moment. It is a very strange sensation, I can tell you. In fact, it happened only a short time ago on my journey here. That is what I thought of when she smiled at me."

"That is not so uncommon. Where I came from we called that *deja vu*."

"Really? I find it interesting that the people of the future give a name to such a sensation." For several heartbeats both men were quiet. Then Enoch continued "Speaking of the future, I can tell you this: despite the success we have enjoyed, it is important to remember that we have not won. Not by a long shot. You must not become complacent. Your role in the events remains incomplete."

"Yes, sir."

"To that end, I believe, there is something I must give you," said Enoch gravely.

"What is that?"

"This." From within his cloak Enoch took out a cylindrical object that appeared to be made of some kind of crystal. Logan could see two compartments filled partially with fluid in either half of the small cylinder.

"This is something the Created One said he had been working to improve ever since he connected with you, but he refused to tell me its purpose. However, he said you would be able to deduce it and, with help, properly employ this cylinder."

"He said that?" asked Logan in wonder as he took the crystal cylinder from Enoch and examined it, turning it over in his hands. "I have no idea what it might be—"

Logan stopped speaking when he looked closer at the stopper on one end and noticed a small but very clear symbol on it. When he examined the other side, his mouth dropped open. He had a good guess at what the cylinder contained.

"What is it, Logan?"

"Where I come from, this symbol here indicates 'male.'" Logan pointed to a circle with an arrow shooting out from the top right. Turning to the other stopper, he pointed to another circle, this one with a cross protruding down from the bottom. "And this indicates 'female.'"

"I do not understand," said Enoch. "What does this have to do with you?"

"I do not think it has anything to do with me—at least not directly," Logan said wistfully. "But it may be very important for someone not yet born."

"The one you spoke of when you first arrived—the one called 'Noah'?"

Startled, Logan looked with surprise at Enoch. He remembered how he briefly mentioned Noah's name when he had first arrived in the Ancient world and had discovered where—or better yet, when—he had arrived.

"Yes. I think this cylinder has a lot to do with the future of the world and the ability to repopulate it."

"Tell me no more, Logan," said Enoch with a wave of his hand. "I know enough of future things. I do not need other knowledge added to it."

"Very well. But—" Logan stopped, unsure whether he should bring up something he had wondered for some time.

"What is it, Logan?" asked Enoch.

"You never shared with me what Adam taught you," said Logan. "What was it?"

It was Enoch's turn to pause to consider his words. Finally, he spoke.

"It is a secret, Logan. One that I will tell you, but you must never tell another soul."

"Yes, sir," said Logan eagerly. "Of course."

"He showed me how to alter or erase the memories of men."

"That is what he wanted to show you?"

"Yes," said Enoch with a smile. "It would be a very dangerous skill in the wrong hands, particularly given our previous discussion."

"Is there anyone else who knows how to do that?"

"According to Adam, I am now the only one with that ability and the knowledge to use it."

"Why would he think you need to know that?" asked Logan.

"Must I repeat myself yet again about how little I know of

the mind of the Created One, Logan?" Enoch said with a smile. "But I am sure we will find out. Now, let us join Methuselah and Logan. We have to prepare for the long voyage ahead of us."

Two days later Lamech and Logan stood with Hemeth at the top of the cliff that looked down on the harbor below. The two had just said good-bye to Captain Lubin and his crew, who were making great progress on the hull of the new vessel, aptly named *Destiny's Tomorrow*. Hemeth had left the construction site to bid farewell to his friends.

"We will see you again soon, Logan," said Hemeth, looking out at the harbor which just days earlier had been so full of ships. Now it was almost empty. "You will be visiting us often during your travels with Captain Lubin. And you will always be welcome to stay in Gallios's residence. I just hope your journeys here will be less eventful than when we three arrived together."

"Yes, so do I," said Logan. He looked over at Lamech. He knew Lamech would most likely never return to Atalànt, and it made Logan sad to know his friend might never see Hemeth again. For several moments, the three were silent. Then Lamech placed his hand on Hemeth's shoulder.

"Thank you, Hemeth," Lamech said simply.

Hemeth smiled. "We all needed each other during this journey," he said. "Who knows, perhaps the Head of Days is not yet finished with us three." With that, the three friends embraced. Lamech and Logan left their friend standing on the cliff as they descended and took a small craft to their vessel in the harbor to begin the voyage home.

# Epilogue

Sara watched as Talaon emerged from a tent in the early morning in a deserted area sparsely populated with trees. He shivered. Scowling, he wrapped his cloak more tightly about himself as wisps of mist floated past him. Behind him lay a cooking pit with the charred remains of the previous night's fire. Talaon took some wood from a pile near his tent and quickly lit a new blaze. Then he turned and walked over to a second, more elaborate tent, scowling again.

"Lord Tubal-Cain," said Talaon in a gentle tone.

"What?" cried a voice from within the tent.

Talaon rolled his eyes before answering. "It is the time of the morning you wished to be awoken, sir."

"Very well. Make my breakfast."

"As you wish, my lord." Talaon walked away from the tent and began putting together the provisions for the morning. A few minutes later, Tubal-Cain emerged from the tent and sat down on a log near the fire. Talaon gave him a warm drink along with some bread and meat. After this, he stood behind Tubal-Cain and waited patiently. When Tubal-Cain had finished eating, he handed the cup back to Talaon and then stood up and stretched.

"Lord Tubal-Cain?" said Talaon tentatively.

"Yes."

"We have remained several weeks here on the outskirts of the Tortured Mists," he began with a look of trepidation on his face. "How long do you think we will need to wait here?"

Tubal-Cain eyed him with irritation. "I do not know."

"But you trust this Zior girl who told you to come here?"

"Have you become so bold as to question my judgment?"

Talaon turned pale. "No, my lord. I would never question your judgment. I only question her intentions."

"Well, do not!" said Tubal-Cain gruffly. "There was something about her that I cannot quite explain. But I know she spoke the truth."

"If you wish, my lord, I could move our tents closer to the

Sacred Cave where it is not so cold. That way we will certainly be the first ones there if something emerges from it."

"Do you know nothing of the past, Talaon? The first time a metal creature came out it killed several of our greatest warriors. I would not wish to be there if such a thing were to happen again. If I could spare you, I would send you there to wait, but as it is I have only you to serve me now. No! If events occur as before, we will know when something happens, and then we can approach with caution. Besides, no one is around to make it to the Sacred Cave before us."

"I understand, my lord."

"Good, see to it—"

Both men stopped and tilted their heads as if they were listening to something. Together, they gazed in the direction of the Sacred Cave.

"It is time!" shouted Tubal-Cain. He started running down the path to the Sacred Cave, Talaon following behind his master. Sara found herself following behind them and considering Talaon's earlier comments about the distance to the Sacred Cave, because it took quite some time before the two men approached their destination. Tubal-Cain slowed his breakneck pace as the two entered a region where the foothills began to increase in height. They were near a mountain range Sara had never seen before. Tubal-Cain signaled to his companion that he should proceed with more stealth. As the two walked silently forward, they approached an area with several cave openings. Hiding behind some brush and rock formations, Tubal-Cain and Talaon looked up at the caves. From the direction of Tubal-Cain's gaze, Sara could see there was one opening high up in which he was particularly interested.

"I can still sense the disturbance from the cave. So, whatever happened, it is still going on," whispered Tubal-Cain. "Yet, it does not appear that anything has emerged from the cave."

The two watched from their hiding place for several minutes. Finally Talaon said, "I think the disturbance has stopped."

"Yes," said Tubal-Cain. "I sense that too. Now, let's see what comes out."

A moment later, an eccentric-looking man stumbled his way out of the cave. He was rather fat, and to Sara's eye he looked to be several hundred years old and wore outlandish clothes. On his face, he wore a light metal contraption that held round pieces of glass in front of his eyes. In his hand, he held something that he was studying intently.

"Have you ever seen such strange garments before, Lord Cain?" whispered Talaon.

"Perhaps I have," said Tubal-Cain with a thoughtful look on his face. "About thirty years ago."

The man looked up from whatever he was holding. When he did so, he must have been very surprised by something he saw, because he gave a brief cry of shock. He began to look more closely at the thing he was holding.

"I think it is time we met this new visitor," said Tubal-Cain with confidence.

"Do you think it is safe, my lord?"

"Does this one look like he can hurt us?" asked Tubal-Cain incredulously. "If we could not get answers from that young Zirci mongrel, perhaps we can get some from this one."

"You think he is connected with Logan of the Zirci?"

"Oh, yes," said Tubal-Cain with a malicious smile. "I think this one is very connected to the whole confusing labyrinth of questions surrounding that young man." Tubal-Cain stood up and walked out with a regal gait to meet the visitor. Taking this as his cue, Talaon followed his master. The man from the cave did not notice their approach until they were very close to him. Hearing them, the man finally shifted his attention from what was in his hand to Tubal-Cain and Talaon. With another look of shock, he waved his hand and proceeded to make a series of unintelligible sounds.

Tubal-Cain frowned as he heard the sounds, but he mimicked the man's wave and spoke to him. "I am Tubal-Cain, Firstborn—er—Noble Born among the Cainites."

In response, the man made even more strange sounds, to which Tubal-Cain shouted, "Stop your nonsense!" At this command, the man ceased making noises. Tubal-Cain tried again, but more slowly. He gestured to himself and simply said, "Tubal-Cain." The man nodded and copied Tubal-Cain's gesture, saying, "Geiger." Tubal-Cain nodded back and smiled. He continued to approach the man, who backed up a step. At a cue from Tubal-Cain, Talaon sprang upon the man and held him fast.

"Let us see what you can tell us, my new friend," said Tubal-Cain. He reached out and touched the man's temple. Immediately, the eyes of the man rolled back in his head and he went unconscious.

Sara could not help but feel sorry for this man, whoever he was. A movement in one of the lower caves caught her eye. Shifting her focus, she saw an older man quietly slip out and around the side of another cave opening. He was only visible for a moment before he ducked back into the darkness of the cave. However, he was not so quick that Sara missed the mark on his arm. This silent visitor was another Zirci!

At this moment, the image before her eyes began to ripple and dissolve. Sara felt as if the ripples were moving her back and forth in a swaying motion. When she opened her eyes, she found herself in Geber's private quarters in the ship returning her to Nod. Sara sat up fast, almost hitting her head on the ceiling of the berth in which she had been lying. Frightened, she made a move toward the door, because she did not want to be found alone in Geber's room under any circumstances.

"Everything is fine, sister." Hedred came over to her and pressed his hands on her shoulders, preventing her from leaving. "There is nothing to be afraid of. I am here."

"Oh, Hedred," she said with a gasp of relief. "I must have fainted from all the events recently. I am sorry."

There was a short laugh from behind her.

"My dear Sara, we both know you are much too strong a woman to faint," said Geber as he walked up and stood next to her. "Now, tell me. What did you see?"

# Concluding note From Author

Thank you for reading *Atalànt: Beginning's End*, Book 3 in the Future Perfect series. I hope you enjoyed the third installment of the adventures of Logan, Lamech, and Enoch. If you did, I hope you will pause to write a review where you purchased this book.

Please join my mailing list *carlsonwriting.com* so I can let you know when Book 4 comes out. I promise not to give your email to anyone. The next installment of the Future Perfect series will be written in "first person" from Professor Rudy Geiger's point of view. Should be interesting!

Steve Carlson
August 2017

# About the Author

Steve's eclectic background ranges from working as an Au Pair in Germany to drug testing athletes for the Olympics, to also serving as a high school youth pastor in Colorado. In his twenties Steve lived and studied in numerous locations around Europe and in the United States. During this sojourning season of life, he developed a keen interest in history, politics, cultures, and languages. More than that, he gained a framework for engaging these subjects in the context of faith. In writing the Future Perfect series, Steve has been able to use this framework to creatively explore how morality, faith, apologetics, fate, and free-will might have intersected in the ancient past and how such intersection might relate to the present and future of our own world. Steve enjoys living in the beautiful state of Colorado with his wife and children.

# List of Characters & Terms

**Abel**—Biblical figure; son of Adam; murdered by brother Cain; sired no children and thus not counted in the official thirteen sons of Adam; *only* mentioned in the story

**Abijam**—Adoraim Firstborn; deceased; father of Lubin; son of Eshean; *only* mentioned in the story

**Adoraim**—Ancient male; sixth living son of Adam; sired the Adoraim Line; built a city with a major harbor that has his name; *only* mentioned in the story

**Atalànt**—Island to which Adam and Eve moved to allow their children to fill earth. Also, it is a place of art and knowledge where the Elder Born live after siring children

**Bete**—Zirci female; daughter of Eshet and Abilene; *only* mentioned in the story

**Cain**—Biblical figure; first born son of Adam; murdered his brother Abel; sired the Cainite Line; possesses multiple Gifts

**Callos**—Elder born Zimmah; Atalànt resident

**Chanokh**—Biblical figure; first born son of Cain; in English his name is "Enoch;" to avoid confusion the author chose to use the Hebrew transliteration of the name

**Cherubim**—Biblical figures, angelic beings guarding the Garden of Eden with a flaming sword

**Chul**—Ono Firstborn; son of Chul

**Churios**—An ancient and intricate type of sculpture cast in the shape of a perfect sphere

**Eglaim**—Adoraim captain; second son of Eshean; uncle of Lubin

**Eshean**—Adoraim Firstborn; grandfather of Lubin; no gift

**Enoch**—Biblical figure; Sethite male; first born son of Jared; fifth grandson of Seth; Gift of mind reading and influence; Prophet of the Most High God

**Elijah (Eliyahu)**—Biblical figure; Prophet in northern kingdom of Israel during the reign of Ahab (9th century BC); was taken from earth in a flaming chariot

**Enos**—Biblical figure; Sethite male; first born son of Seth

**Ether**—Sethite male; brother of Enoch, father of Talaon; *only* mentioned in the story

**Geber**—Cainite Firstborn male; grandson of Tubal-Cain; Gift of combat

**Gallios**—Elder born Ono; Atalànt resident

**Geiger, Rudy Dr.**—Modern-day German/American male; physicist

**Haal**—Ono Lowborn male; father of Hemeth; *only* mentioned in the story

**Hedred**—Ono Lowborn male; brother of Hemeth

**Hemeth**—Ono Lowborn male; sent to artisan camp; gift of the mind

**Heshbon**—Adoraim Firstborn; great-grandfather of Lubin; gift of "weather reader;" *only* mentioned in the story

**Huppim**—Adoraim sailor; First Mate on *Tomorrow's Destiny*

**Janice**—Elder Born Cainite; daughter of Cain, sister of Xavier; Atalànt resident

**Jared**—Biblical figure; Sethite male; father of Enoch; fourth grandson of Seth

**Joshua Doss**—Modern-day Jewish male; Logan's father

**Kedar**—Zirci male; first born son of Zirci and Lois

**Kenan**—Biblical figure; Sethite male; firstborn son of Enos; third grandson of Seth

**Lamech**—Biblical figure; Sethite male; first born son of Methuselah; seventh grandson of Seth; Gift of combat

**Logan Doss**—Present-day male; protagonist

**Lois (of the Zirci)**—Zirci female by marriage, (Sethite by birth); wife of Zirci; Gift of ; *only* mentioned in the story

**Lois Doss**—Modern-day female; mother of Logan; archaeologist; *only* mentioned in the story

**Lubin**—Adoraim Firstborn; captain of the ship *Tomorrow's Destiny*; son of Abijam; gift of "weather reader"

**Mahalalel**—Biblical figure; Sethite male; firstborn son of Kenan; fourth grandson of Seth

**Methuselah**—Biblical figure; first born son of Enoch; father of Lamech; sixth grandson of Seth; Gift of healing

**Milali**—Cainite female; married Jared (Enoch's father) after his first wife died

**Naamah**—Biblical figure; Sister of Tubal-Cain

**Okra**—Ancient male; eleventh living son of Adam; sired the Okran Line; *only* mentioned in the story

**Ono**—Ancient male; third son of Adam; sired Ono Line; *only* mentioned in the story

**Sara**—Ono Lowborn female; sister of Hemeth

**Seth**—Biblical figure; second living son of Adam; sired the Sethite Line; possesses multiple Gifts

**Sula**—Zior female

**Talaon**—Sethite male; son of Ether; nephew of Enoch

**Tipharah**—Town on Atalànt located near the harbor

**Tubal-Cain**—Biblical figure; Cainite male; son of Lamech (Cainite) and Zillah; forger of all implements of bronze and iron; Gift of the mind reading and influence

**Yarad**—Ono Firstborn; father of Chul

**Xavier**—Elder Born Cainite; daughter of Cain, brother of Janice

**Zior**—Ancient male; eighth living son of Adam; sired the Zior Line; *only* mentioned in the story

**Zirci**—Ancient male; thirteenth son of Adam; sired the Zirci Line; deceased at beginning of *Commencement*; *only* mentioned in the story

Made in the USA
San Bernardino, CA
20 August 2017